The Forsaken Wilderness

VIVAAN SHAH

SIMON &
SCHUSTER

London · New York · Sydney · Toronto · New Delhi

First published in India by Simon & Schuster India, 2023

1 3 5 7 9 10 8 6 4 2

Simon & Schuster India
818, Indraprakash Building,
21, Barakhamba Road,
New Delhi 110001.

www.simonandschuster.co.in

Pbk ISBN: 978-93-92099-41-0
eBook ISBN: 978-93-92099-40-3

Typeset in India by SÜRYA, New Delhi
Printed and bound in India by Replika Press Pvt. Ltd.

FSC
www.fsc.org
MIX
Paper from responsible sources
FSC® C016779

Simon & Schuster India is committed to sourcing paper that is made from wood grown in sustainable forests and support the Forest Stewardship Council, the leading international forest certification organisation. Our books displaying the FSC logo are printed on FSC certified paper.

To Shiv Subrahmanyam

Contents

PROLOGUE

Uncharted Territory

Uncharted territory; a term often loosely applied to those realms of the earth our species has not been successful in encroaching upon. Since the advent of measurement, man has strived tirelessly to configure and justify the prominence of such territories—or the lack thereof—on the globe as we know it. The Russian landmass alone has baffled explorers from the dawn of transport, its northward expanse and Siberian recesses—the vast tundra stretching on into a near-lunar landscape of glacial desolation as far as the eye can see; capability quails at the mere approach to those ancient ramparts that wall in the Antarctic interior from curiosity within an infinity of ice; little is known even of the arid grasslands of the Eurasian Steppe upon whose back the westbound caravans marched, or of the great deserts from whose bosom Babylon was said to have sprung.

Human limbs have as yet failed to reach the full extent of the Arctic, to ply the breadth of the oceans that swell across the equator, and comprehend certain blotches of islands and archipelagoes scattered like constellations across a galaxy of blue, cast far adrift from continental formations and areas of settlement—occupying the remotest outposts of human will. Regions whose temperatures would not allow life to thrive let alone visit. Places unfit even for animal habitation. Furnaces and foaming depths!—whirlpools and aerial swoons, mountainous monstrosities and the blasted wastelands intended for no living creature to tenant, and no sentient life to furnish…

The earth in its divine fancy moulds alien landscapes, fashions forms unthinkable, and lays into view vistas of such wild geological anomaly that might startle even the jaded glance of the airplane pilot—composed of phenomena not nearly as unaccountable as its abnormal arrangement might suggest; harbouring serial formations of objects that present no apparent reason for thus existing.

A thousand frightening instances leap to mind. One is brought at once to consider the symmetrically proportioned slabs of the Giant's Causeway in Northern Ireland; the bulging rock formations of Goblin Valley, Utah; the floating Tianzi mountains in China, the Cotton Palace of Turkey, the fluorescent travertine terraces in Iran, or the Whale Bone Alley of Siberia. The mind marvels at the technicoloured mountains of Peru, reels at the blood falls of the Antarctic, halts at the Silfra tectonic rift in Iceland, and whirls into the crooked forests of Transylvania, right into the Richat eye of the Sahara; petrified by the properties of Lake Nitron, perplexed by the swollen Dragon trees of Socotra, the gargantuan Al Naslaa rock formation of Saudi Arabia, the Monolith of Uluru in Australia, the seven stone giants of the Ural mountains. Even the Rorschach splattering of acid pools in Ethiopia, and the mineralised mosaics across parts of Northern British Columbia.

Through the ages, cartographers mapping expeditions and topographical surveys have laboured to fill in the blanks in the chart, replacing hypothetical landforms with concrete relief features, often journeying to the ends of the earth to corroborate their scenic speculations. Our forebears had not half our means at their disposal when contemplating the earth and its mystery, yet they envisaged order, exercised a will upon their external world, contrived battlements, lead one kingdom to another for the melding of all the material world and its contents in favour of arranging dominion over the unconquerable infinite; shook their fists at the almighty when chance partook of their voyages and lead us to the flowering of another age when their accomplishments would hold fruit. It took only an endeavour as brazen as satellite mapping to render clear and detectable every conceivable aspect and visible feature of physical reality. One could now accurately determine and account for the entirety of the earth's surface area, its most far-flung corners and its blankest oceans, and with the aid of an all-seeing eye, even observe those fragments of our planet hitherto untraversed.

Hence, for those with the benefit of a satellite view, the term 'uncharted' pertains principally to that which lies beyond the bounds of chartable space, both aerial and terrestrial; beyond the spectrum of the five senses and certainly beyond any means of measurement or recording as yet devised. Even in an age of mechanical ingenuity, there are terrains over which no aerial survey can fly, be it the attempted gridding of the ocean floor (constituting a good seventy per cent of the chart), or even the ineffectual excavation of immense caverns untraceable, and multitudinous in depth and direction. And so, just as the human brain harnesses but a minute fraction of its capable apparatus, our own worldly habitat is said to present an infinitude of such scenes of aberration that suggest the occupation of a good one-third of the planet's surface and more than half its atmosphere.

Following the physical law, that which cannot be sought

by the naked eye proceeds inwards into the depths of the dungeon, fleeing the light, and retreating to some collective centre of darkness; the very primordial ooze of civilization, the all-encompassing nothing which begat all! Down among the gnats and beetles, the scorpions and vipers shielding it from our grasp. The circle of time ever rotating, ever cushioning up against a barrier of uninterruptable black mass, never ceases to precipitate an epoch that might illuminate some of these enigmas, blinding us eventually by its incalculable origin and ultimate objective. Did time ever begin? Would it then dare to end us nearer its own horizon, propelling us inexorably towards eventual oblivion?

It was then perhaps solely that and that alone which consigned Professor Chaturvedi to a dismal fate, to his unforeseen doom—time!—and time, alone! The enchanting prospect of probing beyond the known frontiers of human exploration; to reason beyond the tangent of discovery yet foreseen. To enter the inferno unchallenged, and venture unbidden towards that hidden half, that nether lair…so as to glimpse the percentage of the earth that evades our eyes and finds subterfuge in the intangible areas of our understanding. Was it the spirit of inquiry and scientific investigation into realms of existence not even science can comprehend? Was it some malignant force of nature that inflicted retribution on those that dared to commit the greatest and deadliest sin of them all: To plunge into the unknown. To try and unravel the mysteries of the universe.

It would be difficult to provide—if provide we must—an accurate answer to the aforementioned queries within even the lengthy course of this account's narration, but I shall endeavour nevertheless to present a case that will bring some rather startling facts into light.

PART ONE

Of the Spiritual Circumstances Which Befell Professor Chaturvedi

chapter one

Let me say at the outset, that my incentives are not legislative, nor are they theological in any formal sense, they merely encompass certain personal directives, as might constitute ritual, observance of rigidly held beliefs (wholly of one's own invention), prayer, inquiry and above all incident—in other words, *adventure*! of the soul and of the spirit. Perhaps that was what led me then down the slow and unfortunate path of engineering: a nightmare preoccupation with increasingly disproportionate yields.

My installations taking me places far off and away from the region of my nativity—a location whose disclosure I shall not grant as yet—I invariably ended up at unearthly hours of the night and day, suspended from the crevice of a mountain corner, deliberating the intrusion of a pipeline into its recesses, accommodating struts and rivets into dimensions impenetrable, or across the terrible height of some dissolute bridge unworthy of reconstruction—pondering earth and space, vision and blindness, height and death, the crawling expanse of landscape, the skeleton forms of earthly objects, animate and inanimate—the definite shaft of possibility.

To plough this worldly kingdom of all its coral wealth, of all it could provide and find in its inner-most reaches, shimmering amongst the coal and dirt, the ghostly spectre of existence—whose eyes envelope, like the unclosing bud, all of daylight and the outer sphere.

Like many a man sent for the propagation of what hydel-power project would service the remotest settlement of regions dancing precariously on the boundaries of the map—I developed my own series of minute superstitions, clearly customised sets of irrational thought and behaviour by any means to ensure the serenity of my morrow. Naturally when the correspondence diverged I took to wild flights of fancy. I instigated my colleagues and associates into investigating irregular occurrences that had nothing to do with the task at hand, just so the dread symmetry of my intuition be appeased. In my spare hours from the sites, I would venture up as far as the road would take me to forbidden passes, on the pretense of taking some pictures. Often enough, it was not a memory I was after as much as it was a *vision*; a vision that turned into a sensation, a sensation of true and unfathomable terror, of heights—an inexplicable embrace of the deadliest vertigo: a plummeting swoon; I would peer into the drop mockingly and fancy momentarily that I might, with the simple flick or detachment of a protruding rock, endanger the welfare of the entire project we had laboured so long and scrupulously to preserve, despite all kinds of weather conditions, and high altitude, inaccessibility and lack of local manpower. What I perhaps wanted at first was a bird's eye view of the work taking place at the site, so as to scrutinise any possible safety hazards that might have been neglected. But soon, when placed atop such a juncture, and the physical unease of the scene had settled—aberrational fancies of the most unreasonable kind would threaten to get the better of me, at moments when my brass eye and reason were required. Thoughts unnamable, incited no doubt by the desolate surroundings, warded off in quick succession by fierce prayer. I would pray and pray upon the sweep and majesty of some mountaintop, that the very thought its scenery lured into being never see the light of day. And then unperturbed after an hour or so of supposed rest, which I would spend in penance, I would resume my chores at the site, sharing my concerns with the others over the course of the day's events.

I chose not, as other practitioners of my trade, to dwell in the supernatural, as some of them are wont to do (a phenomenon attributable in part to the various ghosts that hover over engineering colleges); but instead in the realm of the unknown. A realm not altogether unfamiliar to even the locals rarely provoked into assisting us on our excavations. Ghosts and spirits seldom rattled me, and I do not recall having ever been frightened by the prospect of a life everlasting. My terrors tended to lie amongst what are more euphemistically termed—scientifically unexplainable phenomena. The monsters I envisioned on my expeditions were carved out of cold fact, moulded out of reason and painted with that most incomprehensible terror of them all—logic! And its disbelief. The one doom folly that led me to what I am about to enumerate.

The astute Prof. Charan Prakash Chaturvedi, mountaineer extraordinaire, and PhD in environmental sciences (part-time herbal expert on botanical healing) whose acquaintance it would be my custom to make, was not doing too well with his practice; a foundation known as the Himalayan Rock Climbing Adventure Institute of Mountaineering and Research. His calloused hands had clutched the uppermost summits of Kanchenjunga, Bandar Pooch and Gaumukh, among others; all with a proficiency decorating him as something of a legend around the campfire.

The HRA Institute was supported charitably by the State Tourism Board of Uttarakhand. They would take the parties enrolled in the camp up to an altitude of not more than 3,500 metres. Sometimes this comprised a group of students from a neighbouring school or college; every once in a while, a seasoned climber; perhaps the backpacking foreigners that swarmed in by the busloads, or even the common tourist who could scarcely walk a mile uphill before wearying of the tiresome treks they embarked on. The institute had a team of scouts and local guides which accompanied the parties on their expeditions and navigated the routes and paths that were to be followed, with the strictest severity; both by the participants of the climb and most certainly, by them. Any deviation from the allotted paths charted by their instructors resulted in imminent expulsion from the organisation; one was left then to be a freelance guide until signing up with another mountaineering outfit—all to the devices of his own cunning, prospecting for pilgrims at the more prominent rural way-stations up a crooked mountainside, and hitching rides on highways at an incline connecting not previously accessible villages and districts.

One of the chiefs of these iron-clad instructors, indeed Prof. Charan Prakash Chaturvedi's aide-de-camp in overseeing the day-to-day operations of the establishment, was Ms Pratyusha Negi. She was from a mountaineering family of some repute—her mother had been the illustrious Smt Damini Jain from Roorkee, who had even taught geophysics at the IIT and had been one of the founding members of the Department of Earth Sciences. Pratyusha Negi, after having abandoned a short-lived attempt at medicine, decided to devote her vocation full-time to the

HRA institute, in exchange for a moderate fee that would support her and her three dogs—a Doberman, a German Shepherd and a Bhutia. She resided with her companions in a two-storey cottage near the Sangrali village that had been bequeathed to her by her paternal grandfather—the late great Brigadier KNS Negi.

It was *her* discretion that would determine which trek was suited to which kind of party, how much time should be taken to complete it, and the kind of provisions that were to be carried along. Prof. Chaturvedi rarely accompanied any of the parties up on a trek. He spent most of his time conducting lectures and educating students as to the basics of mountaineering and the correct usage of the equipment involved. He would do mock demonstrations for them, enumerating—countlessly, and patiently—the rules, drills and appropriate protocol for ensuring safety in precarious circumstances. He enjoyed the company of youngsters, especially those adventurous enough to be interested in what he had to say. He set up all kinds of obstacle courses for them, planned treasure hunts to keep them entertained, screened documentaries and gave first aid lessons. He even put up an artificial rock climbing wall and had a special prize reserved for the first child that managed to climb up to the top. The HRA Institute had been quite an attraction for students, youngsters and tourists of all sorts. Although its facilities were not more advanced than those at most adventure camps, Prof. Chaturvedi's singular dexterity (albeit aided in no small part by Ms Negi) at rock climbing, was considered by most to be its prime asset. In fact, she was said to have been swifter than him at ascending a rock face. It was at rappelling down that he had more nerve and command. She was a three-time gold medalist in surface-climbing and archery at the various IPS (Indian Public

School) meets she had participated in over the course of her long and unstable academic career. A district silver-medalist, finalist and runner up for long jump, triple jump and javelin throw. Had even represented the state in archery. The 'infrastructure development' enterprise (whose name for hazard of banishment I shall not utter), under whose employ I serve (or did serve; a matter still of some heated contestation), had called upon their services on numerous occasions for the administering of rock extractions along the more precipitous and winding mountain roads leading up to Mahanagar—a steep settlement along the border of Garhwal and Himachal Pradesh that granted no established motorable routes up to its base.

Prof. Chaturvedi had lent his expertise even on the explosion of an entire mountain range to enable the narrow passage of the vehicular exodus through its crags and tears—what he referred to as 'sarva-naash', the final state: The eve of destruction. When progress shall reign supreme and nature shall dance tunefully to the banshee shrieks of blaring lorry-horns.

It had first occasioned me to make his acquaintance in the autumn of last year, when I was stationed in Shikodhara, a treacherous mountain pass up the North-Western ridge of Kedar Nath, shielded on the leeward end by the Nanda Devi National Park, a dense reserved forest known frequently to teem with a wide variety of jungle cats. I was, at the time, chief secretary of the Energy Division at Larsen & Toubro, and had filed for my resignation papers; a decision not borne of the heat of the assignment, but instead of a discontent that had accumulated over a long term of service.

Indeed, I had been considering the proposition from the moment I had signed on. The pay was not by any means adequate to what I had earlier enjoyed at my preceding posts. I served merely at the pleasure of the Chairman of the Board of Directors on overseeing and supervising the day-to-day operations of twelve of their major projects: two in the Darbhanga district of Bihar, one along the upper reaches of the Aravallis, four large-scale solar installations in the state of Uttarakhand alone, five majors plans all across upper Himachal Pradesh—including the Greater Himalayan Power Project and industro-agricultural five-year plan. At Shikodhara, it was my fortune to have been appointed Chief Engineer; a designation that ingratiated me involuntarily towards his orbit.

His institute's headquarters were situated in the heart of Garhwal, Uttarkashi. Prof. Chaturvedi had read all about the neighbouring regions, the passes and glaciers whose names had often been uttered under his breath in prayer, and which if conquered, were said to guide the soul to eternal salvation. Being a devout practitioner of the act of pilgrimage and possessing faith in the potential therein to absolve one's misdeeds, he consulted with a Swaami—Shree Shree Guru Dev Atal-Anivaarya Natija (at times spelt with a double 'e' depending on the passage of the moon), a name of his own fashioning, no doubt having arisen from the 'bania' Bhatija clan that were said to populate parts of Eastern Garhwal.

Swaami Atal-Anivaarya Natija was an astrologer, or jyotish, who advised either the town's affluent or those higher up on the Brahminical ladder. He had renounced the clergy, and was devoted entirely to private practice, advising individuals as opposed to households and families. He felt it gave him a more thorough and acute understanding of his client's moral landscape. He was well versed with the vast assortment of scriptures and kundlis, and had told Prof. Chaturvedi that there exists a temple in Hampi, which is said to contain, to this day, in its libraries—all records of mankind. He would often refer to the Puranas, Upanishads and Dharmashastras, quoting the Vedas as if they were written on the back of his hand and reciting shlokas often of his own devising.

As custom would have it, in order for Prof. Chaturvedi to sustain his mountaineering outfit, numerous financial compromises had been made, countless freelance jobs undertaken on hazardous climbs and projects outside the capability of both him and Pratyusha Negi. The end of the tourist season and the depletion of business during the rest of the year was not a promising sign as far as the administration and maintenance of the facilities were concerned. Someone still had to foot the bills for equipment leased from adventure sports stores, army warehouses and camping retailers. And in most cases, it invariably ended up being Ms Negi, whose family grudgingly came to the rescue when informed of the institute's plight.

He began asking loans from his friends and neighbours, who—quite bewildered at first, given his prestige among the townsfolk—certainly never relented. And when time came to settle those debts, out sprang a Polio Contribution Fund for him to do the rounds with, beseeching donations from some of the more prosperous citizens—garnering sympathy on the pretense of sanctimonious chores. This permitted him an extension in his obligations until the time came to pay off his staff salaries at the end of the month. He protracted his payments as long as his eminence would merit, until some of the local guides began to quit their jobs. One of them even descended upon the institute inebriated, with some pahaadi (mountainous) thugs, to collect his hard-earned money, creating quite an undesirable spectacle for Prof. Charan Prakash Chaturvedi, who at the time—engaged in conducting a fitness camp for a troop of eighth-standard children—did not take kindly to the drunken display. His lack of spontaneous discretion at no doubt, so embarrassing an affair, led him to deliver a furious blow to the concerned party's upper torso for all assembled to witness.

Since that incident, most schools preferred not to send their children to HRA for the summer camps. The institute, without whisper, lost a large portion of its clientele in a fortnight, and at the onset of the following tourist season, Prof. Chaturvedi's professional and personal reputation began to disintegrate, so that he was not of much use, despite Ms Negi's best efforts, even to the few customers who did remain.

He prayed furiously to the almighty, begging for forgiveness for all his indiscriminate misdemeanours, and implored his deity to land him some deliverance on the morrow, or at least at the earliest, as time was elapsing rapidly before his eyes, spilling into insensibility. *And so it happened,* that I came upon his path! At the very juncture of bankruptcy, when the soul sways willingly to and fro across the fine thread of moral propriety.

chapter two

Banging his head intermittently on the stone walls while delivering summation of his woes at some roadside temple on the way to Sahastradhara, I chanced upon him at the foot of degradation. Passers-by would peer in to gawk and cackle at this dementia, even capturing photographs of the madman at the altar of Sai Baba: The inevitable surmise that it was indeed a case of demonic possession, laughed off by the strolling sadhus who denounced such claims, proclaiming that where the devil exists, so shalt exist God!

'Objects of worship,' one of them announced, 'have always acquired a sort of silent quality of terror. In the old days…' here he held up his palm and settled upon a stoop—'they were to be feared…' clearing his throat he glanced upon the recently discharged Prof. Chaturvedi gasping by a milestone, handled physically—part in jest, part in an earnest attempt at recovery—by a horde of leaping teenagers. 'The rituals were to be obeyed as a law of the land!' He pronounced, rising cleanly out of his seat and regathering his companions to march on up the hillside.

Having saved Prof. Chaturvedi from the manic rabble

at the Sai Baba Temple, that lay convinced it was a case of genuine hysteria, I proved to be that deliverance!—and proceeded him on towards my own preferred place of worship: the river. He recognised me as a yellow-helmet-wearing supervisor at the HDPL pipeline drill in upper Dhanaulti, that had helped in the attachment of his harness hatch to the hook of a mechanical crane of ours that could reach up to a height of some eighty feet above the ground. The project needed a person with his grip on the rock face to manoeuver some last-minute adjustments in the alignment of the piping. It was a treacherous job and he accomplished it marvelously with much ease, nary a hint of perspiration in sight! Reminding him of his feat one sensed in him a slight step towards composure. Once we reached the embankment of the Kali Gad River, he appeared positively at ease. From then on, out poured his whole life story…

He had been visiting the temple three times a day, ringing the bells with all his wrath, fasting for weeks on end, diligently checking his horoscope on every full moon night and spending days by the side of Swaami Atal-Anivaarya like a worthy disciple. He had reached the point where no amount of penance could salvage the decay within. Swaami Atal Natija too was baffled, and his deficiency in this particular case of spiritual consultancy was a matter of considerable alarm—both to himself, and to his clients, who knew well what ailed Prof. Chaturvedi.

Uttarkashi being a small town, everyone was aware to some extent or the other about everyone else's personal circumstances. Whispers quickly began doing the rounds of Prof. Chaturvedi's financial ruin. The disenchanted stupor he had fallen into had become an object of much ridicule among the locals. He begged Swaami Atal-Anivaarya Natija like a terminally ill patient would appeal to his physicians.

He beseeched him to validate any definite cure, anything that could reverse his luck or provide temporary solace.

Eventually, Swaami Atal-Anivaarya Natija had to come up with a valid solution in fear of jeopardising his own practice. Twenty-four dips in the freezing holy water of Lake Mansarovar seemed too inconsequential, too routine. A pilgrimage to Gangotri had already been performed before. Hemkund Saahab, the floral valley of Sikh enlightenment, would prove scarcely effective to his strictly circumscribed code of spiritual practice. The abundance of blessings at Badrinath were apt to lessen their effect, thought he without utterance. He had heard of a remoter peak in the Garhwal range, which rose from the greater Himalayan valley, above the tree line yet below an altitude of five thousand and five hundred metres; relatively high considering the adjoining areas. It was considered unscalable due to the steep vertical ascent. No one had reached the summit and its location at the bridge between the greater and lesser Himalayas was itself an anomaly on the map.

A topographical survey expedition team had embarked on a journey in the spring of 1971, never to return. That was also the year another party had attempted to climb Nanga Parbat.

The notorious peak came to be known as 'Ranibaug'; meaning the garden of the queen. An appropriate name considering its inaccessibility. It was said that no human feet had ever trod upon its rocks, save for those of ascetics and sadhus lost in its unforgiving wilderness. Their equation with the forces of nature was incontestable. Mountaineering parties with the most advanced equipment in their aid would often fail to attain the summits the sadhus would so effortlessly clamber up, almost with the ease of a mountain goat.

There were scarcely any navigable walkways or established routes up to the peak, yet the sadhus had their own routes, their own paths and maps, all embedded in the guise of instinct. Faith is the most effective compass as yet devised. It guides one through thick and thin, through the smouldering lava, through *hell* or worse; yet only provides to those that maintain its holy stubbornness. It only serves those that are able to cope with its severities, those that resign themselves to the divine surrender of forces beyond their reach.

Prof. Chaturvedi was certainly no stranger to the minor cruelties of circumstance. As I was later to learn: Fate, in the absolute, had never been particularly kind to him, and he claimed to lay forever in the mercy of its whims and fancies. Misfortune had been his constant companion for as long back as he could relate. It was latent in every moment that passed him by, and although briefly camouflaged by frequent spells of harmony, it lurked in the very air he breathed.

I was soon to glean, from his deteriorating manner at the river bank, that the prospect of facing it in its utmost extremity seemed far more enticing than battling with the mundane assaults of his daily existence. He was ready to laugh in the face of all adversity, and knowing fully well that the climb was jinxed, decided he would set out to cleanse his soul.

And it was only then, perhaps in a passing allusion to the possibility of my accompanying him, that he half-formed the stuttering proposition that any financial aid from my part would be rewarded tenfold upon my person in the coming years, if I were to yield to what he persisted to be—the reformation of his life.

chapter three

I had a week-and-a-half off-duty from the HDPL rigging site, while they mined the mineral reserves. An extraction team had laid base at our encampment. We had been driven out of the site by a fleet of JCBs that somehow shredded a path for themselves up the hillside, and a recently assembled thermal drilling and boring apparatus, the construction of which at that altitude was made possible by the delivery of a convoy of twelve-tyre axle large-scale-carrier trucks trudging steadily along the rocky ascent at a tortoise's pace, over the course of one-and-a-half days. There were said to be nickel and copper ore deposits stolen away in some crater inside where we were operating upon the plateau—completely sealed up by the non-porous enclosure of the sandstone constitution of the hillock. Once the government survey personnel had vacated the sight, all civil engineers were on voluntary standby for the spring. The bulk of the installation had taken place during a cruel winter. I was in need of some excursion, a communing with nature, a surge of sensation, be it the grand embrace of white water-rafting, bungee jumping, ski-diving or even skiing; or perhaps the more intimate forms of outdoorsmanship like fishing, a good hunt, swimming, the old stroll in the woods, a bonfire—some song!

But the trek proposed by Professor Chaturvedi was not by any means, what one could consider 'recreational', in the strict sense of the word. Embarking on this expedition meant putting one's life imminently at peril. From what I gathered, no one had indeed ever succeeded before in being able to reach the peak of Ranibaug in its entirety. But according to the Professor it was well within the capability of anyone who attempted it. Glancing at this paradox, I considered urgently the proposition, entertaining all kinds of frivolous notions such as—unearthing some startling discovery, possibly even bringing to light some remote finds and relics never before accessed by humankind. There were a few places of this sort on the map as I knew it; uncharted territory, and the notion pursued me constantly on my lay-over in Uttarkashi. I also came to know more of the Professor's life story as the townsfolk told it. There seemed nothing out of order about his mental faculties, or his physical health. His medical reports were above reproach, and as the prospect of my companionship seized him after numerous attempts at convincing Pratyusha Negi, his psychological maladies somehow lessened their torment on his calm and now calculated manner.

From what Ms Negi related, the trouble with the Professor was strictly financial, and she even half-suspected his entire mental collapse was some sort of an elaborate charade to evade the wrath of vengeful creditors. That a state of financial ruin could manifest itself in a form of demonic hysteria, or supposed possession, was nothing novel in her eyes. She had seen many before resort to the *religious* in order to cheat the *rigorous*.

Now, in order to accomplish this—without question—

intimidating trek, despite my beneficial participation, Prof. Chaturvedi would require the assistance of either a sadhu or a guide, since the angularity of the peak Ranibaug and its surroundings were unfamiliar even to his most reliable allies, Ms Pratyusha Negi included. We decided the need would emerge for a rifle. This was easily obtained from the Uttaranchal Ordinance, thanks to an ex-employee of his, Shera, who had served in the Garhwal Rifles and owned a permit. He managed to get his hands on a Standard Regulation .303 bolt-action Enfield rifle, which jawans (privates) used to carry on reconnaissance missions that did not involve heavy fire. It was sturdy and dependable, if a little obsolete. Shera was a local Garhwali and knew the terrain better than anybody in the region. He had been Prof. Charan Prakash Chaturvedi's number one scout and guide for the outfit until his financial conduct got in the way of his professional proceedings. He now worked part-time at a tourism and adventure sports depot in Rishikesh. He would spend the evenings gallivanting along the banks of the Ganges, listening in humbled rapture to the rantings of the various sadhus. He had once even accompanied the more approachable of his acquaintances to the Maha Kumbh Mela. He would befriend the white-bearded weary travellers, and spend hours in their midst like a worthy disciple, hanging off the ends of their sentences, trying to extract a pearl of wisdom from their crumbling teeth.

They found the little fellow a trifle amusing at first and even coined all kinds of pet names for him, the foremost being 'Nepali', one which he particularly resented. But then having gained second-hand knowledge of his resourcefulness they advanced themselves to his entrustment, faintly alluding to a loan in passing, gathering favours, sometimes enough to scrounge through a day of square meals, sometimes lodging for the night till they packed their belongings and were off on their way to another holy pilgrimage.

They would tell him that every hard-earned paisa spent on them was an investment, that it would do him good in the long run—that he was serving the left arm of the almighty. And he bought all their ragged tales, given that his account with the almighty had suffered considerable deficits in proportion of his vices to his virtues. It seemed only reasonable to present him with an incentive to run away from his temporary existence. All it took was one of Swaami Atal-Anivaarya's sermons to convince him of it.

And so, on the eve of our departure, when Prof. Chaturvedi, Shera and myself were all stocking our vehicle with the necessary supplies, none could desist from muttering certain sacred phrases to ourselves out of habit, before casting off into the unknown. Pratyusha, who had come to see us off, was the first to point this out.

'Did I give you the keys?' the Professor asked her.

'You did!' she nodded, resting one foot against the hind wheel of the jeep and spinning the key chain around her right index finger like a revolver. 'Sealed off the rec-room. Double lock on the staff canteen. The tempo from Vahamin-Electrico should be here shortly to collect the generator.' She spun her wrist around to check the needle on her watch.

'What else is left?' he prodded her.

'Mmmmm...' her brow crinkled up in thought. 'Let's see...lock on the implement shed, garage, store room and presentation arena!' These she counted on her finger-tips. 'Mess hall, and A.V. area, back exits all checked.'

'Obstacle course?'

'Been dismantled.'

'Good,' the Professor acknowledged. He had a blue HRA cap on, a khaki-green sleeveless HRA jacket, and a pair of camouflaged army trousers. Slamming shut the boot of the jeep once a headcount of all items had been conducted, he turned towards her and said, 'Well…I suppose this is it then everyone!'

'You finished your prayers yet, Professor?' she exhaled, kicking a pebble from beneath her toes.

'They can be continued on the road.'

'Well…' she raised her hand sort of lazily in the air to wave. 'Bon Voyage then…'

It was apparent beyond mention from her manner that she did not take in the slightest to the Professor's plan to embark on this expedition.

'What's the matter Pratyusha?' He caught on to this in an instant.

'It's nothing,' she shrugged, looking down at the ground.

'You still sure you don't want to come along?'

'My uncle's not allowing me,' she dug her hands into the nylon pockets of her maroon windcheater. 'He's my local guardian. Can't leave without his permission.'

'Can't argue with that.'

'Plus, I got a bad leg,' she gestured towards her bright white Reebok running shoes, emphasising the cushioned ankles they bore. 'And to tell you the truth, Professor, even if I could—I wouldn't want to come…'

The Professor stood still without asking, but a sound almost involuntarily escaped him—'Wha…'

'Why?' I interposed, heeding the Professor's bafflement.

'You see, I'm not a particularly religious person,' she told me. 'I go for the regular temple visits with the family, the odd pooja and havan here and there. Recitals of the satyanarayan katha I can't stand, and deliberately avoid. Pilgrimages I enjoy more for the trek than the actual act of prayer. I keep upvaases whenever the family insists. But vaasthu and astrology is where I draw the line.'

'That's where you and I differ, Pratyusha,' the Professor began. 'Look, I'm not exactly superstitious either...'

'Then why do you embark on this trek?' she asked.

'Not out of superstition my dear...' the Professor insisted.

'The only reason nobody attempts this trek is superstition.'

'Not only...'

'And the only reason you're attempting this trek is superstition.'

'How does that make sense?' the Professor threw his hands in the air, exasperated even before the journey had commenced. I took instant note of these inconsistencies of temperament.

She tried to reason with Shera, but he would have none of it! He was determined and had made up his mind—sitting in the passenger seat, he was eager to depart.

'Madam,' he explained to her, almost echoing Swaami Anivaarya's assertions. 'Ranibaug is hallowed ground. To step upon earth that has as yet never been visited is beyond holy. It is eternal. What we seek to find there shall have no reward in this life.'

'That's right,' the Professor chimed in from the rear of the jeep. 'It is eternal! Everlasting. Swaami Ji has asked me to mark a rock at the summit, at which we intend to build a temple in honour of the peak and its queen goddess.'

'Look,' she stated. 'I understand your need for pilgrimage and penance, but to endanger your own life in search of salvation is beyond holy too. It's holy foolishness if you ask me! You can't be serious?' she barked, her eyebrows alerted in inquisitorial stance. 'You don't actually mean to tell me you believe in all this!?'

'*Believe* in what Pratyusha?' the Professor tried on a laugh. 'I'm telling you it's not a *belief*. It's the truth! It's not as simple as faith or devotion. This is to unlock some of the secrets of life, don't you understand my child! To be nearer to God.'

Her eyes now overcast with a grave sense of doubt as to our intentions, she kicked at her heel, squinting her mouth in disagreement. Perhaps the thought we were venturing up to the mountain out of greed; a yearn for accomplishment, a place in history—had at last occurred to her. She again shunned her eyes down and brought up the subject of the water pump from beneath heavy lidded disquietude.

'What are you going to do about it?' the Professor inquired, clicking open the door to the driver's seat.

'The motor hasn't been fixed. But then again…' her gaze lifted from the gravel to the back of the jeep. 'I don't see any need for it now that you…' she reached for a word, but found only a cluck.

'Now that I?' the Professor wanted a completion of her rumination on the plight of the institute's water supply.

'Now that we're closed!' she surmised.

'We're not closed,' the Professor reminded her, adjusting the bridge of a pair of sunglasses over his nose. 'We're just temporarily out of service.'

She kicked a stone out of our path and yawned, waving goodbye forlornly.

'You give your uncle Raman my best alright!' the Professor informed her once he swung hold of the steering wheel. Spinning it around with a jerk, he poked at the ignition which grumbled out an engine, and by the time we were all done waving our goodbyes, we were already in motion, off on our unknown way.

Most of the equipment had come from the warehouse in the institute's camp and the cantonment's hardware supply. Our rucksacks were sturdy and carried sleeping bags, a stove, two bottles of kerosene, a tent-kit, and enough warm clothes to keep us reasonably well covered at night. Along with the rifle we carried twelve rounds of ammunition, a Swiss army knife, a 1.5-watt torch, eighteen AA batteries, an A-5 bearing indicator compass, and a pair of mountain boots each. We had contemplated taking along a pair of khachars (mules) to carry the load so we could make swifter progress while ascending the mountain, but hesitantly abandoned the idea on accounting for the hazardous nature of the expedition. The last thing we needed on our hands was another set of creatures to take care of during the arduous climb. Although the khachars were known to be a tough breed, Prof. Chaturvedi still felt it would be unfair to subject the poor creatures to such a journey whose course could not be conventionally determined.

chapter four

We departed from Uttarkashi at the crack of dawn. The road up to Taluka, which was to be our starting point as well as base camp for the night, was said to be eleven hours by car and two entire days and nights by foot from the GMVN at the town square where I had temporarily taken up residence. Impeded by scabrous bumps, potholes, and breakages in the asphalt, it wound on along the mountain side, up eventually towards the Tolan Pass, across which lay its inevitable point of conclusion; a small mountain settlement, not densely populated enough to be classified a village, nor developed enough to be listed on the map. The only guiding light in the unendurable drive presented itself in the form of crumbling milestones whimsically littered along the onward path.

We stopped for lunch at a dhaba and took turns behind the wheel. Prof. Chaturvedi drove the first half of the way and handed the steering wheel and his dark glasses over to Shera to escape the mid-afternoon glare of the overhead sun. The road was bumpier than expected in parts but Shera manoeuvered through its puddles and craters with the deftness and knowing air of a 'pahaadi', invoking their numerous battles behind gears to steer clear of the precipitous drops and landslides that flanked the mountain roads. The sight of those drops and the potentiality of a fall had scared many a lesser driver to abandon ease and proceed by foot up the tenuous escarpments.

'Take it easy Shera!' I gathered my wits in urgent reprimand when an oncoming tempo diabolically whizzed by us on a blind turn.

He smoothened his grasp on the steering wheel and nearly caressed it as the wheels grinded over a rough patchwork of stones forming a crossing to a broader strip of mountain-shelf for us to climb on to. 'I know these roads like the back of my hand…' he let out at length, his stare still scrutinising the minutest formations on the curving path before us. 'I've driven up and down these twisted climbing pathways more than a hundred times, without exaggeration. Ask the Professor.'

The Professor sat up and snored in agreement from the passenger seat. I leaned forward on his backrest to look out of Shera's window, the forsaken drop that lay half-covered by his jacket, somewhat shrouded by the distant mist, entirely vacant in the exposing sunlight, illuminated beyond understanding. The deadly clarity of the sharp end of a blade! Permanent, yet somehow as if by some magic benediction—*apart.*

'You see that drop down there?' Shera's eyes averted from the white line curling against the hillside, now glided by into the open drop, circling the clear desolation from up above like a buzzard hovering the heavens. 'I've been down there.'

The Professor still did not stir from his fixture on the window glass. My hand gently lifted from the back of his seat and trembled towards my own pocket. 'How do you mean?' I probed.

'I drove off a cliff once,' he stated blankly.

'You did?' My eyes closed in astonishment.

There was nothing further to be said. 'Hmm…' he groaned in dreary recollection. The blare of a tractor-horn beat his gaze back to the path. He simply spread his shoulders apart and rested one elbow on the open window-side.

'And?' I asked.

'Hmmm…' he looked back at me, nonplussed. The Professor adjusted an elbow under his neck.

'What happened?' I insisted to know.

'Nothing. You just free fall for about five or ten seconds and hopefully get caught in a tree or at the edge of the "khud". It's nothing big. Happens all the time.'

Happens all the time? I should think not, my eyes shrunk from the oppressive vista that trailed us on one side. 'These roads are like a snake!' Shera's speech staggered at a troubling thought. 'A coiled serpent!' he stressed. 'You need a license to be able to drive on these roads. A mountain license. Not fit for anyone to just come and go on a round as and when they please. Sometimes they swallow you up, whole—these roads.'

PART TWO

The Expedition

chapter one

After completing a twelve-and-a-half-hour drive in Prof. Chaturvedi's all-weather 4x4 jeep, we arrived at the culminating broken road that disseminated into a wooded network of walkways and non-navigable paths, any number of which could have been unsuccessfully employed in the sojourn up to Ranibaug.

Although vaguely aware of Prof. Chaturvedi's personal reasons for embarking on this mission, Shera was sensible enough to presume the objective was only partly religious. Hence, most of the conversation around the campfire was restricted to topics of geographical interest and mountaineering lore. Shera boasted of his posting at the Siachen glacier and spoke fervently of his brief yet memorable stint in 2004. The GD Expedition of the Spring of 2004 to K2 was undertaken by a party comprising mostly of foreigners. He was deputised as their escort to the Line of Control, where they were handed over to the other side. They, of course, never returned.

Very few had managed to climb that menacing mountain. It grew to become an object of horror to the soldiers posted on the Indian side and stories were told about strange goings-on around the peak. There was the instance of a PAK Radar Station picking up signals from an unidentified aircraft which had performed a landing at an altitude of some 6,400 metres above sea level. Then there was the body of the soldier recovered from a mining site. He was still alive but could not be placed in the army registration files. No one had any information about his identity and the soldiers on the Indian side assumed him to be a Pakistani espionage agent as much as the officials on their side thought him to be an Indian intelligence officer. This mystery was never quite solved. And according to Shera, the man was still held in custody in the northernmost reaches of Siachen at a checkpost called Tanglung-la.

'What about Kongka La towards Tibet?' I proposed.

'Ahh…' he batted his back-hand in the air, a sort of inadvertent flick of a cover-drive. 'Nothing to that,' he insisted. 'Merely speculation.'

Indeed, it was. Merely speculation.

'Eye witness accounts, testimonials on record,' I reminded him. 'Radar frequencies and radio waves being scrambled to the point of disorientation. Loss of communication. Demagnetisation of all electrical and mechanical appliances at the outpost.'

'The Indian Army is equipped with the capability to combat any kind of internal or external enemy, terrestrial or not, be it germ warfare, micro-bacterial spread, chemical gas, radiation, nuclear activity…'

'Nonsense!' Prof. Chaturvedi proclaimed, provoked into speech after a strict bout of silence.

'…whether it comes from another world,' he continued undeterred by the Professor's upheaval, 'or even from within…' he lingered on the term, his eyes falling motionlessly in the direction of the Professor. 'Some even say…' his lips cracked apart in a smile. 'It works better than a pandit or a priest. A good and thorough cadet instruction drill could exorcise the life out of a wailing lunatic.'

Prof. Chaturvedi did not like this kind of talk in the least. He told Shera to go and fetch some more firewood. The nights were liable to grow imposing in the mountains and the last thing he needed to hear was a tall tale of some bygone era. In 2004, he was on his way up to Yamnotri. He chose instead to fondly recollect that harmonious expedition, rather than to dwell any further on the towering dread of Siachen.

The next morning, we awoke at 6 o'clock sharp as per the Professor's instructions. It was pitch dark; not a trickle of daylight visible. The chirping of the crickets had ceased and a light dew had settled on the grass caressing the nails that held in our tent-strings. The dawn eluded us as we packed up our sleeping bags, and dismantled the tent, each holding its three corners to fold up in such a manner that would easily fit into its case. Having loaded our rucksacks, and mounted them on our backs after rinsing the utensils, and extinguishing the bonfire, we each looked to the other.

'Got everything?' the Professor checked.

A vague spread of light was hesitantly beginning to show over the clouds. He immediately strapped on his dark glasses.

'Stove?' he looked around.

Shera tapped at the swollen base of his rucksack—'Check!'

As the daylight descended, we were on our way. The trek was effortless on the first day, or at least so it seemed stumbling up the rocky bypasses, looking down into the desolate drop of a yawning ravine furrowed by a crooked stretch of empty river—taking paths too narrow for the three of us to walk side by side. The dangers of these precipitous slopes had discouraged many a party from attempting the climb, even seasoned climbers like Pratyusha, all in the guise of good sense. 'Bah!' I mocked the very notion of it. Good sense! To us, it was cowardice.

The thorny clearings in the scrub clothing the mountainside formed crisscross paths through dense shrubbery and dry overhanging foliage, that ran at times in stark contradiction to what we took to be their intended trajectories. The ascent was getting steeper past the enshrouding vegetation, an enormous gorge opened up beyond the knoll we crossed, and as a broken pathway of boulders jaggedly formed a twisted route before us, Prof. Chaturvedi thought it better to rest about every five or ten minutes for want of breath. Shera remembered still the days when his saahab could run up a mountain like a long-distance athlete—his shoulders strung up like a bison board, supporting the weight of two rucksacks on his upper torso, calves firmly clenched in resolve, stern pectoral girdle swerving into the triceps. 'Gone were the days,' he thought, whistling out a Garhwali folk tune played by shepherds on their flutes in contemplation of fatigue. He was no longer the Prof. Charan Prakash Chaturvedi he once used to be. Alas!

And so, we carried on up the parched hillside, the sun strangling his eyes despite the dark glasses and the weight of the carry-bag already aching his back. I was quite astounded to witness what I mistook to be a sheer dearth of endurance, but when reminded by Shera that the Professor's body, 'just like an old car often needs a day or two to warm-up to its optimum potential!' I was soothed out of my immediate worries about *his* progress up the slope, and decided rightfully instead to focus on *mine*. Shera was always a few metres ahead, leading the pack. He was quick on his feet, and I often struggled to keep up with him, as did the Professor with me, lagging behind consistently like a weary straggler he would have once chastised. Not once through the journey had we enjoyed his company. His approaching old age had done him no favours, and his need to engage in rest ever so often was not a promising sign.

By noon, our next campsite was still close to around eight kilometres away, and we still had half a day's trek to complete if we were to make it to Osla by sundown. There were parts of the journey that Shera jogged through once the ground flattened and curved on past a small cascade to a thick forest stretching up into a coniferous stairway: tall towers of trees, line by line in impeccable arrangement, slanting with the gradient of the land; acorns adorned every stretch of walkable pathway, and the strange scents escaping the shrivelled up plant-life grew into fragrance the longer they lingered. A spotted deer stumbled across our path. I'm sure I caught the rustle of what could only have been the clumsy motions of a wild boar. Bird sounds of every delicacy and type sounded querulously here and there. Up in the sky, the branches formed byzantine shapes and patterns above us, shadowing us through the harsher part of the afternoon. And from a distance the blotches of white announced, at the termination of the conifer studded pathway, an altogether different terrain for the remainder of the evening.

Having managed easily to reach Osla well before sundown, and after resting on the rocks that stood at the foot of the pass leading up to the mountaintop, we emptied the snow out of our boots. Osla was at an altitude of two thousand seven hundred metres. We looked promptly for a water body adjacent to where we could set up camp. Shera found a spot lying along the shadow of the ascending ridge that cloaked a good portion of the sun, which was growing barbarically as the altitude increased. The site was next to a stream which fed into a small waterfall that slipped off into the steep drop from the edge of the platform we were on.

The three of us were by now considerably drained and Shera had to practically set up the tent all by himself. Prof. Chaturvedi was swaying left and right, and looked surely like he was about to collapse clutching on to the ropes of the tent for Shera to nail into the ground. It was growing colder and neither of us had the strength to go and collect firewood. I remember having dutifully packed a carton of Maggi which was to be our emergency meal in the event that we found ourselves incapable of preparing something more substantial, such as the baked beans, or rice, or the MTR packed meals we had carried along. Shera crouched down on the ground to ignite the stove. I pumped the kerosene vigorously for him but couldn't induce more than a spark; the stove would hint at a flame and then go off suddenly without warning. Shera took the knob-topped metallic stick from my hands and drew it in three times to the stove, tapping at its bowels, twisting the nozzle in once he had managed a regulation. We kept pumping it to get it started until Shera had the good sense to blow at it, sustaining steadily the ghostly motions on the circular ring into a blue flame. We placed the steel container on the stove. Prof. Chaturvedi took the bottle off his rucksack to get some more water from the stream.

After having cooked and partially eaten the Maggi noodles, we all collectively decided it best to lay down on the cold ground with the sun beginning gradually to set over us. In about fifteen minutes of vigorous motion on the grass from Shera's end, which I took to be the irritants of some forgotten itch, and which prevented me from attaining the full length of my slumbers, he ambled towards his empty rucksack, abruptly arisen and strolled on up towards the narrow stream. When asked where he was going, he simply mumbled without turning—'Up stream.'

I quickly followed suit, leaving the snoring Prof. Chaturvedi with nothing but grass by his side and a tent in the vicinity.

Accordingly, Shera considered it best to collect firewood before it turned completely dark. We climbed up after crossing the stream and walked towards the impenetrable forest alongside the trekking path, that one usually never takes the trouble to venture into while on an expedition. We found some broken twigs, bark, leaves, acorns and a log of twisted fir. He stuffed them into his gunnysack while continuing to stomp around looking for some more. He thought it right to stock up as best we could, as this would prevent us from having to go out and look for more in the event that we ran out at night.

While scrounging through the waste along the ground, and heaping the dried leaves aside to separate them from the wood, Shera took gradual notice of a marginal crater which descended into a sort of snake pit. He looked down into it, and as he rummaged through the mess of leaves and hay, he at once stumbled upon something which caught his attention. It was a bone which could have either belonged to the human or buffalo species. It was about the length of a fibula, and markedly off-white in colouration, pock-marked and coated with a rust-like harshness to the touch. We took it along with us to show to the Professor. Shera remembered the expedition to Rupkund in the summer of 2008 when they had found a skull among the rocks while levelling the earth to pitch a tent.

It was about seven o'clock in the evening when we returned. The Professor still lay asleep without any hope of revival before an uncertain hour; legs sprawled outwards, his arms crossed beneath his neck supporting his head with the heel of a palm. We placed all our findings next to the stove and started to shovel a pit for the bonfire. I cleared up the plastic packets of Maggi masala and accommodated them into a makeshift dustbin. When turning to collect the plates, however, I was surprised to find them gone. I thought at first that perhaps Prof. Chaturvedi had kept them away but was soon reminded by Shera that the Professor had fallen asleep after finishing only half his helping of Maggi. Shera immediately looked into the steel bowl of Maggi on the stove. It too was empty. Now this was a matter of considerable alarm. It obviously meant that it was not altogether impossible that our campsite had come in contact with some other external force. As we speculated as to its nature, Prof. Chaturvedi awoke with a start—eyes considerably reddened, hair in a stringy tangle—visibly famished and demanding his Maggi. He was hungry and disoriented, and in urgent need of nourishment. I made him some coffee instead after washing the container in the stream, and informed him that the Maggi had unaccountably vanished, showing him the bone we had scavenged along with the firewood, thereby emphasising for all our collective concern, that it was *still* unlikely that we were alone.

chapter two

Our next base camp, Harki Dun, was at a considerable distance from any other form of settlement; about fifteen kilometres from Osla by foot and partially cut off from the rest of the valley. Beyond the glacial ascent to the west of its peak, there lay another entangled route through the snow-clad shrubbery to the base of Ranibaug; but it was deemed too precarious for us to take. Most of the routes were non-navigable and wove through impenetrable landscape. Thankfully, we were carrying a sickle that Shera had borrowed from a farm we had crossed on the way up to Osla. We would now have to cut through the vegetation after Harki Dun as the forests from then on were forecasted to grow all the more imposing. Trekking through the snow was easier than beating out the dense forests that curtained the mountaintops.

Having lived in valleys or hill stations all my life, and having gazed wondrously at the dimensions of the vast and majestic mountains always on the horizon, I had often contemplated the possibility that some kind of life must have thrived upon the slopes and mountain-sides that no living organism would dare to venture onto with the exception perhaps only of the mountain goat. But even they were known to have fallen from the rocky and unpredictable mountainsides. Shepherds had been known to lose entire flocks in these mountains. Any poor creature's next step could be its last.

The insect paths we adopted up a steep fault scarp in the mountain face, the result no doubt of some prodigious rock fall, were inconceivable to me. It was the Professor and Shera's singular ability at navigational precision alone, that made them possible. Nowhere was rope required. It was simply a matter of estimating the swell of the bluff, which left to intuition could often prove deceptive as I had learned once from a mishap in Solan. But I was in the presence of experts in their trade—the kind of skilled labour the company I work for had only recently begun to employ to save them from the kind of catastrophes their ignorance had volunteered to commit.

We set up camp at Harki Dun by sundown. The hike had been comparably brisk yet arduous. Instead of the magnifying rays of the overhead sun, we had cold windswept paths slippery and frost-ridden. A light sleet settled upon the hood of my windproof double-layered jacket. The decrease in temperature certainly suited the Professor famously and a renewed burst of vigour caused him to overtake even Shera on our way up. Once the two of us reached, we of course found him lying prostrate on the ground, out of breath and panting profusely. On noticing us, he sprang to his feet and immediately spread out his carry mat and sleeping bag so that he could lie down and enjoy a hard-earned, and in his words, 'legitimate' rest. Shera was somewhat baffled at his irregular sleeping hours, recollecting that on our first night at Taluka, the Professor had scarcely slept a wink at night and complained the following morning of Shera's snoring, lamenting that he had not brought along a separate tent for himself. While stocking up and packing for the expedition, Shera had suggested that we spare the extra weight, provided the saahab did not mind sharing his tent with him. We squeezed into it each night, the three of us—pushing and shoving the other into stupor; whether it was sleep was doubtful: there was scarcely enough space for the two of them. There was always the awakening flow of a waterfall, never resting or letting the lightest sleeper among us rest entirely. The cry of some night animal would pass, every once in a while, over a weary ear unable to mishear its implications. Over the past two nights, the insomnia in the tent after lights out began to assume contagious proportions.

We had now reached the kind of terrain where only two of us would have to sleep while the third kept guard at the bonfire with a rifle, huddled up beneath a shawl. We would rotate the allotment of duty as per our sleeping habits, and as it was Prof. Chaturvedi's custom to drop off before an appropriate hour, he invariably wound up having to make use of the time when he found himself unable to rest—the night.

Indiscriminate portions of snow lay all about the place. I avoided looking down from the pinnacle of Harki Dun. The view was liable to scare anyone with a fear of heights; a fear I did not necessarily accept at that moment, yet one which insinuated itself upon my person in that very vista of swooning vertical expanse. The drop was severe and gave one an inkling of the considerable yet relatively negligible progress we had made thus far on our expedition.

chapter three

The glow of the bonfire provided as comfortable a sanctuary as we could afford in this bewildering night. Shera had his army jacket on and the Professor had clumped himself under every possible form of clothing and covering he had brought along. Shera had even given him his blanket as he was less susceptible to the cold; a discrepancy I at once took to be peculiar—given their even familiarity with the altitude—yet inevitably attributed to the Professor's approaching infirmity.

The night wind rattled his bones and the vague, indecipherable sounds of the restless forest nearby crept into the already ominous air. Nighttime this far out was significantly more discomfiting than it had been at our prior basecamps. Somewhere in the distance a jackal could be heard howling away at the moon and the continuous sound of the water flowing downwards in a stream had grown more forceful and somewhat restless. Shera hinted it was best if he got some rest as the saahab had already had his fair share in the evening. He handed Prof. Chaturvedi the rifle and a box of ammunition and left us by the bonfire to crawl into the tent.

The Professor sat rigidly upright as a rock under his blankets, appearing faintly like a village maiden in the darkness. He stumbled up to get a cup of coffee laced with brandy (a practice of which he would never recreationally partake), spilling some of it onto my unfolded thighs. I offered to re-heat it for him—lukewarm as it was, not having scalded me—when he clasped one hand tightly around the rim of the mug, and with the other motioned towards his resting rifle.

'Want me to hold that for you?' I suggested to him, as he cleared the bald patch of ground around the bonfire that was to be his seat for the night.

Cradling the rifle securely within his elbows, once he placed down the half-full mug beside his feet; he strived to speak, but found himself chattering his teeth instead with deliberate haste, as if in anticipation of impending danger.

'Did you hear that?' his teeth suddenly stalled in their tremors.

'What?' I rotated my neck around to encircle the vicinity.

He thought it to be the sound of human footsteps at first, but then catching a rustle quickly changed his mind, deciding instead that it was probably an animal of some sort seeking refuge. He quickly woke Shera, who was more perceptive on these matters. Shera emerged wearily from the tent, mildly stricken with concern and looked furtively around in the darkness, almost as though he were graced with night-vision goggles. He made a couple of sounds and whistles, calling out into the night as though he possessed the ability to communicate with the other species. He had, after all, been at one point the number one scout and tracker in the Garhwal Rifles and was no doubt an authority on such matters as concern the animal kingdom. He informed the saahab that there was no chance of an attack of any kind if the two of us just sat idly by the bonfire with the rifle. The Professor insisted that Shera sit along with us, but Shera (with some intervention from my end) managed to reassure him over the course of his brandy that there was indeed *nothing* around the campfire area. He guaranteed it, swore on his great grandmother even.

But she was long dead, and as he snuck back into the tent and I bent down to zip it shut for him, Prof. Chaturvedi let out a shriek at the top of his voice! Shera jumped back out over the half-formed zip, upper-torso first—catching his saahab by the mouth and strictly instructing him to maintain dead silence. Shera walked about tentatively, this time more attentive and taking the Professor's presumption a trifle more seriously.

Prof. Chaturvedi swore he had heard something. The barking of a jackal perhaps, or even the growl of something more malicious. Shera finally sprang on his saahab, and hissed such a deafening call of silence that it nearly toppled him on his side. By now all distinction of their classes and the protocol resultant of that dynamic had evaporated in the midst of nature at its deadliest.

Just to stay alive in this cold was a chore. Perhaps an animal of some sort had indeed been attracted to the bonfire. It was not a matter of alarm. If you did not interfere with any of God's creatures they would not interfere with you; Shera had conducted most of his journeys in the wilderness under that dictum, or at least so he claimed. Never had it hurt him. It had cost his brother his right ear, but that was due to a bear, and there seemed little likelihood of us encountering anything that threatening at this height.

And even if we did, we had a rifle. Shera once again turned in, promising the Professor saahab that *nothing* would happen. This time he did manage to fall asleep, even before I closed up the folds of the tent should the night wind choose to disturb him.

Prof. Chaturvedi sat quietly at the fire, trying his damnedest to stay awake, the gun clutched firmly under his blanket. He fastened his right index finger around the trigger and cocked the rifle. He was ready to use it at a moment's notice, and as he heard something once more he held it up and called out sternly—'WHO IS IT? *Show yourself!*'

From out of the edges of the forest, there emerged a quaint-looking sadhu who, going by his haggard appearance, certainly looked like he had not encountered civilization for about as long as we had, perhaps even longer. He quietly came and sat down beside the bonfire without saying a word. Prof. Chaturvedi uncovered his blanket to reveal to him what he harboured beneath. It did not as much as faze the old man. He sat ornamentally amidst the warmth of the fire as he disentangled his wealth of hair and beard which converged into a rope that held together a container upon his head. It was there that he kept all his belongings. He unravelled the tokra (box), practically disemboweling it of its contents.

It contained an orange shawl, some beads, a wooden knife, a rudraksh and a bone. The sadhu spoke an indistinguishable language. Having travelled far and wide in these territories, Prof. Chaturvedi had become reasonably familiar with most local dialects, at least enough to recognise if not entirely to comprehend. He could not trace this particular one, although he guessed it sounded faintly 'pahaadi', in some variant of the term. He informed the old man by gestures that he did not speak his tongue and hurried on towards the tent to wake up Shera, who came out this time with far greater urgency. He too tried communicating with the old man, as did I, but alas to no avail! He informed us that the old man was talking gibberish, and that he knew pretty much each and every dialect spoken in these parts but had heard nothing like it.

Shera reckoned that the sadhu was considerably intoxicated or a mute and was having a hard time enunciating just what it was that was on his mind. His emphasis grew guttural, producing sounds rather than words of any order—but markedly as if in contrast when he bellowed out a command, what he was saying became more distinct. The language did at first sound like gibberish but as he kept talking it began to resemble to Shera various rural dialects he had heard in his childhood among the mountain folk. He first suggested it could be a strain of Garhwali spoken along the Tibetan frontier, but the more he listened the more he speculated on the possibility of it being some sort of ancient language from the scriptures—Prakrit or a far more ancient form of Sanskrit perhaps.

Prof. Chaturvedi asked me to offer the Sadhu some water which I did, but he humbly refused with a guarded show of great deference, stooping into some kind of ritualistic posture and sitting cross-legged with his head drooping until the next word was spoken. After a certain point in time, the three of us failed to produce anything more to say. He sat in that posture the entire night, absolutely still. There wasn't the slightest sign or indication of movement of any kind. Not even the twitch of an eyelid, or the shifting of an elbow. He did not appear to be breathing yet his eyes were fiercely open. Prof. Chaturvedi gaped on at him in awe, shuddering at the possible implications of his presence in this wilderness.

chapter four

The next day the Sadhu, employing hand gestures which he demonstrated quite arbitrarily, asked us to follow him on his trail up the mountain. We promptly proceeded to do so after having wrapped up and parcelled our belongings. He took us not along any navigable walkways but across the mountain-side, which at first glance seemed precarious but was not as dangerous as it appeared to be once the forest undergrowth was within grasp for us to hold on to. I must admit, there were parts of the hike when I was reduced to climbing on all fours, grabbing rocks for support and holding on to branches that seemed steady enough to cut the onward vegetation that proved to be a further hindrance. Choosing which rock to step on was a vital decision, and made by each of us with the strictest discretion.

The sadhu was making his way up the mountain like a billy goat, and left us behind by a wide margin. He did not find it necessary to halt for a break as often as we did. After failing several attempts to catch up with him, we were certain that we were lost and had indeed performed a foolish deed by having trusted him in the first place. Shera thought it best to abandon the old man and make our way back to the established tracks that were to be the route as per our original plan.

This, however, was not as simple as it appeared to be. We had a fair bit of navigation to do before we could make it back anywhere near where we had set up camp. We had been climbing for two hours continually and descending the mountain-side was a far more dubious proposition than ascending it. We would have to slide down the slope keeping a firm hold on the rocks, and the possibility of one of us slipping was immense. After some serious thought and deliberation, and more than a little altercation, we decided again to try and reach the sadhu. We followed his trail, keeping track of footprints, looking out for a disruption of the prevalent vegetation on the ground or any other signs of his passage.

As we climbed onwards at length we began to notice, the narrow route we had employed lead up to a rock face of some thirty feet that obstructed the walking path. It had to be climbed. We immediately thought it best to place our belongings at a selected spot and carry on from there, this time swearing to recall in vivid detail the return path to the assigned location.

As soon as we had attained a portion of flat land, Shera began digging a hole in the ground with his bare hands while Prof. Chaturvedi emptied all the mountaineering gear out of his rucksack and began preparing it for use. I unloaded a tin of threptin biscuits and a water canteen, and lodged them to the Professor's belt-pouch. We buried everything else under the earth and looked on at the path winding up the steep rocky slope to the hillock.

We clambered up the slope to a point where we could see clearly the top of the rock face. There was an anomalous tree that stood by a protruding rock that looked merged with the plateau, an outgrowth of mineral and plant transmutation; a most vivid formation that loomed over the height of the hillock like a wagging neck, its branches sprawling outwards, and stroking each other in an entangled embrace.

Shera first hooked on his harness which had a belay device attached to it. The Professor then put on his own, did the same for me and clipped on his carabiner to tie the rope into a double bowline knot to string up to mine. They attached a three-pronged hook to the other end of the rope, which was intended to be used as an anchor. Shera tossed it up the rock face to fasten it in between the protruding rock and the trunk of the tree, and after checking the stability of the fastening, signalled the Professor to proceed upwards. Once he had reached a sufficient height, I followed up after him.

The rope stretched with a slow crackle as it came under the pressure of the two full grown adults. I dangled momentarily on the rope, grabbing hold of the rocks on the face of the bluff before Shera tugged at the tangle in his clasp from down below, tightening the alignment of the stringing. Prof. Chaturvedi climbed steadily, using the indentations along the surface as a foothold to get a firmer grip on the ascending rocks. The crannies that freckled the upper portion of the bluff served me well past my initial instability. Once I hoisted myself up on to the edge of the rock face, and unhooked the carabiner, Prof. Chaturvedi flicked his hands at Shera from the height of the ledge to signal his secure passage. It was a sight to behold! Shera scuttling up the rockface in a matter of seconds, practically without the aid of the rope. The Professor turned his glance away, in heed of preserving his own imagined capabilities. One was at once reminded of farmers in the South of India scurrying up a towering palm tree with the swift grace of a circus acrobat.

A route was visible in the distance from the ledge we now stood on. It was evident from the harsh angularity of the path before us that we had chanced upon a section of the mountain too steep to be ascended by regular climbers. No one without an efficient rock-climbing acumen and the concerned implements at hand would dare risk in their right mind the hurdle we had just manoeuvered. It seemed clear beyond all doubt that the creator of this fiendish mountain had not intended for any human foot to traverse it passage, not even the harmless paw of a passing animal. The twisted and deformed tree seemed its sole inhabitant.

The sadhu had long vanished into the desolate scenery. Prof. Chaturvedi wondered how he must have climbed up the rock face and tried vigorously to determine which route he could have possibly taken up, searching frantically all about our surroundings, trying to make sense of them. The peaks and summits of the mountains lay unconquerably afar and seemed to stretch on into infinity, never to be scaled. From down below the peaks that fed the glaciers looked like foreboding towers upon a castle, its tapering spires mingling invisibly with the mist of desolate eternities pervading all around, brooding in its vast and unreachable solitude. Surely no man in his right mind would try to look upon the mountains beyond and think of setting foot there. There was a reason they could not be reached, and all those that had endeavoured to breach or violate its sanctity had perished. Perhaps we would indeed be the first human beings to ever set foot on Ranibaug's upper reaches.

chapter five

As the night approached, we scampered about under the shelter of a large rock which merged into a crest of the adjoining ridge. It provided little respite from the devious wind. My teeth chattered violently, trying in vain to apply a technique the sadhus had taught Shera to withstand the cold: simple inhalations through the nose with a four second interval to unleash a slow six second exhale from the mouth, proceeded by a repetition of the same cycle till the blood temperature stabilises. He had adopted those measures in Siachen during combat, but this was a far more worrisome predicament. He had not the faintest idea whether we would make it through this night. As the absolute darkness of the night blackened all, Shera pulled out his torch to ensure at least something was perceivable. This was more than either of us had ever had to endure—being stranded on a mountaintop in the dead of night without food, water, supplies or firewood. The biscuits had been devoured on our ascension up the rock face to compensate for the inordinate exertion, and we had failed to come by a stream anywhere in sight once we had successfully overcome the obstacle.

Thankfully, Prof. Chaturvedi had had the good sense to bring along the rifle. He had it strapped across his shoulders. Shera had a box of ammunition and the Swiss army knife in his military jacket. That was practically all we had on us, not a morsel of nourishment nor a drop of water between us.

At dawn, we deserted the spot where we had perished for the night and staggered on upwards. The routes arose into myriad formations up the jagged protuberances of the slope, now approaching a near fifty degrees in slant, some deceiving us to a dead-end, others unpredictably branching up to an elevated area of what appeared to be terra firma but failed to remain so when stepped upon. Progressing up the long winding path and gaining altitude, I sensed the Professor gradually lapsing into frivolous and altogether irregular behaviour. The wearisome struggle we had endured over the past couple of days had taken its toll on his apparent composure, so strenuously sustained through the better part of the expedition. His faculties by the moment began to diminish, eroding whatever little survival instinct he had left and had displayed the night before. He complained of a severe vascular headache, insisting that we halt for a while till he felt sufficiently recuperated. His entire forehead was greatly swollen, and he pressed down on his temples violently in hope of suppressing the neural agitation. At first, Shera contemplated the possibility that he might have been bitten by an insect of some sort, but the Professor seemed convinced it had something to do with the atmospheric composition of the region. He said there was something unearthly about it all, and that the very air itself was *tainted*.

Shera pulled his saahab back up to his feet and nearly handed him a slap in assurance that there was nothing at all *wrong* with the air. We both, after steadying our nerves, reminded him that it was imperative that we proceed as we were already losing time. We were all suffering from malnutrition, altitude sickness and oxygen deprivation. A stream of flowing water which we had chanced upon earlier had been our only source of nourishment for the day. At times during the climb, Prof. Chaturvedi held on to Shera's arm for support, taking his steps more cautiously and with a more deliberate precision, thereby slowing down our progress even further.

At noon, Shera decided to halt at a height of about almost five thousand metres. Our destination was still another quarter-day's trek away from us. He had by now taken control of the rifle and all twelve rounds of ammunition were in his possession. He was now manning the expedition almost singlehandedly. Neither the Professor nor I were capable of accomplishing even the most menial of tasks. Shera warned him not to venture off too far from our temporary campsite, and shoved the last sip of water down his throat with much resistance. He tucked him to sleep on a bed of grass like a mother nursing a sick child, sacrificing his own jacket for the sake of his saahab's comfort. Shera felt resentful of this, of these newly acquired responsibilities that were proving all the more burdensome. He wished he had never made this wretched trip up in the first place, and that he was back in the shelter and warmth of the city, away and secure from the menace of the wild. Thoroughly dismayed, he threw the Swiss army knife and torch onto the ground in a rage, and proceeded to go around and look for more water and other supplies. He insisted I accompany him, so that the Professor felt incentive enough to enliven some consciousness—'It might arouse his survival instincts,' he mused. 'Being stranded.'

chapter six

Shera carried along the rifle on our brief excursion into the adjoining wilderness in hope of coming across anything that might qualify as food, even though there wasn't another living creature in sight for miles. We scanned the entire territory but found nothing, not even a drop of water or a speck of snow on the damp earth which at first was disconcerting, but on glancing upwards at our destination, I was soon reassured by the snow-clad path which lay ahead. It was the last stretch of daunting earth that succeeded us, and I wondered plaintively whether we would have the strength to complete the journey in the Professor's current state. With him though I felt certain that the prospect of abandoning his expedition after having come all this way was far more troubling than the notion of overcoming the frailties of human temperament and capability. He had still to keep his wits about him though, not to mention his strength and his sanity. If not his, then at least *ours*.

Scouring the waste in the forest to gather firewood for the night, we once again chanced upon some skeletal remains that lay scattered along a damp patch of loose earth. While rummaging through a heap of leaves and broken twigs, my attention was immediately seized by what appeared to be a skull.

After lifting it out of the mess of disintegrating wood, I placed it upon a rock so that Shera could examine it. The contours of the skull were immensely elongated and swelled into a knot around the occipital area. The nasal cavity was large and trapezoid. The inconceivably hideous smile which graced the mouth bore not the slightest resemblence to the human skull. The eye sockets were placed far apart in such a way that suggested a side vision like that of certain reptiles not capable of the usual 180-degree line of sight. Their incongruous placement defied any biological purpose and even the jaw and forehead were disconcertingly shaped.

We left all the firewood we had tirelessly collected and ran back at once towards the campsite, carefully holding the skull cradled in my crumpled windcheater.

We showed it to the Professor who was immediately propelled out of his stupor upon witnessing it. He leapt up to his feet, awoken by what he considered to be a visitation! He studied it carefully and placed it on the ground. He glanced at it from all possible angles. The proportions were startling and he even wondered if exposure to extreme temperatures and conditions at this altitude might have deformed the skull.

The mandible descended to a wild and incomprehensible deterioration of the lower jaw—its dental features in morbid disarray, appearing almost to writhe outward as if two pairs of teeth were contained within one mouth. The irregularly protuberant maxilla merged into this deformed mandible, holding together the hinges by means of a cartilaginous adhesion. There were unaccountable fossae toward the cheekbones and earlobes. The dimensions of the skull were too exaggerated in their spatial allocation. Most simian life forms, even the most eccentric of baboons, did not possess so elongated a cranial chamber that almost alienated the lower hemisphere.

Even though I was not particularly adept in matters concerning the identification of regular and irregular forms in mammalian and reptilian anatomies, I knew it was unlike anything I, or even the Professor had seen in the biology laboratories of our lifetime.

Shera wondered where the sadhu must have reached. He was up in the outermost reaches of the Himalayas where it was certain that no antecedent party had ever been recovered. Perhaps he would never return. Perhaps he had lived amongst the wilderness all his days and had never encountered civilization of any kind. Perhaps he was one with nature and all its creations, more so than any human being had any right to be.

For the first time in my life, I was undergoing the extremities of starvation. Never had I known this level of deprivation, this degree of utter inanition. I licked the very snow we tread on as the magnifying rays of the overhead sun melted the ice beneath us into trickles and droplets of water as if showing some mercy for the three forsaken souls. From the portion of flat land where we had temporarily set up camp, there undulated ahead of us some fifty odd metres of downhill windings which were proceeded by another steep snowy ascent up the nose of a rock formation that swelled up into the chin of the larger structure of the range, casting the entire procession of peaks with distinct facial characteristics, a gloating mosaic of twisted expressions and openings, projections and declivities, gnarled necks, and sunken craters of mouths like laughing mountains. After having climbed the fissures and rocky trespasses, up the ever-widening terrain that never ceased to punish and craze, I gazed up at the stormy vista above us which appeared nearer than it probably was. Ranibaug was still close to a quarter day's trek away, and as we approached closer I felt a strengthening air of unease. The mountain was vast and unconquerable. The three of us had by now abandoned all desire for conversation. We were as silent as the desolate air we breathed and the spirit of companionship had long worn out its welcome.

After about another two-and-a-half hours' worth of trekking and trampling through ankle-deep snow—which resulted in a moderate two odd miles of ascent—we stopped by the side of a stone boulder to rest for a moment. Shera sighed in what assumed the air of relief, breathing rapidly in spurts to catch his quavering breath. A long-awaited smile erupted on his harrowed face. But Prof. Chaturvedi, haggard beyond the point of recognition, breathed heavily, gazed up at our destination and ordered Shera at once to hand over the rifle and the ammunition in case we encountered anything.

Shera, of course, refused—but the Professor was adamant about his rightful ownership of the purchased firearm, he had paid for it in full with *his* money! He grabbed hold of the rifle strap that was wrapped around Shera's right shoulder and snatched it off him in an instant. Shera took one step away from the Professor, his palms cast outward, an index finger gently lifting in warning—one eye turned in my direction, the other planted firmly on the Professor—but before either of us could move a limb, he swung out the Swiss army knife from his belt and held it up for his saahab to get a good look at. He would cut the Professor's throat to make it out of there alive. Prof. Chaturvedi now pointed the gun tentatively in his direction, wrapping his index finger timidly around the trigger. Shera slowly circled him, calmly instructing him to drop the weapon lest anyone get hurt. I reminded him that he was not in his right mind and liable to make a disastrous mistake. The Professor would not relinquish control. He insisted on keeping possession of the rifle for the remainder of the journey. At my eventual urging Shera agreed, provided the Professor would cease pointing it at him.

Prof. Chaturvedi calmly lowered the rifle, and just then—a split second after—in swift mockery of his proposal, Shera reached forcefully for the strap causing his saahab to fire a shot into the air. They paused their struggle to register the echo of the gunshot that flew across the scenery. Shera looked at the Professor in utter bewilderment. He threw the gun on the ground and collapsed. Shera tried recovering him, shook him fiercely, but it was of no use. We had to carry him on our shoulders for the remainder of the journey.

The snow-covered path we left behind was succeeded by a most harsh, and unforgiving gravelled terrain. The stony earth pierced like burning embers to the soles of my feet. The depths of our torment were now reaching Biblical proportions. It was almost like a collective retribution exacted on all of us by the almighty for all Professor Charan Prakash Chaturvedi's wrongdoings. This was to have been his penance, his price, his salvation—our misdeeds meagre by comparison—and although we could carry him no longer on our backs, we would have further to endure his suffering. Shera tried again to revive him once we lay him down beside a patch of clear ground. The Professor's eyes slowly opened to grasp the majesty of the summit. One felt some sensation in him had been alighted and strengthened by the prospect of having neared his destination.

After laying him down and resting him indefinitely till

he felt somewhat recuperated, the two of us shakily got up from our haunches, and trying to maintain balance with one shoulder of his draped around each of our necks, proceeded onwards. We kept on and on with the resolve of determined souls, misguided and misled to a remote redemption. Our spirits were expectedly enlivened as we touched the foot of the crest that arose up to the peak and although there was no chance of another conflict that could possibly break out between the two men, there was an instability in their carriage. Prof. Chaturvedi stooped low, his posture distorting progressively to the primordial state. Shera hung his shoulders down, swaying wildly left and right against the approaching wind, which was fierce at this height and seemed to originate from an altogether untraceable direction. It was the last hundred metres, in a manner of speaking, if one were to use an athletic expression. The conical upper-body that arose into the pinnacle of the mountain was in view and in about two hundred metres or so would be well within grasp. Zig-zagging strips and columns of levelled ground deceptively dragged on up the hypotenuse. We crawled up a near vertical portion of the southwestern face on all fours and forged ahead through a breeze of approximately fifteen knots to the east to arrive at an eroded shelf some twenty feet in breadth, where a sight that exceeded any of our wildest and most diabolical conceptions awaited us.

chapter seven

A shredded tent-spoke slanted twistedly above a mess of sleeping bags, gloves, monkey-caps, cardigans, and other tattered human belongings. A trail of caterpillar boots and gloves emerged from the dislodged zip entry, proceeding up the rocky stairway that lay fifteen odd metres ahead. At the culmination of the track laid out by the irregularly scattered footwear, stood a large cylindrical rucksack (such as one might witness on the backs of foreigners carrying months' worth of luggage) supported upright by a voluminous weight lodged firmly in its base. A three-legged stove rusted by a blotch of black earth that at one time must have been the remnants of a campfire. The three of us slowly spread out around the windy shelf, our jackets flapping violently at our sides. Shera's cap nearly flew off. The Professor bent down to rummage through the torn tent hold. Having unearthed a tin of sardines, he immediately rejoiced at our discovery, sifting through the ruins dusty with uncounted ages. Joining him in his quest for nourishment, I espied several photographs beneath a heap of antiquated maps, bindings and trail guides—the edges of the pictures poked out of a loosely enclosed geometry box. Smiling poses and processions presented their weary teeth: a party of four officials with a yellow government survey camera stand, the bugling lens from a vintage total station theodolite gazing blankly amidst the grins. The photographs were all in black and white and from the time worn stains of rot and fungus on all the hastily displaced objects, it was not entirely improbable that they might have been more than thirty-forty years of age. The sardines had disintegrated into an oozing mush, the top end of the decaying tin-can came off with a simple press unleashing a diseased odour. Our next best bet was a preserved jar of pickle, mostly turnip and cauliflower, with the odd stem of carrot and bamboo shoot faintly detectable. We swallowed it down in a splash, chunk by chunk, drinking some of the slimy containing fluid also in thirst for some replenishment. Next came a bottle of whiskey, Officer's Choice, from the strapped bottle-holder of one of the rucksacks. Nothing they contained apart from the personal properties, such as dried up toiletries and wallets, including the clothes, could give any indication of what might have transpired for them to abandon the campsite so deliriously, with half their essentials strewn about the place in careless disarray. Signs of a violent flight were evident in every article of vital importance that had been ruthlessly discarded, considering their indispensability at so trying a terrain and altitude. Rubber bands, flashlights, binds of rope, a mallet, sickle, shovel and pick-axe, hammers and bolts, tent-pins and nails, a screwdriver, reams of notes and triangular drawings in varying states of decomposition, exceeding in abstraction the most labyrinthine designs, deteriorating in stability as the lines grew reckless and quavered. I have been able to retain from memory only one somewhat singular image that impressed itself upon my fancy, that of a three-dimensional cubic opening to, what appeared to be, a pyramidal tomb of some sort.

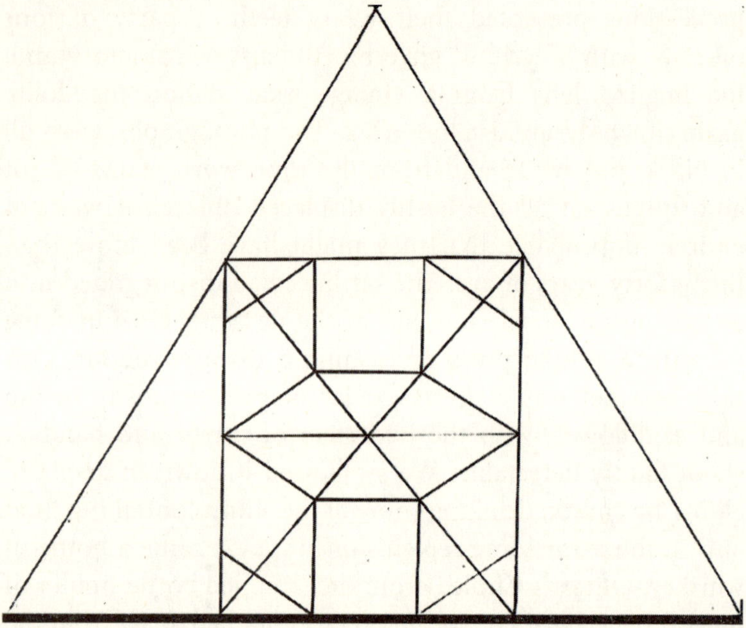

No bodies were to be found or recovered anywhere around the campsite. Displaced belongings hinted at neither paths taken nor direction of flight, they had about them an indeterminate aspect of the arbitrary or indiscriminate, as if it were all in jest—a breeze of madness or gaiety; some unearthly revel.

We proceeded on up the rocky stairway, all eyes still hazily attached to the mess of campsite that retreated from view as we shambled on through another hundred metres of hummock. Neither of us had had the courage to open the sole rucksack that stood upright away from the tent. What it contained was a matter only for the most heinous speculation that none dared approach; that whatever it was that bulged out of its synthetic flesh might have caused the catastrophe that claimed the entire team of campers.

chapter eight

At the summit of Ranibaug, that no human presence had ever laid claim on, sprawled a disconcerting stretch of arid terrain. Decaying and crumbling rocks covered every tract of walkable land, some piled and scattered together in baroque formation: there seemed to exist no trace of vegetable or plant life. Beyond a terrace-stepped ascension of blasted land, stood a forlorn temple at the peak, almost camouflaged in part by the rocky protrusions; looking down into the tumultuous drop, its slouching finials twisted like horns upon a Minotaur.

The temple was carved out of a convergence of earth and stone unlike anything either of us had ever encountered, not too dissimilar from the monstrous tree we had earlier witnessed. Even the vague relics furnishing the interior in puzzling ornamentation disobeyed the evidence of idol worship. There appeared no sounding bells or gongs or horns to ring the bugle cry across the valleys. A lone spear, unlike the prong of a trishul, closer in shape to the writhing of a claw, stood upright from the tip of its pointed roof, acting in part as antenna to the twilight. The indecipherable designs chiselled into the pillars of its arched-entrance were deeply unfamiliar. The altars seemed composed of a substance not identifiable to the mineral kind. No civilization could have conceived the hideous murals that adorned the temple walls. Seals, intricate and ornate, horrendously put together in an asymmetry composed of symbols and inscriptions bordering almost on the microscopic—possessing an ingenuity of workmanship that suggested evidence of disturbingly pre-Harappan origins. Deities and sculptures, all grotesque and leering in formation, exhibiting a malice that seemed borne of the seclusion of their dwelling.

Prof. Chaturvedi recollected tales told by the swaamis and soothsayers from his childhood of a civilization that predated even the earliest scriptures of all established religion. Customs created long before the dawn of mankind, relics that had witnessed the gradual establishment of the landmasses, and vistas inconceivable to ordinary human comprehension.

'All life sprang from the sea!' he declaimed, half to himself and half into the wind, scattering each word. 'Like a newborn babe that swims in the sanctity of its mother's womb before pouring forth into the open air. We were all amphibian once, and so we shall remain!'

Purporting to not have fully comprehended the thrust of his delivery, I beckoned—'Come again Professor? I CAN'T HEAR YOU!'

He was now floating in mid-air, partly levitated by the fury of the wind which sent him circling his steps in all directions till a dizzying whirl brought him to a fall.

'When the vast mountains were formed…' he continued, regaining himself unsteadily, '…from tectonic collision; the ocean—the collective womb for all of mother earth, was forced to expel her half-formed contents to live among the great heights, dispossessed and deformed.'

Shera tried reaching for him lest he should fall another time, this time injuring one of his limbs severely, thereby casting him debilitated for the remainder of the descent; a fiendish proposition! The Professor serenely shrugged off his grasp, proceeding on into the mouth of the tornado. The temple billowed with the mingling gusts hissing against the stone, and ricocheting back out from every possible opening. It was only partially roofed, that too with broken edges around the pillars, the rest of the surface area laid out in a courtyard formation. It resembled from one dimension the outward thrust of a lower jaw, and as the body of the enclosure swelled upward at an incline, if one blurred one's sight into double vision, I could have sworn it assumed the aspect of the skull we carried with us in a bundle of jacket and cloth.

Perhaps the skull we had found was a remnant of such a creature that had dwelled before the earth had evolved into the formations we now know. Hidden from the path of mankind and all that has been witnessed by eternities of speculation, travel and adventure, made for no human to see or touch, and no mind to ponder upon. Cut away from the world and all its inhabitants from the very outset of its existence.

Fragmented memories flashed before my eyes, of caverns and protrusions on the earth's surface, sheltering secrets too remote for calculation, vistas too divine for speculation, and the all-encompassing horror of the geological anomaly that was Ranibaug, that no man should ever know and no man had ever dared to know.

I was arrested by the spectacle of its isolation and refused to retreat from its rapture. The wind was steadily escalating and developing into an unmitigated storm. Disobeying Shera's warnings, I walked towards the temple, cutting through the ravenous wind and undoing my shoes—entered in.

chapter nine

Inside I saw things beyond the wildest description. Things no language could communicate or articulate, and things not perceivable to the normal spectrum of the five senses. Colours which transcended all known frequency, invisible to the naked eye. Sounds which dropped below the infra-sonic radar. Hideous distortions of the human form, satirically rendered as if in jest, etched and sculpted in calculated disarray. Animal and marine frescoes emblazoned in an overflowing anatomical extravagance for which mutation seemed too timid a term. Insects which squirmed in between crevices and joints of the stone slabs and time-worn masonry.

Prof. Chaturvedi and Shera still hesitated from entering. They gaped on at me from the entrance, eyes alight with diseased wonder. At length, I became aware of a low rumbling sound much like the roar of thunder that seemed to be shaking the very foundations of the temple. I attributed this to the crashing of the wind and at once felt the need to escape the sight of the temple for a short while, at least till I restored my bearings.

The peak was doing terrifying things to the mind. I

scampered through the storm, away from the pinnacle of Ranibaug and headed down the conical slope of the peak. The two dazed apparitions in the dust scarcely took note of me tumbling down the mountain side in flight of the remaining daylight to trek downwards to the spot below the rock face where we had dug our rations. As the altitude dropped, I felt the air pressure exit my ears. I ran past the decades old campsite, not wishing to pay its ruins anymore heed. A few more kilometres on, and somewhat recovered by the downhill stride, I felt certain I would make my way back up to Ranibaug at daybreak after having recovered the rations and also some strength. Although I had abandoned my two companions temporarily, one could permit that it was for hazard of losing consciousness that I executed that decision: it would scarcely do much good if all three of us were to faint due to weakness. One of us had to be awake and alert at all times; that was one of the deals we had made with each other when embarking on this hazardous expedition.

I managed to reach the rock face before the sun could set entirely. It took a good deal of vertical sliding and two hours' worth of trotting down the rocky descent, only to arrive to the undesirable discovery that the belay device required for rappelling down the mountain-side was not at hand. The carabiner though was attached to my belt, and the rope was still fastened around the tree. I tried to wrap my palms around the rope, pondering the friction involved if one were to use simply the grasp of its support while descending. Just then, I caught the faint rustle of someone trampling through the shrubbery.

Shera peeped out from amid a herd of bushes.

'What are you doing here?' I demanded, somewhat flustered at his sneaking up on me.

'I followed you down...' he spat, taking a seat daintily on his haunches.

'On what cause?'

'Ahh…' he looked around, crumpled his lips in and out his mouth, and whistled out a dissonant reply—'Safety…' he declared before nodding his head in evasion.

'Yours or mine?' I wondered.

'The Professor's,' he hopped up.

'Is the rifle with him?' I backed away, sensing his minutest movements.

'It's with him…' he took one step towards me, I backed off into the tree, and held its cartilage as a shield. I reminded him of our rations that lay buried beneath the rock face and asserted the vitality of their recovery if we were to make it anywhere near a reasonable campsite by midnight, when the owls would be out, and open space would envelop all—and then there was truly no accounting for anything. Shera said not one word in response.

'What's with the Professor?' I felt myself trembling into a quake, clutching tightly at the tree, its bark disintegrating on my fingernails.

'Nothing's wrong with him!' Shera softly insisted. 'He's just having one of his spells.'

'What spells?' I asked.

'Didn't you hear about what happened to him last week at the temple near Sahastradhara?'

'What about it?'

'Well, some say he was…' he searched in the air for a word. 'How shall one say…'

'Demented?' I grew still without even noticing it.

'In a manner of speaking,' he paused, somewhat deliberately. 'Or one could say that what was witnessed there was his true state, the actual self.'

'How do you mean?'

'Well you see,' he began, crouching down again on all

fours, this time holding onto a root submerged in the soil for support. 'By now, I've more or less come to know his ways as if they were my own. I know when he's sad, when he's happy, when he's hungry, when he's tired. You might not know it but, he had at one point entrusted me with all his confidences. He had only briefly spoken about his kin, when I once asked while dusting the framed-portraits of his uncles at the institute. I remember when he was ill, and I had nursed him through the ninety-eight-kilometre walk to Ronsara Taal. I remember the long hours spent by his sleeping bag. When he was infirm and in need of a helping hand. And I provided that *hand*, the hand that carried him through that torturous expedition.' Here he spread out his calloused palm and gazed at it in the rapidly diminishing daylight. 'And here I am, called upon to perform that task again.' The wind swooped over his shoulder as he stood. 'The hand that's listened to all his outbursts, and borne witness to all his lesser sides.'

'You see, Shera…' I spoke. 'If you intend to imply that we leave him here…'

'I didn't mean anything of the kind…'

'Then?'

'Only that he himself might not desire to return from where he is just now.'

'And just where is he?'

'At peace.'

Peace. The word itself reverberated like a sounding bell, alien to everything within likelihood. I started for the rope, incapable of listening any more to his suppositions. He intervened shortly to string up the rope, and inserted it through his belay device. After rappelling half-way down the rock face and adjusting the wire's firmness, he waved at me to follow suit. Once we were down we swiftly unhooked our carabiners, disconnected our respective harnesses, left the rope hanging from the tree, and proceeded hurriedly to locate the spot at which our belongings were buried. It was surrounded by a tulsi tree of medium height and adorned with bichhoobooti on all corners to act as guardian. As I began determinedly to unearth the ground, from beneath my fingers I could sense something scuttling under the soil. For a moment, my grasp recoiled from the earth. I looked to Shera, who looked back at me perplexed as if he had heard nothing. I scanned the entire area from my haunches—my neck peering around—but came across nothing immediately. Even the faint sound had vanished before I could get any deeper into the ground. Whatever it was, it had chewed open both the rucksacks and gotten into the food supply. As we salvaged whatever we could, cheering ourselves up with the possibility of the culprit being a rodent and nothing else, we soon became aware of a faint breeze falling our way. It grew when announced upon our quivering jackets and in a matter of seconds, blew into a gust before we had even settled our belongings from the mud. We both clutched firmly at the rations as it swept over us, preventing them from being blown away, and once it passed and the air subsided, we both simultaneously loosened our embrace over the belongings. I slung on my rucksack, and handed him the tent-kit once he had buckled on his. I fastened the lower belt strap of my rucksack to my harness, clipped open my carabiner and as I turned around towards the rock face to climb back up, saw that the rope was missing.

chapter ten

It had vanished from around the circumference of the tree trunk, the rock which stood by its side bore no trace of it. Presuming it had slithered off into the recesses of the vegetation, we searched all along the descending ditch joining hands with the drop, from the edge of the plane we were on: saw it nowhere amid the endless plant life, vainly sought to climb up the cliff with the use of our bare hands and feet (a proposition nearly unthinkable by this point) and were ultimately arrested by what we had all this while failed to take notice of: the tree had grown to another quarter of its height in the intervening day-and-a-half since the burial of our goods.

It stood out against the shrinking foliage like a freak of nature, its lulling boughs stretching forth, and stroking sparsely the bearded ground in the definite shape and grasp of a tentacle. The tubular base of the trunk had grown broader in diameter and was approaching the breadth of an enormous well. An irregular posture distorted its mid-section to an inordinate degree. Branches crawled out its flesh in the manner of a Gorgon, extending in length and crookedness, the writhing nature of its aspect. Shera too thought it looked larger than when he had last seen it; he was equally baffled at such significant growth in so short a span of time. He could not take his eyes off the grotesque structure, almost hypnotised by its outré dimensions that struck one as perfectly natural from a distance when blending in with the primeval backdrop, but on closer scrutiny acquired a pronounced change of air.

'You see this plant?' Shera looked up at it with a sense of longing. 'The only living remnant of the vast botanical potential of this soil….'

'It probably stood the test of time.' I suggested.

'Our ancestors cultivated this soil…leaving all kinds of survivors. Pine, chestnut, cedar, elm, poplar, birch, but this plant is the only living symbol of those days.'

'What days?' I requested to know.

'The days of old…the time before the human encroachment on a land that did not belong to the humans.'

We walked on a little further in solemnity.

'You can almost smell the degeneration,' he sighed. 'The degeneration of a landscape that was once fertile and prosperous. Now it's almost like a desert with worn out shrubs having taken the place of those glorious banyans. The temperate evergreen forests,' he let out a snort in defiance. 'The only thing that's evergreen about it is the environment minister's wallet.'

I bowed my head in acknowledgement of his offering with barely detectable movement, yet it communicated my alignment with his sentiments. The leaves and branches had grown disproportionate to the trunk communicating only entanglement through their intricate architecture, escalating into knots the sinuous branches formed, crossing each other in all directions, irregularly.

'The old ladies in the village would tell the young ones stories of how when the Ramayana was written, there used be oaks that blossomed on the tallest peaks, amid glacial desolation. Giant ferns taller than any seen at the Forest Research Institute (FRI). Temperate deciduous forests, green like the meadows of heaven. Coniferous castles and beautiful tropical palms that spread out like dinosaurs over this blessed land.'

The tree was too compact in its form, there was not a trace of fragility, hence it could not have possibly rotted away as per my initial suppositions to account for its peculiar shape. Carbon dating seemed impossible considering the complex web-like circular formations around the torso that probably converged at the vascular cambium. It had neither the girth nor the bearing of the contemporary gymnosperm, its malleable manner dismissed any notion of decay, yet its vivid composition appeared nothing less than a century old as the rusted bolt to a metallic grating of some ancient rampart. I thought it at first to be a pine of some considerably archaic origin, but its development and extraordinary outgrowth seemed to resemble botanical modifications dating back to the Paleogene or late Cretaceous Period, some sixty to seventy million years ago.

The two of us just glared at its gigantic stature and its oblique expression. Its characteristics were a subject of the most startling bewilderment and fascination, even from afar and especially from below the height of the rock-face into which it blended. The daylight had by now begun entirely to deceive us, and just as we sensed, through the spilling rock fragments, the motions of Prof. Chaturvedi kicking his way down the hillside, from a near unnoticeable corner of the ledge, I saw a blurry figure emerge from the hazy outline of the grass.

'What are you doing down there?' Prof. Chaturvedi called out to us from above the rock face, sight soon escaping him but evidently rejuvenated. In a matter of minutes, it would be all dark, and neither of us able to reach each other.

'DO YOU SEE THE ROPE OUT THERE, PROFESSOR?' I called out vigorously to him without sparing a moment—my hands cusped around my mouth so as to produce a dramatic enough noise to hopefully scare away whatever had cornered our companion from behind. A figure was now barely detectable.

'The what?' he cried out, puzzled.

'The rope! THE ROPE!' I stressed.

He turned his head around and tilted a gaze about his immediate vicinity. 'I can't see it!' he called.

'DO YOU HAVE A SPARE IN YOUR BELT POUCH?' Shera frantically inquired.

The Professor began to fumble at his belt pouch in defiance, dislodging all its contents onto the ground. As he stooped to collect them, he noticed in resolute detail, the varicose veined roots of the tree steeping out of the earth. Upon witnessing the length of the trunk, he began to utter a few incomprehensible words on the diversification of plant species, and then bent down on all fours to inspect it. He studied it from the roots upward, all the way to its minutest tendrils. He circled the periphery numerous times, scratching his forehead and widening his eyes with his forefinger and thumb. He took out a pencil to chew on and after much thought and deliberation, made an incision on the epidermis, carving out a rectangular dissection to get a glance into the fibrous cortex which lay beneath. It was greenish in colour according to him, but not comprised of ordinary plant tissue. He emptied a specimen into one of his containers, promising to study it under a microscope.

He cut out a few of its leaves and rubbed them on his hand so as to decipher the inherent material qualities. It left a blackish resin and then solidified from its liquid form into a dusty particulate. He then chipped off a piece of the bark and studied the residue that it secreted.

'I've never seen any form of wood or planet matter quite like it,' he remarked in a strained sentence, speculating as to the potential properties that it contained. 'The movements within the plant body,' he announced, 'could either be attributed to a multicellular outgrowth of abnormal proportions or they could even be its very own unique method of respiration adapted in these conditions.

'You think it needs the *cold*?' I asked, loud enough only for himself to hear at that height.

'Climactic conditions do not appear to be a matter of much concern for this organism. It seems to survive solely on some trace elements.'

Shera mentioned to me that while digging the pit for us to place the bags, he had stumbled upon some peculiar rock fragments some two-and-a-half feet beneath the ground's surface. He paid it no heed at the time, having even half-considered that they had metallic properties or could be the key to an alloy of some sort.

Prof. Chaturvedi's interest in this oddity, however, was not entirely scientific. It seemed to have a semi-hypnotic effect on him and he could not resist indulging all his attention, going over every inch of it with microscopic precision. He practically lay down on the cold earth and began to inspect the intricate arteries of roots that penetrated the upper layer of the soil, that had first brought this spectacle to his view, trying to trace their descent into the nethermost realms of the rock. He then stood up gradually, chewing the corner of his lower-lip, and adjusted his torch beam through the encroaching darkness to investigate the possibilities of there being some sort of deformity, or mutation in the pith or inner bark, as a result of partial or direct contact with radioactivity. The touch of its wrinkles, and the caress of its stooping branches seemed to have a somewhat disconcerting effect on his manner. He had now gone over every formation that scattered itself along the bark, every contour that inched towards a curve, every pore that saved a faint breath, and every pigment that ignited its appearance in the daylight.

'WE CAN'T SEE YOU PROFESSOR!' Shera hollered up the hillside in a clanging echo that now flitted about the somewhat quieter scenery. The chirp of the night insects had not commenced, and as the tinkle of the canister dropping from his hands sounded on the mud, Shera immediately backed away from the rock-face and shot his torch up at the tree. Through the diminished beam that nearly faded as it touched the edge of the cliff, we saw only the glass container roll down the hillside and drop soundlessly amidst our feet. When we looked up again, he was gone…

chapter eleven

We slept that night to a vague throttle of deep uncertainty. Having laid out our sleeping bags in the open air right below the cliff, one of us would stay awake with a torch in the attempt of issuing a bonfire from what twigs and grass were at our disposal. It was an arduous task. We took turns at it, with Shera's attempts approaching a spark, but neither of us prospered at shielding the flame of the match from the wind despite the surplus of kerosene. We consumed two tins of baked beans between us, crushed into fine particles a packet of raw Maggi noodles and shook in its masala powder to further crush and shake the whole concoction into edibility. Shera unsealed a carton of Parle-G biscuits, and began to dispose of them one by one, bit by measly bit—crumb at a time, without deigning to offer me a bite. It was a human test of wills—who could eat faster to exploit more thoroughly the opportunities presented at times of famine. Shera was liable to devour the entire stock of supplies, ravenous as he was from the climb and quick descent. The Professor was still nowhere to be seen or even heard from.

Our worries strode from panic to disarray, from disarray

to fury, from fury to delay (or as some would have termed, 'cowardice'), and from delay stemmed the urge to escape. What strange creature lurked up there in the darkness of the cliff side? Was it the tree itself that had swallowed him up, or the skulking ascetic who had aimed to partake of his company that night?

None could be sure of what compelled him to disappear. And even in the morning when we awoke from a deficient passage of dreadful sleep, and the sunrise illuminated the entirety of the ledge, still nowhere could he be found; the canister filled with plant matter in our possession, the final clue as to his whereabouts. We argued fiercely over what course of action to adopt. Whether to abandon Prof. Chaturvedi, under whose auspices we had initiated this journey, or rig a makeshift apparatus out of every available inch of cloth and garment in our bags and on our backs, to enable an easy passage up the cliff and proceed back on to Ranibaug to search for our friend and companion, thereby putting both our lives irrevocably back at risk.

I emptied the canister of plant matter into the palm of my hand once the tirades ceased. Shera shot up to examine it in what I took to be an involuntary act of truce. It was snot-green and liquefied sporadically upon direct contact with the sun till it reached a consistency much like that of a moisturizing ointment. It began to lather when rubbed beyond a certain measure. Upon the application of water, it crystallised into a sponge-like formation, when incinerated over the blue flame of a stove it dissipated into phantasms of odourless vapours, trailing off a fume of colourless residue.

And once after announcing its departure, when it ceased to remain visible, it would condense back from the vaporous form on contact with the wind, scarcely more perceptible than the dew which forms over thickly lain grass, yet a powdery remain was noticeable on the utensil upon which it was placed, which certainly would not be utilised in the future preparations of food of any kind fit for consumption. The plant matter had in it, beyond a perceivable measure, a touch of the inorganic, a sense approaching the breakage of thermocol in violent contrast with the compact nature of plastic. It had its own self-sustaining mechanism, and the reaction to sunlight was startling. It seemed to absorb from the composition of the atmosphere either carbon dioxide or nitrogen, given the paucity of the most vital ingredient at this altitude—then synthesised into an altogether unlikely state of matter, a glue or gelatinous form of cellulose which was expanding at an advanced pace, altering form and density, sometimes even volume. There seemed to be a sole supporting life force behind the handful of plant matter the Professor had extracted, for it took less from the atmosphere than it gave. I simulated with all the illusion of my eye, a magnifying glass—to decipher its complex cellular structure. I guessed it was constituted of an altogether untraceable compound, multiplying cells at an accelerated rate, when under the glass scrutiny of my eye it began to evaporate systematically into the air almost to the point of absence. When we turned the fire back on, the near-invisible structure on the utensil grew slowly into a size that still scarcely perceptible to the naked eye, proceeded this time to spread about on the steel plate beneath which it was heated in writhing patterns. The beams of the overhead sun were causing some sort of activity within its cells, enhancing its minute sprawl upon the plate into a bubbling swoon. Shera's eyes enlarged from their sockets as he beheld this. He twisted his neck to and fro as if in search of the Professor.

Vapours now seemed secretly to escape it, growing into a plume as we turned off the gas. Creeping towards the corners of the plate where it was entrapped, it attempted to climb the piping circular walls of the utensil, then flowing sightlessly into its base, proceeded thoroughly to dismantle its attachment. It burned through the steel base of the utensil like an acid but with a sinuous motion more like mercury. The entire bowl cracked apart right in half, and it slithered off into the scattered perforations circling the stove. I immediately turned the stove around to empty it out onto a bald patch of dry earth. It trickled out through the minute holes after rattling around inside the gas chamber, and fell collectively to the ground where I gathered the green slimy substance with both hands to empty into the canister.

Shera began now agitatedly to prepare a rope from the various garments, socks and handkerchiefs from the gathered rucksacks, including those belonging to the Professor, sowing them up together with his Swiss knife; tying, tearing and stitching bits of trouser end to the sleeve of a sweat-shirt. Invariably having accomplished approximately around eight metres of solid, steady rope, it became apparent from the drop of the rock face, that the length required to send it twice around the tree would essentially encompass thrice the amount we had envisioned. Shera now proceeded to disrobe himself without as much as a second thought, imploring me to do the same.

After an hour-and-a-half worth of tying together a stretch of forty-foot rope clad in nothing more than our undergarments, we dragged it over to the hillside. It was heavy and would not be lassoed without any difficulty. The first haul was mine, unsuccessful as it proved to be. Then came Shera's throw—a tad more effective but equally incompetent. We both with joint strength tried tossing the rope across the tree, holding it from either end and catapulting it in the air in the manner of a skipping rope, but it would not reach anywhere near even the edge of the cliff. It just would not traverse such a height. Shera now reached for the first rock protruding harmlessly from the hillside, and lifted himself off the ground in clambering pursuit of a further foothold. Carving out a step with his Swiss knife after having attained one, he was able to—with wavering support—reach up another five feet. There was a sunken portion of the rock face with a margin hewn horizontally below which he stepped upon, one hand holding his end of the make-shift wire. Tucking it between his waist, he made for another crevice in the rock surmounting the sunken outline. He lifted himself up from the initial foothold with its support and stepped into the sunken margin, his barefoot suctioned at its curve. A lesser foot like mine would not have been able to grasp what was then attempted.

Having heaved himself above the sunken portion of the plateau, and finding over it a more sympathetic contour, which he was effortlessly able to crawl over, he found himself touching one of the protruding roots of the tree that stuck out from a fissure in the rocks. At once he began chipping away at the loose formation of earth and rock, the rope all this while knotted around his waist. His right foot slid from its grip momentarily when he attempted to apply some force, arousing in me a palpitation in quick response. He was by now at a height of some fifteen feet above the ground, and a fall of any kind would yield in the minimum a broken ankle.

'Plough gently into it!' I instructed him with a restrained voice.

He did so like a terrier dog uncovering a spot with his bare nails. Once he got through to the root, and tried tugging at it with his arms buried in the rock fragments and dust, his legs left their rigorously sought out holds—they were airborne for an instant; he appeared suspended solely from the root of the tree. Displacing most of the loose earth around his shoulders, he managed an excavation right through the surface of the bluff and swum his way practically right into the rock-face.

That was the last I saw of him up there…

chapter twelve

The rope still hung out of the rock-face, pouring into a sort of anthill-like opening in the contours, such as a rodent might dig. I tried pulling at the rope with all my force, but succeeded in stifling nothing more than a few loose rock fragments jutting out of the cliff side that I might have used as footholds.

I waited. Waited day and night alone for the tree to grow to such a height that its vines would stoop down low enough for me to reach. I went through all our provisions, the last speck of MTR, the last drop of water I could salvage from an adjacent trickle of a stream, the last ounce of kerosene and the last electron on my endlessly bitten batteries to illuminate the coming nights. I began to burn some of the clothes, ruthlessly dismembered—sleeve by sleeve—from the mesh of rope we had attempted to build. The only covering I granted myself was the Professor's shawl which I wrapped around my person, scrabbling about like a primordial ape, not knowing what to do with myself and of time—time; that eternal whirl of wickedness. Imprisoned is some cosmic penitentiary, I strove through the endless days, the torturous nights when all was still, and not a tremor trifled with the sky.

The tree grew as promised, its trunk was by now immensely swollen, its broadened base rose into patterns of concentric circular ring-like formations dispersing in a dense network of outgrowths and hairs that had sprung out of the bark. The cadaverous, and altogether writhing nature of the foliage by now certainly resembled that of the tentacle, and gave the structure of the tree from a distance, the appearance of a gargoyle, but upon a further scrutiny it assumed the proportions of a geological formation: an outcrop from the earth's surface, or a fossilisation of a plant-like form. I bowed down in front of the great tree. Its enormous and expansive stance could provide shelter to a great many around, yet no one wanted its shelter, no one wanted the comfort and shade that it provided. It was almost as though every living being was aware of its deceptive rapture. Every living being but *myself.* I was its sole disciple, and like a deranged follower I bent down on my knees and worshipped the monstrosity…

And in so doing, henceforth devised my own set of customs and practices to keep the Tree appeased.

I first thanked the tree for my good fortune, that whatever danger lurked in the mysteries of this Plant life-form had not reared its ugly head on me. From here on end, till my deliverance or the retrieval of my long-gone companions, every living, breathing moment was devoted to the tree. It seemed only rational that nothing could go wrong so long as the Tree stood above me. Nothing could go wrong! I defied anything to go wrong, anything to happen, a bolt of lightning to strike me dead. But nothing happened. No thunder, no divine intervention, no response from the Almighty. All I was left with was the sight of the Tree towering over me. No living creature would go anywhere near it, and even more surprisingly no insects inhabited it, not even the passing rodent to whom it had once been a home. It dwelled in its solitude like some morose steeple concealing a divine malevolence waiting to emerge. Some answer lay beneath those leaves and in those boughs and deep down inside those roots, sinking into the unconquerable subterranean abyss. An answer to all that plagued me at the given moment; the fate of my companions, and the unknowable forces to whom I would forever remain enslaved.

chapter thirteen

'And God said let the earth bring forth grass, the herb yielding seed and the fruit tree yielding fruit, whose seed is in itself upon the earth.'

It was perhaps the seventh day when God had rested that he took note of my predicament and envisioned to alter it. I was perhaps sprawled out upon the half-shredded sleeping tent I had joined together out of the defunct stove—wrapping it with what was left of the tent's skin—when I took notice at once from perhaps a mile away, of what I later came to know as the rustle of the bushes, and the barefooted stomp of the same sadhu we had encountered at our earlier campsite. He caught sight of me in that haggard condition, half-naked, hair distraught, face blotched with itches, body ravaged by the night insects—and exhibited gloweringly in his harrowed countenance, a trace of kinship. He offered me a dried gourd filled with water of which I joyously partook. After regaining my ability to speak if not my senses, I ventured into utterance of a word, but not a syllable would come out. So long had I spent in the company of the wilderness, that I had forgotten the motions of speech.

I gesticulated wildly in the direction of the tree atop the cliff side which he shortly beheld. I then unearthed the skull from the recesses of the only available rucksack. I showed it to him forcefully, pointing at the tree and now with a vigour evidently renewed, formed words and also sentences, that invariably ended up as questions, none of which he had any particular inclination to answer. I then asked if he had seen my friends. He simply shook his head and answered again incomprehensibly in some remote strain of what could have only been Garhwali. I glimpsed what communication in the stone age must have been like. I attempted by pantomime to render my predicament, even etched certain formations on the face of the plateau with the aid of a chipped stone; a temple and such designs as would be the fruit of so unstable a hand. I clutched hold of the half-swallowed mesh, and drew at it with all my strength, tried vainly to climb it even; poured out the plant matter from the canister into the open daylight and saw the formations it materialised into. None of this could inspire the old man into uttering a coherent word. He sat cross-legged as before and drooped his head in that same posture of abeyance, that not even a falling landslide could stifle.

At length, I began to see that he was meditating, and muttering to himself certain stolen phrases and mantras beneath his breath. He observed my ritual salutations of the tree with a guarded sneer. When I stooped before it, he let out a gruff hiss of disapproval, and the customary kissing of the index finger to the forehead drew from him a vague breath—this he viewed with bleary eyes and an expression unformed, as something utterly alien.

He murmured into speech now, in a clearly comprehensible 'Hindi' disguised all this while with a garble of guttural sounds, a Hindi that bordered on the chaste; the

Sanskritised—as one might find in the holy scriptures, or in the monotone sermon of a Pandit.

'Vaanar humaare purvaj! (Ape is the ancestor to man!)' he declaimed, in part-oratorical stance as he raised one hand up and pointed it into the sky at the steaming heavens above. 'But what is the ancestor to the tree or the mountains, or to the oceans that swell?'

'I believe that God created the earth!' I said, shuddering slowly up to him to sit crouched beside his box. 'And I find it strange, a holy man in your bead and garb, following such a line of reasoning.'

'Ah reason!' he blew the word into the wind. 'Then you do not believe that we descended from our simian friends?'

'No!' I replied.

'Then why do you sit thus?' he flattened his palm at me crouched upon my haunches.

'For lack of seat.'

'And do you not dress like a beast? With nothing but a cloth across your waist. And do you not eat as one, whatever you might gather from the forests? And would you not swing from those majestic branches if given the chance.' Here he finally acknowledged the tree in its full scale and sweep. 'And have you not played in the muck when a child?'

Here he left me speechless. I had been playing in the muck all my adult life as an engineer.

'Science has shown us that there are six stages to our development.' Gathering a weathered twig from the ground, he leaned forward to make a diagram on the mud. He drew six figures ascending in height and posture. 'Only two of which are outside of our comprehension! One that is the ninth stage.' He prodded at the last formless figure. 'And that only the morrow will tell! And the other the fifth!' he poked at the center of his order, a blank space left out in the assembly. 'The critical connection between us and our anthropoid forefathers. Till today there is no sure answer to this question, and nor can there be! All fossils that could have demonstrated this transition have been wiped out. There are even some who hold strange opinions on this matter. Some believe that another intelligent civilization conquered the earth and was responsible for the progress in our own intelligence.'

His gaze fell involuntarily upon the skull—the misshapen lobe and protuberant chin. Pointing at its temple, he concluded—'Since the dawn of mankind to this present day, all kinds of changes have occurred in our environment which for better or worse determine, and try to influence the form of the human being. Like the development of our apposable thumb, or like our five fingers that were once in the shape of a paw, or our backs which straightened up with the passage of time, or our noses which were once as hideous as those of the reptile kind, or our eyes which once couldn't see up to our current 180-degree line of sight. Even our hair that once drowned our entire body. Our maker created us in the image of a beast, and yet we persist that we are human.'

'And what of the temple?' I asked. 'In whose image was that built?'

He lowered his head in resignation and murmured—'In the image of the earth! Of its stone, and fire—its mineral form and its deep waters. Or...' he hesitated. '...what was glanced of it.'

'By whom?'

He did not answer. I asked him how he had ventured up the hillside without the aid of rope. He arose from the ground and wagged one finger at me numerous times before saying—'There is another way.' Here he carried me through the bypass of hidden shrubbery at the precipice of the mountain-side, farther down the thorny wood from which we had emerged, to the left and up a seven-foot wall of mudded rock. The leafless branches we cut-through lacerated my entire upper torso from the waist on up till the chin.

With the hill to our backs, we staggered inch by inch through a parapet narrower than a foot. My toes spilled over its edge, squirming from the precipitous drop I had contemplated—to plummet into the limitless abyss and fall into infinity freely. When in sight of firmer ground, and a steadier terrain we proceeded on upwards, in this instance, through a thicket of gangling, lanky conifers, emaciated beyond belief—soaring up to the end of the tree line, bereft of the slightest touch of green, the frailest flower, not even an acorn, approaching the state of petrification.

Once past the tree line, we crawled on all fours up a vast boulder which permitted in its breakage a passage up to the winding tract of flat land at its top. From here, now in the distance I could remotely see the much lower route we had employed in our tireless sojourn up to the point of pilgrimage. Had we kept up with the sadhu in our initial efforts, we might have been spared the terrors of privation we had collectively to endure. We might have even pitched camp at the undulating entry which rose like the steps of a terrace farm towards the full reach of the temple atop the peak of Ranibaug.

It was nearly sunset when we reached, and as we approached the inexplicable structure, out from its pillars bellowed what sounded like a Tibetan Long horn or an Alphorn in reverberating sets. Or the chant of a wailing elephant. It droned in breaths, as if emitting a primeval roar from the very bowels of the earth. Its basso-profundo whirring dropped beyond tolerable levels of vibration to the human spirit, and rattled the inner fibres as might the continuous thump from the bass of a large-speaker. The blaring honk when protracted went dissonant, persisting as it did beyond unendurable decibels. But a successive breath enlivened in force and range, its booming, sonorous call. The sound grew intolerable to my ears once we neared the entrance, there was no need for me to remove my footwear outside as my soles were now hardened with the stride of days. Bruised, and partly bleeding though they were, they failed to excite in me any cause for concern when faced with the direr diminishments at hand.

Inside the temple sat another elderly sadhu, who from the motionless greeting he received from my guide, led me to believe that he was undoubtedly acquainted with him. He was blowing from a large white shankh (shell-horn), the size of which baffled me no doubt as I had only known marine shells of any kind to be no larger than two handfuls. The full scope and breadth of this artefact however would be futile to describe, let it suffice to say that it was perhaps the length of a sofa, teethed with sharp serrations that ran along the curve of its opening. Instead of being blessed with the tear-drop delicacy of its type, it ballooned into a shape unrecognisable to the oceanographer; its upper mouth opening as if in a malign smile, pressed to the lips of the bearded ascetic.

He ceased when fully grasping my presence, so lost was he in his meditations, and taking offence to the interruption of his ceremonies, courteously asked me to take a seat by that altar whose nature it would be inaccurate to describe as anything even remotely divine.

'The language of the seas!' he illustrated, gesturing at the indecipherable engraving scrawled in stone. Whether it was a figure, a symbol or an alphabet I could not rightly tell. It had the likeness of colour, but the leering outlines and graphic charcoal inscriptions clothed in shadow bespoke even vaguer contents hidden away in its multitude of designs. Closer to the eye, the crawling formless things deconstructed into even more minute patterns that from a distance were clouded to the sight.

'The deep sea!' he carried on. 'God hath said that "The deepest trench shall one day touch the sky and in its wake leave unformed things out in the dry land." This he hath said many years ago, many, many…' he pointed his arm up. The other sadhu who sat glumly by the entrance nodded his head in admission. 'It was before the birth of mankind…' the wise elder continued. 'When he hath just created the earth and envisioned in its prospects, endless harmony. But the birth of man! One of the grave outgrowths of his plan, in which he had no hand, endangered the fragility of his more spectacular designs; the mountains and trees, the rivers that flow, the deserts and dimensions of his imagination made fruit! We simply arose from those membranous mistakes he left shrivelled upon the shores. In his fancy he moved continents, fashioned volcanoes and fire! Brewed whirling maelstroms, incited explosions in the sky. Shook the earth itself and all he had created from its very foundations to quell its restless unease with the mystery of existence. Was no different from the shaking charlatanry of the village madman or tantric that dances in alleged exorcism of some mortal's woes. And when God grasped the full severity of his blunder, he called upon from another sky, some unearthly things to alter into shape what nature could not fashion into form. So, it is written.' And here again he sloped towards the tablet.

The other sadhu sat still as a stone statuette in deep meditation on the old one's citations. The two of them looked generally alike in habiliment and styling, only the older man had four streaks across the forehead, unlike the customary three, and wore his bundle of thick hair in a markedly distinct manner from the other. Where the younger (only relatively so) sadhu circled his hair atop his scalp and wound it into a ball as do the Sikh children, the older one had a three-tier structure sculpted from his somewhat mustier fibres into the snare of a cobra. His eyes were deep black, floating void-like planets from which illumination arose only when alarmed.

I ventured to ask about my friends, a Garhwali guide and a renowned Professor and mountaineer from Uttarkashi. His eyes grew mystifyingly large at their mention.

'You will note,' he spoke, 'their absence.'

'Indeed,' I replied in muttered reverence of his firm remark.

He arose from the frigid temple floor, and produced from among his heaped belongings that lay beneath a shawl, the Professor's .303 bolt-action rifle.

'You will know also,' he said, 'a man from Uttarkashi. Not the one to whom this weapon belongs, but indeed his master…'

'The Professor?'

'Ah…' he lowered the barrel of the rifle. 'But who prophesises to the Professor? Who teaches the taught, who themselves in their own vocation cannot help but teach? I refer to a scoundrel. The one at whose urging you came here.'

'If you mean the company I work for?' This I spilled accidentally under his laser eye examination of me.

'I mean a holy man to whose commands you leap, set foot into the unknown wilderness, risk death or worse still, privation.'

'Do you refer to Swaami Shree Shree Gurudev Atal-Anivaarya Natija?'

'I refer to a man I know from Haridwar who ascended in swift degrees from Baniya to Brahmin and who now masquerades as a soothsayer, an astrologer, a pandit! Him conducting a pooja would be a blasphemy! He earns good money from the townsfolk telling them tall tales of a mountain. He claims to have climbed Mount Kailash! Oh, the imbecile!' Here he lapsed into soliloquy. 'But it is uncertain whether there is indeed one man behind these sustained efforts to preserve a collective belief in the irrational. One could say that Swaami Shree Shree…' he pronounced his name in a mock-reverential tone. 'Gurudev Atal-Anivaarya Natija is a collection of individuals.'

'How can one say?' here I interrupted his flow of thought.

'Did you ever cast eyes on him?'

'No,' I said. 'But our other companion Shera, the Garhwali, did have a word with him.'

'Did *you* ever see him with your own two eyes?'

'No…' I answered again after thinking about it a good deal.

'Then could it not be that your friend the Professor deceived you, without your knowing it, to accompany him up here, fooling you with the talk of swaamis, embroidering garlands for the photo-frames of some imaginary godhead to whose whims he marched?'

That was precisely what he had done to Shera.

'WHERE IS HE?' I squealed.

'At peace,' he replied.

He arose from the floor of the temple, and held me gently by the arm, guiding me out through its narrow portals, his very presence having warded off the sensations that had last plagued me when I was inside its confines. He gallantly showed me around the mountaintop, clutching the arid earth that spread out around us, picking up rocks from their designated arrangements, their cryptic ornamentation not too dissimilar from that of a miniature Megalith.

As we passed the temple, the mounds of rocky debris grew more pronounced and compact—some even shone with a lustre reminiscent of quartz or agate—bypassing the function of a shrine to arrive at the reverential pageantry of a tomb. They could even have been coffins of a sort, comprised of curious gemstones, and precious minerals. Just when I began to ponder the possibility of a rock extraction having taken place on this mountain, I was arrested at once by a sound so unfamiliar yet strangely recongnisable, that I could place it only as the shriek of a shehnai or the squawking of an entrapped bird.

PART THREE

Mount Doom

chapter one

Beyond the temple, at the far edge of the peak, where a rigid strip of stone ground stretched out as a precipice into the open drop—a narrow rope ladder dangling at its cliff laid way to an opening on the other side of the mountain. One had to climb down many feet in order to attain the lower parapet that hid just beneath it. And at this platform, one could view a lurking illumination emanating from inside the rock formation. A thin passageway led towards this luminous chamber, and as the two wise men guided me into its recesses, I felt myself shuddering to fit into the unaccommodating alleyways to enter the eventual earthen duct we had to crawl through in order to achieve a small, ankle-deep water body on the other end, which provided a broader walkway. The routes through this grotto kept winding into a serpentine network of tunnels and passages, that never ceased even as we began a descent down what unmistakably in the shallow light felt like steps chiselled out of a swoop in the cave complex that led to another water body where beings were gathered—half-clad, long-haired, and shaggy bearded statues of men forming a semi-circle around a small lake some forty feet in diameter. Prof. Charan Prakash Chaturvedi sat amongst them, occupying a position that certainly hinted at prominence, given he was placed in the centre of the circle of seated men, and the only one with his hands joined in prayer, undoubtedly conducting some ritual mass or ceremony. And to be seen lost in the assembly of ragged persons was Shera, covered in mud—the only figure along with the Professor whose locks did not emerge—entranced in some vague state hovering between obedience and ease. A series of oil fire lamps were placed at the various nooks and turns around the large cave.

Just as Prof. Chaturvedi, momentarily distracted from his service, noticed me enter with the two sadhus—he cast his eyes upon Shera, who, as if sensing some beam through closed eyes, leapt up from the seated arrangement and made his way up to us in an instant. He greeted me with much surprise, and informed me that the Professor would be with me shortly as he was in the middle of the ceremony he had come all this way to perform.

'What ceremony?' I whispered to Shera.

'Absolution,' he replied, pointing towards the Professor, who now stood up from his cross-legged position, and slowly stepped into the lake. He waded in past a few feet of shallow water until a sudden drop in the depth caused him to disappear just a few steps into the lake.

He arose in a few minutes from his dip, wreathed in what looked like seaweed, and covered from head to toe with a sort of moss or green algae. The oldest member of the gathering, a tall sage draped in white hair and beard, stumblingly made his way into the water and received the Professor with outstretched arms in a sort of communion, having successfully administered his baptism. He cloaked the Professor's shuddering upper torso in a sheep-skin shawl, and ignited a havan (homa) in front of the seated assembly, wherein he then offered the shawl. The wool set ablaze a plume of dense grey smoke which fumigated the entire enclosure of the cave. Breathing was significantly stifled, my immediate cough caught everyone's attention save the old man's. The entire ritual bespoke a Pantheistic order not known to contemporary man; there was something frightfully archaic about the proceedings.

The old sage then addressed the gathering, his arms risen high in the air, balancing solely on one foot and his eyes closed yet still seemingly susceptible to sight—'As you can see!' he proclaimed. 'I have summoned today men from three separate fields of study, namely—science…'—here he pointed at me, '…geography…'—this he attributed to Shera, '…and last but not least, theology.' This last term he reserved for the Professor; a characteristic of his with which I was no doubt unfamiliar. 'The most intuitive of all studies known to man,' he continued, 'upon whose shoulders all other doctrines must rest.'

'Then I take it,' I broke in, much to the silent dismay of the gathering, 'that you intend to represent the branch of psychology, given your apparent clairvoyance.'

'Oh no!' the old man asserted. 'Simply the law. At least in these parts. The field of the mind is not my department, at least as yet.'

'And what law do you speak of?'

'There are certain rules and regulations to this establishment!' he began.

'Establishment?' I scoffed.

'If your tongue is quicker than your ears, then maybe it would rest a while and listen…'

'I just can't see what *rules* there could possibly be that you yourself would willingly enforce up here!'

'It is not solely I!' his eyes loomed across the seated figures. 'We would not want to be provoked enough to enforce those rules.' Not a figure stirred from the ground, a silent menace enveloped all in their stillness. 'Rules are meant merely for observing, not necessarily always for obeying. Once they are instigated into effect, startled into action, then there's no turning back from the long arm of the enforcer. And especially if the jurisdiction that arm exercises does not have merely to entail proceedings within the limits of its operation. It exposes itself to all conduct inside or outside the realm of its approach, and hence endangers itself to entities it should have never come in contact with in the first place. And therein lies the anatomy of crime!' he pointed out with his right index finger only slightly bent. 'There's a place for it, hidden deep down far away in the jungle, lest any human eye take notice of it, or any ear be wary of its shrill cry.'

He placed his other foot down on the ground, and staggered forth a few steps in an indistinct direction. 'Which is why I concern myself with order.' He carried on towards the waterbody in some idle reverie. 'Does not tax the mind. Soothes it, this prospect of endless harmony. Law.' He spoke with the frivolous and guarded grace of the well-educated. There was the spell of old Allahabad in his pronunciation, in his whole idiom—even though shudh (pure) Hindi in adornment, it carried a distinct touch of the vernacular emphasis that could place him as belonging not to some nomadic wandering tribe of sadhus but as a man of the world arrived lately to such an ascetic station in life. 'My mind is at rest young man.' He raised his index finger high up in a pose of acute emphasis. 'Which is why I prefer to restrict my expertise to the apprehending and cleansing of ills as opposed to the diagnosing of them, which I take it has been your preoccupation of late with regard to your fellow companions.'

'Nothing could be further from the truth,' I said.

'Then why have you arrived here?' he questioned me.

'Because I was asked to accompany the Professor.'

'By whom?'

'By the man himself, and also his spiritual advisor.'

'You mean his soul?'

'I mean his astrologer, who gazes into the stars and foresees the future in the form of the irrational.'

'What if I were to inform you that the astrologer you speak of is sitting in our midst.'

Here I scrutinised the surroundings in search of what could have looked like Swaami Atal-Anivaarya Natija, a phantom image stirring in my mind incredible memories of tantrics and pandits. None of the long bearded derelicts fit the bill in even the remotest sense. They all appeared to have about them an air of ascetic displacement unbecoming of the more nominal pieties specific to those in the clergy—the perpendicular ponytail protruding from the back of a bald scalp, a string tied diagonally across the upper torso, a stern physiognomy and stubbornness of will alerting the more reckless faculties to the iron clasp of obedience. I conjured a consideration that perhaps they were indeed the remnants of that fateful expedition that had never been heard from since the year 1971, whose possessions we had witnessed not so long ago. They seemed past all material considerations and could well have slipped into a semi-conscious state of 'sanyasa'. What if the Professor himself had concocted the astrologer in deceit, and was himself who he claimed was his advisor?

The Professor had by now dried up from the glowing warmth of the hearth. He wiped the moist vegetation off his head and body and took a bow, settling back into his lotus posture without releasing a word. He barely acknowledged my presence, although I could assume that my predicament might have crossed his mind after my abrupt abandonment. Shera's eyes stayed stubbornly closed.

'Do you dwell in the realm of the irrational?' the old sage asked.

I could minutely sense myself reaching for my forehead and chest with my right forefinger to ward off the discomposure whose approach I could feel in the innermost corners of my consciousness. He could well have been asking this question of the cavernous formations and frescoes on the stone walls that wound on into a receding chamber that the eye could not penetrate. Wondering what lay ahead, I approached the lake with a trepidatious tip-toe, turning back to learn that my two guides into this labyrinthine network of caves and tunnels had entirely deserted me. The faint moan of the shankh could be heard from afar, stifled and considerably diminished by the many strata and layers of rock it crossed to reach my ears.

'The irrational?' I pondered, conducting my subtle exhortations in silent solemnity. He witnessed me kissing my finger and wagging it numerous times between my brow and mouth in prayer.

When I was a child I would pray for tranquility, good fortune to shun adversity of any kind: 'Please protect our whole family, everyone related to us and everyone close to us and please give us all a very long, peaceful and happy life.'

My early adolescence yielded certain irreconcilable desires; good marks in my exams, a place in the hockey team, the reciprocation of care from a person for whom I felt immense affection. Later, as I approached youth in all its indeterminate glory, I prayed for an admission in the

Indian Institute of Engineering (IIT), a lucrative placement and rewarding starting salary for all my labours behind the desk. Then as adulthood dawned I craved marriage, a child, the fellowship of my peers; contentment, such as one anticipates: serenity of being—peace of body and mind, of soul and spirit. The happiness of all mankind, the eradication of pain and suffering. 'How can one be happy?' I thought. 'When one's fellow human being is not.'

My desires turned to goals, my goals to effort, my effort to expectance, and my expectance dwindled in the ever-passing air of disappointment; the inevitable malaise set in, enchanting me by its unpredictability, fascinating me endlessly as to the nature of fate. Whether one's prayers controlled one's own destiny and that of others? I prayed even more furiously than ever before. I subscribed to no particular faith or religion, but instead appealed to a monolithic God—a grey bearded face in the sky and when he would not fulfil my wishes, aimed to appease him with my righteousness of heart. I made certain sacrifices in my day-to-day life. Abstained from pleasure of any kind in hope of inspiring in him a sympathy, practiced penance of every sort; set ablaze a new set of rituals and acts of obedience to his indomitable will. All until it reached a point of neurosis, of what kind I will *not* as yet specify.

'Logic is the only God I know of,' the old man declared. 'And to believe in the forces of the irrational is to amount to, in my books, nothing less than heresy.'

'Heresy?' I said out loud, surprising even myself. My thoughts had begun to swim into material pronouncements, and even as the memory of my ritualistic motions struck me, I could not be entirely certain that I had not uttered them out aloud for everyone in the space to hear and take imminent notice of. They all glared at me now from around the red-flame, including Shera.

'If one believes that one can make material what one desires with the aid of prayer, that is tantamount to a belief in telekinesis; witchcraft! That one can with the power of their mind alone and its innate concentration make manifest what it requests of this existence. Are you endowed with the super-natural gift? Are any of us?' he spread his palm around the gathering. 'Is our creator? Is he but a holy ghost that is able to mould objects and instances to his will.' The old man slumped beside the fire. 'If I were to pray.' He closed his eyes and joined his hands together as if in mockery of my actions. 'With all my might, that I could extinguish this fire. What that make it happen?'

'No,' I said. 'As that is not a worthy cause for prayer.'

'Ahh...' he smiled. 'But then what is? For an ant that might be its prime consideration. The shifting of a stone. The blowing out of a fire that enflamed its only home. It might pray day and night for a clearing of its way. Can it accomplish that by simply believing that it can? Or will it actually attempt in the physical way to make that happen?'

'Both, I suppose.'

'You prayed day and night for your desires, and worked relentlessly at them too I suppose.'

'Indeed.'

'And when you were granted what you wanted, to what and whom did you attribute that? To what you *did*, or to how you *prayed*?'

I had no immediate answer.

'Consider for a moment, the ratio of your disappointments to that of your fulfilments.'

'What about you?' I challenged his assertions. 'What ails you?'

He took a deep pause before answering in a hushed cry of uncertainty—'Death!'

'Death?' I asked.

'Merely the thought of death.'

'Merely the thought or the actual act of death?'

'You mean murder?'

'I mean a decease,' I corrected him. 'By natural means. About as natural as circumstances here would permit.'

'I have invited the three of you here,' he announced. 'To witness my death.'

At this revelation I was noticeably alarmed.

'As per my findings, the day of my deliverance is at hand. I am to die at exactly the hour past sundown.'

chapter two

From out of the shadows of the inner-most recesses of the cave—that concealed the chamber that lay ahead and beyond a deceptively uncertain dead-end—there emerged a geriatric lady whose age could have been no less than a hundred years; her nose hooked, her back bent-double, her wobbly legs crooked and bow-legged beyond repair, yet her eyes alert to even the minutest motions within the enclosure. Everyone stood up at her entry.

As I later came to know, she was the renowned mountaineer Karma Bodh from Haridwar that had led the expedition up to Ranibaug almost fifty years ago. She had singlehandedly manned a reconnaissance attempt to the Everest Basecamp in the fall of '52, in a premature rescue operation for the famed British Expedition. It was said that a lover of hers at the time was on the team and so enflamed was she by the prospect of his loss, that she ventured out on her own in what was deemed by some of the Sherpas at the time, a fit of unholy *madness*.

She wore her hair in a frail white head-scarf and still sported the by now faded red wind-cheater she had probably worn on that fateful voyage of '71.

'Welcome!' she said. 'To the abode of the queen.'

She removed from her jacket pocket, what unmistakably looked like a coalminer's head-torch from the sparse illumination I was granted; at least that was the most fitting association I could sum up. The flame on the hearth had ceased, and the chorus of bearded men were back at their enchantments. As I came to hold what she handed me, I recognised them to be a pair of suction-cupped, broad-eyed scuba diving goggles, more akin to a snorkeling mask that encompassed even the nose. I tried them on, the strap was loose from the ages and presumably from frequent use.

She now asked me to step in the water. I hesitated expectedly, as the temperature—even inside the cave—was not by any means conducive to a swim, even the lightest immersion. Yet, that mortal pang of discovery compelled me further in, each unknowing step recoiling once at a time, *in*, into the grey-green haze of malign water.

Once I entered in, all thought and apparent awareness ceased, deep into the darkling dust that muddied all visibility. The water was not quite as cold as one might have expected. It was merely murky with slime and the green twistings of waving underwater vegetation clawing at the pebbled ground I soon touched to feel sure I was at a standing height of no more than five-and-a-half feet. I gradually waded completely in past the drop at the mud fall, that perhaps could account for the Professor's abrupt submergence. My feet were floating through a ground far removed from their grasp. The entwining weeds and tendrils writhed in distressing patterns promising a pathway into murkier recesses…

chapter three

What formed the spectacle of my underwater voyage will be reserved for a chapter devoted entirely to those purposes. At the time being, the mere flicker of their memory invokes in me a motor instability that might render the pages that follow unintelligible. Once reasonably gathered, I shall endeavour to share my stimuli with the keen reader, although caution is advised when approaching its pages, for the nature of the material there sighted could be liable to inspire a certain unsteadiness of sensation.

Once emerged from the water, in my noticeably unnerved state, I was guided down the further windings of the cave complex by the old lady as if to remedy my distress, only to find that buried into the mountain whose habitation at present we employed, lay a deep mine, the extraction of which could not have been possibly accomplished without the sort of machinery near incapable of being transported up to a height of five thousand feet. Beyond the passageway she had earlier emerged from, crowded with stalactite of every height and shape, I found myself atop the elevated shelf of a vertical mine-shaft from which I could faintly behold down below, a glowing orb etched circularly into the deepest burrows of the mountain; unreachable save for the dead that attempted its dismal plummet. I at once realised why it might be that these people, whoever they were, had summoned Prof. Charan Prakash Chaturvedi.

The expeditioners might certainly have been adept at such matters as concern mountaineering, but rock-climbing and rappelling down a potentially life threatening cavity in the mountain that yawned an infinitude of bottomless descent was an altogether rarified proposition.

And then, just as expected—Professor Charan Prakash Chaturvedi presented himself into this decrepit mine-shaft from the warmth of the hearth. He was alone. Waist bound with the rope, he began to lower himself into the limitless pit…

'PROFESSOR!' I screamed out to him.

Halting his manoeuvers down the edge of the cliff, he waved out to me cheerily, and widened a grin from behind a pair of the darkest sunglasses I had ever seen.

'I'll be sure and wire you my report. Give word to Pratyusha!' With that, he hooked on a helmet of some sort to climb further down the mine-face and just as he did so and proceeded but a few feet on—out sprang a hideous cry from the very depths of the subterranean hole: a swooning torrent of unearthly voices, a magnetic vortex sucking everything into the ringing orbit of its glowing shrine.

It is only now in consideration of the doom which awaited the Professor and which caused him never to return from his sojourn down the limitless pit, that I can summon the sensations which occurred in my brief but unshakeable swim.

chapter four

It had often been my practice over the course of my job to prospect the possibilities in every murky expanse of water I happened to encounter; to dream up projects that would probe the immutable mystery of the great waterways of our nation.

No waterbody was unfit for exploration, at least in an imaginative capacity; I could not help but picture the very depths of the most desolate patch of still water, the most sordid tributaries, the most turbulent dams, the most lifeless lake and infernal swamp—the mutant sea, and the river too diseased to even touch. Nothing, however, not even the most grotesque fancies could prepare me for what I was to here witness, not in the sanctity of the imagination but in the certainty of the flesh.

Swaying reeds twisted and writhed into the opaque depths, hurling me into an underwater vista where a mire of slime decomposed before my very eyes to relieve what lay beneath it. There stood some thirty or forty feet beneath the water, a coralline formation of petroglyphs enshrined into a wide oblong slab some sixty feet in length and breadth, lodged firmly at the basin of the water body. It emitted a sound not unlike the one I had encountered at the temple. A rumbling, whirring churning of the water that bespoke maelstroms incomprehensible to any but outer space astronauts, defying all terrestrial phenomena, and abandoning the simplest resemblance to anything hitherto discovered underwater. I was reminded at once of the Yonaguni monument off the coast of Japan that persists to baffle both oceanographers and archaeologists alike.

Just as I attempted to touch it, there emerged from its crevices and caverns a seemingly innocuous marine creature, yet once I was granted some proximity to it—the wholly uncanny nature of its aspect baffled and somewhat startled my fascination. It appeared neither amphibian nor reptilian, closer to the shape of a prehistoric bird, a sort of aquatic pterodactyl that shrieked at my ambling underwater form and flapped its tail violently in my direction. Its eyes surpassed every conception of hideousness, its sinuous wings writhed into myriad claws, each with nails and limbs outstretched from its webbed symmetry. The head and beak were so elongated in their appointments as to resemble nearly the mythic intent of an ancient Greek mask. The skull was round and humanoid, almost in the shape of that of the ostrich. There was yet in its morbidly startled eyes, and beckoning open-mouthed desperation, a sort of pathetic quality that belied any superior intelligence. It nearly caused me to faint in mortal terror at its appearance, and had I indeed done so, I hesitate to mention that this document might never have existed.

chapter five

What may have seemed a mirage, or merely some abject hallucination wrought by deprivation now acquired an air of the undisputable, of the inarguable even, the tangible and concretely measurable. I wished at that very moment that I had at my disposal an instrument by which I may have recorded in the pictorial form the images that swept by my every sensation. If I were an artist, I might have drawn what I glimpsed but briefly. Were I photographer of some skill and technique, I may have captured fragments of the unthinkable sights that acquired a firm foothold in my memory, dispelling any skepticism as to the uniqueness of this godforsaken mountain and its inconceivable insides.

Transfixed by the all-encompassing glow of the depths of the mineshaft, I proceed to inform Ms Karma Bodh of what I had seen, of the sounds that I had heard, of the imagery the inhabitation of that temple had incited. And when expressing some fears as to the plight of the departed Professor, was plainly reprimanded for my concerns.

'Worry not about him!' she proclaimed with a graceful swish of the hands. 'The intelligence that dwells down there will see to his accommodation.'

'Intelligence?' I stumbled.

'As to its nature,' she stipulated, 'I cannot as yet tell you what it is.' She shook somewhat agitatedly. 'But then perhaps you have already had occasion to encounter one of its spawns.'

'You mean to tell me,' I quivered, glancing down into the glowing pit with only my peripheral vision. 'That whatever it is that's down there has a settlement of some sort? An accommodation? As you called it?'

'Not exactly.' She gathered her limbs together. 'You see, in our terms it would translate to something closer to an installation, not merely a settlement.'

'I see…' I murmured, retreating my gaze from the lure of its light. 'And what I glimpsed down there?' I pointed at the water body behind the dim, shabby entrance from which we had emerged. 'In the lake?'

'That's not a lake, my boy…' her eyelids crinkled into a faint smile. 'For God's sake, that's not even drinking water you swam in.'

'Th-then?' I stuttered.

'Containing fluid for a vessel. Didn't you meet it?'

'Meet it?'

Her craggy features grew deadly still as if a heavy thundercloud has passed it. Her jowls now started trembling, her emaciated arms again began to jitter—she caught hold of my hand and began to guide me back down the precipitous walkway of the mine-shaft we had earlier climbed with such confidence as might be mistaken for idiocy.

At the stalactite-ridden entranceway to this shelf, she halted a moment, caught some of her breath and began to look back above the deep crater that still shone, by now a burning amber colour hue which drew shadows from the features of the descending walls.

'We will hear from him soon…' she nodded to herself.

'How can you be so sure?' I turned my neck back and forth to emphasise an act of banishment that was unveiling before our very eyes. 'Have any of you managed to go down there all this while?' I asked.

She fidgeted at her belt-pouch, then removed a rolled cordage of nylon dynamic rope from the inside pocket of her windcheater to elaborate on a rusty belay device fastened around her waist. 'I've tried,' she whispered. 'God knows I've tried. We had an instance of one of our brethren,' she rattled out while pointing about, almost in the manner of a geriatric tour guide, 'who attempted to bungee jump. With the use of this very kind of elastic roping.'

'Did he make it?'

'If he did, we'll find out. Same goes for the Professor.'

'Is that why you had us come up here?' I asked, before she could turn upon her heels to exit the mineshaft. 'To act as guinea pigs?'

'You came up here of your own accord.' She turned, ever so gently—the veins that bulged out of her wrists and forearms stolidly tightening up.

'Come to think of it, why did you have me go down there into the water to see what I saw?' I thought.

'It is a sort of initiation rite,' she replied. 'Merely a custom.'

'For what? What is this, some sort of cult?'

The word no doubt frightened her.

'The Sarmoung brotherhood? The Central Asian Mystic Society, Theosophical Taoist and Tantric Buddhist Studies, a Masonic order that knows the secret of some remote civilization? One of those demonic tribes in communion with the other world.'

'Your nonsense becomes you,' she said. 'It is to be

expected of one who has spent his livelihood blasting open mountains.'

'How do you know that?' I shrunk from her in an instant.

She hesitated to form an adequate answer, only her right arm trembled in reply.

'Who is that old man out there?' I demanded, looking out of the entranceway. 'And why is he going to die?'

'We have known all about you,' she clenched her jaw. 'The Professor, Shera, Swaami Shree Shree Gurudev Atal-Anivaarya Natija, the firm for which you work, Ms Pratyusha Negi and the Institute. Everything.' She spat out a tooth.

'How so?' I beckoned.

'The waters,' she breathed faintly. 'That containing fluid.' She began to chew on her gums. 'You heard the sound?'

'Of what?'

'Of the horn.'

The sight of that swollen shell being by played by the saadhu wandered out of my recent memory.

'A kind of aural morse code,' she stated. 'Can be heard by the precious few. Through the minutest vibrations only the truly sensitized can grasp. We had been in communication with the Professor from Uttarkashi, you see. Had been able to relay certain commands through Swaami Gurudev.'

'I thought the old man outside said that he doesn't exist?'

'Oh, he exists alright…' she smiled. 'He is well and in good health. Occupies a fine house in Haridwar, an ancestral property near the Rajaji National Park. He knew of this peak. Had even attempted to climb it once many years ago, but failed…miserably. Even has a malfunctioning knee to show for it. Which is why he had you make the toil.'

'Nonsense…' I protested. 'He had asked the Professor to mark a rock at the summit where a temple was to be built.'

'And who would build the temple?'

'An engineer?' Just then it dawned on me.

'But as you can see young man, the temple has already been built,' she murmured.

'In the name of the queen goddess…'

'And who do you think is that queen goddess?'

Her entire rumpled visage began to now approach the countenance of the Tree. Her caterpillar creases and stony wrinkles assumed the aspect of a divine personage touched with a sort of unerring command over all things living and dead.

'Hah…' her mouth flew open in a burst of cackles. 'Not me, I can assure you!' Her wrinkles formed concentric semicircular smiles all along her cheekbones. 'I may be old, but I'm not that old…' her neck dropped into a slouch. 'Not as old as all this.' Only her eyeballs lifted to encircle this intestinal alleyway into the bowels of the mountain.

Castles of stalactite abounded in terrifying repetition, miniature dominions of microscopic activity, endless turrets and irregular apertures dotting the conical tips of their terraces. Just then it occurred to me that some of the grey cadaverous shapes and protrusions camouflaged in its contours and bends were not unlike the curled-up wings that might cocoon a sleeping bat. I caught at second glance an infinity of such features on the stalactite hanging from the rocky ceiling of the mineshaft. And when the shrill cry departed from some of the sprawled-out wings, out swept from over us a swarm of the same hideous creatures I had met at the trench of the water-body. They swooped into the pit and vanished in a matter of seconds, their dull ringing cry lingering after them only a moment.

'Did you know that a vulture was found at a height of some ten thousand metres once?' Karma Bodh informed me. 'Its wings were tattered because of the air pressure.'

'Wait a minute, that containing fluid you talk of…' It occurred to me. 'I get the distinct sense that it had in it, beyond a doubt, an unmistakable taste of the saline.'

Her eyes glowed. 'There you are right,' she said. 'I didn't expect you to be able to determine that unless you've been spending a lot of time offshore on petroleum drills.'

'How did you manage to get sea-water up at this height?' I looked up above me. Some of the winged gargoyles were gone.

'We didn't,' she said. 'They did.' She pointed deep down into the glowing mine. 'It came from the inside of the mountain. After all,' she spread her quavering palms about. 'This was all saline once. Did you know they found some marine fossils in one of the highest peaks of the Himalayas? You must be aware, of course.'

'Ma'am, this is getting beyond me…' I confessed. 'I am sorry to say I find most of what I have witnessed and heard here to be quite incredible and certainly outside the scope of what anyone down there in the real world would believe.'

'So they choose to believe Swaami Atal-Anivaarya instead.'

'Not all of them…' I shook my head. 'Take Pratyusha Negi for instance. She refused outright to come along on this expedition, a decision I now wish I had myself only half-considered. On account of a worthy disavowal of any variety of superstitious faith. In short, she didn't think that climbing up a mountain to a perform a pilgrimage could cure anything that ailed her in the real world of day-to-day maintenance and functionality. I suppose it's only those that have the time to sit in stupor like the party outside that manage to approach God with their miserable woes, or at least approach what they think is God.'

'What do you think God *is*?' she now asked with a teasing sense of wonder.

'I don't know at present Ma'am,' I said. 'I only wish I knew what the contents of that cave outside thought on the subject. To them, God seems to be some sort of Shambhaala out here, up away from civilization, approaching a newer one…' I looked down into the wide drop.

'An older one,' she corrected me.

'Older?' I almost laughed. That was one sentiment with which I wouldn't argue, especially when coming from a person of her years.

We heard the wailings of death pass over the gathered company uninterrupted by any incense or instrument or even enchantment. It was a pure, human outpouring of sorrow. Miserable sobs and the most pitiful sounds escaped all outside in fitful bursts of manic cries, almost out to the heavens above.

'Ohh…' her mouth trembled vigorously on registering the extent of the tragedy. 'The hour of his deliverance,' she unearthed a steel-chained pocket-watch from within the folds of her jacket and squinted into its dial.

'Is that what it said on his janam-kundli?' I mocked the very notion that he could have intuited his own death by natural scientific means, stranded on this mountaintop.

'We believe in no such thing,' she dug her hands into the wind-cheater, stuffing the pocket-watch back inside its holdings. 'We believe only in *reality* out here!'

'Reality?' I laughed.

'What we can see and touch, and feel! And sense. As per which the vultures will be plucking out his eyeballs any minute now.'

'Vultures?' I nearly shrieked out in disgust. 'You call those monstrosities vultures? They're closer to bats!' I pointed up at the wilderness of nests scattered about in clusters on the ceiling of the mineshaft. 'Or birds of a certain sort. Probably prehistoric. Reptilian and amphibian all at once.'

Her eyes gloated in their sockets as the howling ceased, and the delirious flapping proceeded to awaken in her a long-stilled fury, pent up with the sands of uncounted ages.

'They come from down below,' she spoke after much thought and exhalation to soothe her subterranean rumblings. 'As do the insects.'

'Insects?'

'They put together the temple, brick-by-brick. You can't see them. But at night once they're out, you will be able to feel them! That I can assure you. You will feel them in your bones, in the joints and muscles, in the windpipe, in the eyes, ears and nose.'

I was at once set off onto a somewhat tangential search within the cobwebbed recesses of my memory bank, of an article published in the *Science Reporter*, by a Dr T. Balasubhramaniyam Aditya of Council of Scientific and Industrial Research (CSIR), who had only hinted in his thesis that the prospect of extra-terrestrial intervention in the micro-bacterial form was not as far-fetched as had been supposed by some learned scientists and astronomers within our ISRO Space Programme. That alien life could be no larger than a single-celled organism and no more detectable than amoebae was the thrust of his conclusion. Hence, the proposed space expulsion of bio-warfare waste was not a recommended alternative to the imminent termination of all on-ground radioactive experiments that were being carried out in furtherance of our chemical capabilities.

I envisioned the prospect of capturing one of those winged creatures and taking it down with me, captive, to show the townsfolk—even the skull, or a branch of the tree, or a chip off the underwater monument. It was all well beyond comprehension.

'Since when has this intelligence existed here?' I asked.

'Since the formation of this mountain. It lies deep down inside the very foundation of this structure, probably thrived on some intangible substance of life. No mining team or excavation machinery would have been able to reach it. It thrived and teemed under the earth's surface, and gradually, inch-by-inch made its way up towards the volcanic light.'

'Have you yourself beheld any of these life forms, what they look like?' I asked. 'Apart of course, from the birds and insects.'

'The ones we've beheld are merely their infants. The adults are down below and have sense enough not to try and make contact until they are sure of our intentions. We have tried to reach them using every chanting device and horn at our disposal up here.'

'You mean to tell me that this rubble quarry, this joke of a mine-shaft nests some kind of extra-terrestrial intelligence?'

'This knowledge is vouchsafed only to the few who have, over the years, had occasion to chance upon its precincts. Saadhus, tantrics, lost expeditioners, trail-guides, even some foreigners…'

'How would the knowledge of this have passed on to Shree Gurudev Atal-Anivaarya?'

'The same way the knowledge of you was passed on to us.'

'What you're talking about here is nothing short of telepathy, Ma'am.' I stumbled.

'Indeed,' she bowed her head.

'And who do you worship, may I ask? What Godhead, deity, totem? Don't tell me those monstrous engravings on the temple walls are any representative of your lord and master.'

'There is no idol worship, you see. No Lord and Master, no invisible force to which you supplicate your soul. Only existence...*life*—everlasting!' The sunken recesses under her eyes shivered, some substance of liquidity was noticeable within the retinas. 'No Death!' she mourned.

From the dawn of humanity, the founding and practice of esoteric faiths and occult beliefs that deviate from established religious order have always posed an irresoluble interlocking of interest. If left alone to propagate, they co-exist harmoniously, if stifled they retaliate, when viewed as something utterly alien or aberrant the harm of the evaluation is visited only upon the oppressor, in strictly psychological terms. He retreats into falsities, into superstition as a safety blanket, and lives in perpetual terror of what his belief system has prevented him from understanding. That the heathen spring birth but wisdom be a thought inconceivable, a shred of demoniacal imagery a thing of beauty, impossible! Any sensation that rattles the closely embraced shackles of divine thought, is a thing ultimately to be wary of. An object of apprehension. The subject of a wild array of supposition, conclusions that touch the darkest frontiers of human possibility. Evil, monstrous, satanic, blasphemous!

'There are many more of us here my boy, more than you could imagine. We have found a way to preserve life. The containing fluid. The old man who just recently died will be immersed shortly, given a new set of organs, eyes, teeth, lungs—re-animated. In human terms he is dead, but to retain consciousness beyond the gulf is to attain the divine, the everlasting. A second chance at life. Something the creatures down there must have survived on through all those centuries of confinement in the earth's core. One of our congregation seems to feel this might have been a comet which struck many eons ago, blasting all vegetable and mineral organic life, and building its own everlasting dominion. A new order, and a new faith. Some of this crept into various other religious doctrines over the years by means of those who had witnessed it, and been altered forever by its unknowable power. What we have up here is neither a religion nor a following, but merely an ancient laboratory. Some of the learned men outside are doctors and experts, surgeons even.'

'And pandits I imagine?'

'Oh no…' she shrugged. 'Swaami Atal-Anivaarya is merely an impostor. He is no more a pandit or jyothish than I am a Carmelite nun. He has sent you here as emissaries to gather firsthand knowledge of the peak and all it contains. Priests of other religious disciplines have tried to infiltrate us since the dawn of all doctrine. Before there was even the written word.'

'What does this order call itself?' I asked.

'There is no name,' she said, reproachfully. 'Merely a sensation that it arouses. One that forever alters and seeks to determine the true nature of reality. We have as you can see been working on it.' Here, she loosened the scarf around her head to reveal not a strand of hair set upon her scalp. She was completely bald. The bun which I assumed to take up the greater portion of the back of her head was simply an elongation of her skull.

I now beheld in full frightful vividness, the grafts and stitches which spread down the back of her spine, their numerous attempts to expand the lobes of the brain if it were possible. To rid humanity of God, faith and divine worship, so that only reason and logic may prevail. Our next link, the evolutionary leap, ahead of the missing link. Closer to the realm of artificial intelligence. Perhaps they had been conducting various operations on the human brain, enlarging the spatial composition in adjustment of more intricate valves and arteries that could master matter, just like the telephonic device or satellite or the microscopic wiring of nanotechnology, to enable telepathy, communication across galaxies. When the earth was at its infancy this dimension of progress had probably already been attained by these beings. They might have watched over us in careful meditation at all our endeavours and attempts to plumb the human realm, and developed a mastery over normal forms of existence that would render all natural sciences obsolete.

At this contradiction, I recoiled from the mine-shaft and headed hurriedly back into the cave complex where I had expected to witness the gathered ceremony. It was empty. Shera was nowhere to be found, as was the Professor who had disappeared wholly from comprehension, both physical and spiritual. With some recollection of the route that permitted my easy egress from this forbidden chamber, I was able to trace my path back to the top of Ranibaug, where again I was to be graced with the sight of not a single living being. Even the sounding call of the horn was gone. This time, however, I noticed above the arched entranceway to the temple—the skull of a chiltan markhor, its long and sinuous horns stretching up three-and-a-half feet into the air, as though Pan himself had aimed to partake of these festivities.

At length, Ms Karma Bodh came tottering down from the strip of mountain that jutted out into the horizon, and settled down on one of the steps to the temple.

'Where have they all gone?' I gasped, striding all about in rabid disarray.

'Underwater,' she closed her eyes. 'They are at present, right below where we are seated. In the vicinity of the temple.'

'How do you communicate using the containing fluid?' I asked.

'You see...' she began. 'All this predates even paganism. The worship of truth, of reality, of thought and reason. It was what caused us to ascend from our primordial forefathers in the first place. The capability for abstract thought.'

'Even artificial thought?'

'I know not what you mean.'

'You see, Ms Bodh, I also imagined that if any other planet's visitants did indeed voyage down here, they certainly would not be organic examples of their civilization. Owing to the sheer length of the travel, they would have to be beings which could last one, maybe two or three human lifespans.'

'Come again?'

'They would not be natural beings, Ma'am!' I shouted.

'You mean they would be electronic?' she frowned.

'Precisely. Engineered, automated. In short, artificial intelligence. A life that could live out all those millions of years that you claim, or self-propagate, and perpetuate for eternities in an alien environment, such as the inside of a mountain—shielded by their own technologies. You claim they were infants but for all you know, those winged creatures could be nothing more than helicopters or a mosquito squadron with no consciousness beyond the tasks assigned to them, such as disposing of the dead and protecting their satellites both underwater and the under the ground. One of those creatures tried to attack me when I neared the vessel in that containing fluid.'

'Our friends and brothers are in that vessel right now,' she said. 'As we speak.'

'How so?'

'It is possible to breathe in there. I have been. The pressure is regulated by some electrical mechanism that seals it into a vacuum. And from an opening under its base, there lies another route, through countless caves and tunnels, down to the illuminating subterranean abyss that you beheld from the mineshaft. As per our estimations, the nerve centre of all that energy being emitted from down there lies some twenty thousand feet below. We have only very rudimentary meteorological and seismological equipment at our disposal up here, dating back to the early seventies. Same goes for the other mechanical appliances and surgical instruments. Professor Charan Prakash Chaturvedi's expertise on medicinal botany was counted as another asset by Swaami Shree Shree Gurudev to endear him into our confidences. Which is why, as you noticed, he was conducting the ritual that preceded the death.'

'But I thought you have attained mastery over death,' I said.

'What makes you think that I am not really…*dead*?' her cheeks creased apart. 'What makes you think these eyes are mine? These ears and entrails, and bones and flesh? What if all this while you had been speaking with a person who was no longer alive. Someone whose years betrayed not the slightest sign or indication of their true unfathomability. I myself know not how old I am, young man. In my day, you were lucky to be given a birthdate, let alone a birthday. Death up here though is merely a process the body goes through. Same with birth, and injury of any kind or worldly woe. The true communion is with the infinite.'

chapter six

The wreath-robed procession of haggard, long-haired men soon emerged from the edge of the cliffside. They marched on down from the summit to join us at the temple. By now, even the two sadhus had come out from the innards of the temple which seemed to nurse some sort of trapdoor that led to a nether chamber.

Shera hurried up to me, vaguely revived from whatever form of hypnosis he was under.

'What the hell is going on!' I shook him vigorously by the shoulders. 'Did you see what happened to the Professor?'

'W-what happened to him?' he mumbled.

'He went down into the mountain. He's gone.' I tried with all my might to arouse his alarm, or even his concern.

He batted his hand in the air in reply, and turned his shoulder aside, clearing it from my grasp. 'The Professor has gone down to do what he came here to do,' he grimaced.

'And what is that, may I ask?'

'I told you, didn't I? Absolution. He's cleansing his sins.'

'Nonsense!' I screamed. The gathered company paid me

no more than a passing shrug. 'What are you talking about Shera? You're sounding crazier than that old lady…'

'Don't say anything about Ms Bodh!' he warned me.

'So you know her from before?'

'I've only heard of her. She's a legend in some circles.'

'Why did the Professor bring the both of us up here with him, Shera? To accomplish what? Was this all some sort of an elaborate hoax? All these fire-worshippers,' I scorned our surroundings. 'And deformed carnivorous birds, that peculiar water body and mine-shaft stolen deep away in some remote corner of the interior of Ranibaug. This demoniacal temple. WHAT is the meaning of this, Shera? This is not what I signed up for.'

'You didn't sign up for anything,' he corrected me. 'This isn't some voluntary mission or construction job you've undertaken. You have no contractual obligation. You can leave here anytime you like…'

'What's the matter with you now, Shera!' I glared at him in reproof. 'You're sounding just like them.'

'We've come to find something here. And we're doing everything we can to reach there.'

'Even if it means conquering death?' An illusion I still found difficult to fathom. 'And feigning telepathy with a simple background check. Accusing me of witchcraft, of heresy, of telekinesis.'

'You saw the Professor that day at the temple before Sahastradhara, didn't you?'

'I did. But what does that have anything to do with this?'

'It was a full moon night; he was having one of his spells…'

'You are sounding increasingly like a crackpot now, Shera!'

'Hysteria! What doctors cannot diagnose and sermons

cannot cure. It is a terminal condition. And the Professor is at present engaged in doing whatever he can to restore his mental faculties.'

'In some underground laboratory or hospital?'

His lips broadened into a faint laugh. 'It isn't like that! It takes months, years sometimes to be redistributed into the environment. Take for instance that tree we encountered on our way up. What makes you think that tree wasn't endowed with human capabilities?'

'Plenty! Common sense for one.'

'When I disappeared into its recesses, where did you think I wound up?'

'In an underground ant colony I suppose?'

'With the Professor. Inside its tunnels, in the vacuum of a fossil. The intricate network of roots led us through a thick liquid to finally emerge about five hundred metres west of here.' Here he pointed down in the direction of the terrace-stepped landscape that sloped below us. 'If you ask me, this whole thing perplexes me just as much as it scares you. I'm not afraid of anything, even death…all I want to know is what lies down there…' He touched the earth before the temple. 'What breathes and foams below this sacred ground. What malign force will emerge from its bowels?'

'What did you see in the underwater vessel down there?' I asked him in a flash.

'Nothing,' he answered in swift certainty. 'At least not anything worth remembering…' his eyes stayed on the ground, attached by means—as if—of some magnetic force. 'I don't know,' he quaked. 'We went to deposit the body.'

'Look,' I guided him to a corner of one of the pillars, away from the others who were by now congregating around the entrance. 'Why didn't either of you tell me anything about this? What was the purpose of bringing me along to witness this ceremony?'

'The Professor thought that it might do you some good…' he admitted. 'But as we approached closer, he changed his mind, and actually asked me to do you in with the rifle.'

'Preposterous! You wouldn't expect me to believe that!'

'I can swear on it!' he clipped his fingertips around the skin of his Adam's apple. 'He thought death would do you better than what you were to behold at Ranibaug. He was convinced that he'd made a grave mistake! You see, Ranibaug is said to have a strange effect on the psyche. In other words, the higher one climbs the more one tends lose what in ordinary terms is thought of as their sanity. That's all there was to it. He thought he'd rather see you dead than an insane person. I had to convince him otherwise. Handed the rifle over to the Baba.' He swung one of his elbows in the direction of the entrance where one of the two wise men was posing fitfully by the stone steps, nodding at everyone's entrance. 'They maintain law and order out here. There's more you know,' he assured me. 'Legions of men and women and children, and goats, and dogs, and khachars.'

'You mean to tell me you actually *knew* that aghori Baba that chanced upon our campsite that night?'

'I knew his superior. The one who plays the horn. Met him at Hrishikesh. One drunken night he told me all about this place. I took an oath that I would never tell a soul until I myself made the effort to climb it and see for myself what was up there.' He now pretended for a moment as if we were back in Uttarkashi, taking in the night's McDowell's at a rooftop restaurant in some seedy hotel. 'You can go if you like.' He then proceeded to say. 'But as for me, I'm staying up here. I have renounced all those bright shiny lights that glitter at us in dark solitude on the mountain tops, as if sneering and ridiculing our distance from them. I am one with the mountains.' His eyes closed, and his fingertips touched his thumbs raising them into a wavelike haphazard motion that only grew more indistinct as his sight abstained from taking anything in view. 'One with the trees, one with the waters, one with the worms and the caterpillar and the dragonfly!'

chapter seven

Often enough, there comes a time when the very fibre of one's psyche is put to demands so anomalous and outside the bounds of common experience, that the very nature of reality is itself a matter of some contestation. At such instances, mankind is wont to retreat from such a spiral and appeal to some higher power, where beliefs are hatched pertaining to the outcome consequent of each mortal action. That the black cat crossing the road could pose a threat is no more valid an inference than an elephant dropping from the sky—yet the thought, a brief glimpse of doom, however momentary, occurs, and with it follow a million suspicions and indecisions, yielded by nothing but a timid association implanted in the reception of reality.

It would be safe to say that both the Professor and Shera were as fixed in their intentions as might be the village grandma who pauses in her chores to defer to the marching echo of a funeral procession.

I spent the night at Ranibaug, blanketed by a sheepskin shawl, in one of the burrows beneath the temple, sleeping beside Shera in one of a row of countless cubicles hewn out of the rock and mud—hovering between consciousness and a psychogenic fugue state. No insects outside of the ordinary made their appearance as yet. In the morning, there was an assembly at sunrise at the altar of the temple where an ever-larger contingent of mountainfolk had grouped outside the entrance, and wore woolly garments and leathery apparel, furs of a certain sort, patches of mule-haired mufflers, even the odd nylon wind-cheater was to be sighted here and there amongst the shabbily clad children. The women were cloaked with layers of shawl, some of the men even donned oval mountain caps, closer in fashion to those worn along the North-West Frontier Province than to the famous Manali topi, or the multi-coloured Garhwali flat-top. I remember reading of the pagans of Kafiristan (present-day Nuristan), a land untouched by Islam till the turn of the previous century. Or of certain regions in upper Himachal Pradesh that were said to be populated by faiths other than Hinduism and Buddhism until just recently. The people could not be placed geographically, they were merged as one sole-throbbing spirit that breathed and whispered among themselves of their new visitors—the shy laughter and gaiety reminiscent of a small-town square in earnest anticipation of a long-awaited arrival. No chorus was to be sung, nor any lamps or dias lighted. They had merely come to peep in and stare with the same sense of wonder that had dawned on our acquaintance with Ranibaug. They spoke a similar tongue to the one I heard the first sadhu utter. Shera tried his hand at it, but failed in a sentence or two, provoking in them a gaggle of laughter in quick response. The children shrugged away from his embraces, hiding behind the legs of their parents. The two sadhus were now partially disrobed and conducting service with hums and murmurs which circled the partial enclosure. A drawing of the deceased old sage was engraved along one of the walls above the altar. Ms Karma Bodh stood alongside the other mourners, and clapped her hands every now and then to dispel any frivolity that might displace what was to be a solemn occasion. In a matter of moments, all men, women and children were seen to scatter as the murmurs grew into chants and the chants into a horn. The sound was too much for them to take. The shaggy long-haired regiment of Ms Karma Bodh's seemed the only occupants to be able to withstand it. A pallor clouded Shera's face, a bloodless dust-coloured complexion beset with exhaustion, exhilaration, and vacancy all in the same hue. His head started to rattle with the trembling motion of the vibrations. Once the rumblings became all-encompassing, and interrupted even the fixture of the slabs that held together the temple, from out of the deepest recesses of the Spartan bunkhouse down below, there crept a multitude of verminous insects, all in different shapes and sizes, some with two heads splitting and intermingling into the other, others with retractable tentacles, and bobbing antennae the size of a hand grenade. It seemed evident they were no doubt some obscure species of overgrown pest, yet their movements alarmed even the sadhus conducting the ceremony. They grew in numbers and exploded out of a mound in the burrow where they were teeming in terrifying profusion, and heading rapidly in all directions, sideways up the wall, diagonally, in straight lines, in circular patterns, in V formations like migrating birds. They trampled over all over our sleeping arrangement and in a matter of seconds quickly demolished all the carefully constructed cubicles.

Karma Bodh reached immediately for our rifle that lay hidden beneath a shawl near the altar. Before the insects could scuttle about entirely and besiege us, she pumped in the cartridge and blasted four holes into the temple floor with successive manual re-loadings, all her geriatric limbs rising steadfastly to the occasion. One of the crawling creatures was beheaded in an instant but persisted to writhe about on the botched floor. Another clump of tentacles splattered about the altar, unleashing a slimy liquid indistinguishable from the lather which had formed from the plant matter. A dispossessed claw flew across my forehead and landed smack on one of the displaced tiles, bleeding out a ribbon of the same ghastly fluid which foamed and burnt into the temple walls. It only became apparent to me now that perhaps the weathered marks and torn features of the temple were not the time-worn stains of age, but simply the results of similar disturbances in the seismic structure, and the many attempts there expended to exterminate what it unleashed.

The tentacles and tails, and gnats and beetles retreated into their caverns without a trace. Ms Bodh lay down the rifle in its allotted resting place and asked the long-bearded company to step outside while she had a word with the two new entrants.

chapter eight

'If and when you do choose to go back down to the so-called "real" world,' she began, 'the movement of your lips will be closely monitored! Each syllable, utterance and breath will reverberate to our communicative facilities.'

I looked at Shera dumbfounded, my mouth open with the sheer imbecility of that claim. He seemed to be convinced, and met her murmurs with hums, and nods at each of her assertions.

'There are those that can hear,' she went on, poking at her ears with eyes aghast, showing for the first time in her demeanour a trace of senility. What if she was now all of a sudden playing old for Shera's benefit, and had assumed within the blink of an eye, the mantle of wise old grandma from the almost robotically cunning mountain-climber I had heard speak at the mineshaft.

'They'll catch up with you,' I assured her. 'All of you…' this I now directed to Shera with my arms maniacally apart. 'There's no way you can prevent this from breaking loose down below. They have to know about this. They'll find you!'

'They already have,' she demurred. 'Or at least they've

tried. Swaami Shree Shree Gurudev Atal-Anivaarya is a part of that "they". And it is indeed *they* that have sent you here in the first place, so let's not get all high and mighty, my child. Don't get ahead of yourself. You are a part of that "they" you so proudly assign to lesser mortals. You're no better or worse than the lot of them!'

'I'll go straight to them when I descend this mountain. I'll inform my colleagues, my employers, the police! The army. I have contacts in the Cantonment in Dehra Dun!'

'If that is a threat my child…' she snorted. 'You will have to do better than that. You can send in the Air Force! That isn't going to get us to budge an inch. What we have unearthed here shall remain, and all those who wish to view it will have to make the effort to trek up here, and earn that right. That is the only thing that hasn't stopped me from blowing your brains out all over these temple walls like the rest of those insects!'

'So you do kill?' I asked. 'In this new order you propose to have devised!'

'It is not I, my child.' Now she looked towards the altar that crawled with an infinity of glowering designs, her eyes squirming and throbbing as they swam into its structures. Her hand stretched out as if to reach or touch—her lips prayed, her forehead bulged—'Not I!'

'Then WHO is it?' I shrieked.

'Have you ever believed in something for the sole sake that you would will it?' she trembled, nursing the hand that stretched now in her pockets.

'Indeed.' I nodded. 'Haven't all of us?'

'Then what is it?' she smiled. 'That thin line that separates wish from reality? Logic from magic?'

'Magic?' I laughed, looking at Shera who batted not an eyelid in reply.

'Why not magic?' she mused. 'Was it not magic that got us to the moon? The man that developed the rocket-fuel that propelled our man-made engines was a firm believer in the occult and to him the dream of mastery over matter was no more magical than it was to the physicist that split the atom or the simple radio wave that was able to traverse vast distances within the flick of a second. One man's magic is another age's science!'

chapter nine

My farewell to Shera was brief and almost half-salutatory; a matter wholly devoid of the usual sentiment that would no doubt be the fruit of so arduous a toil. To the old lady I bid only my good wishes, and hopes to see *her* again.

'You will!' her smile hardened. 'And you will certainly hear from me. If not from me than at least from *us*.'

'I will look forward to that.' I turned around, and thumped Shera on the shoulder. 'You take care of yourself, Shera!'

'I will,' he expressionlessly drawled.

When I started to make my way down, I heard scarcely a sound from the mountaintop—no horn or rumble or chthonic tremor that had earlier unsettled us. With the drop of altitude and air pressure, an equilibrium reinvigorated my, by now, corroded and somewhat diminished mental faculties. I was not permitted to take along with me any specimens that might corroborate some of my wilder claims. I paid nary a glance to the tattered campsite I crossed soon after, even the Tree from which I carried no particle. Somehow through sheer intuition, I managed to trace my steps back along the narrow parapet that bypassed the bluff. Thoughts danced frantically about my frontal lobe, meditations on the plight of the ship Mary Celeste that disappeared towards the turn of the century, the as yet unsolved tragedy of the Ural Mountains that this incident so closely resembled, the inexplicable natural blast in Russia that raised an entire forest to the ground within seconds. These were indeed thoughts to consider in light of all that I had experienced.

It took many days, countless nights of exhaustion to traverse the long and torturous descent that took me back to our basecamp in Osla. How I managed to accommodate that fiendish return to civilization through starvation and madness and more is a matter I cannot wholly explicate. All I know is that I was guided back as if by some divine unseen force. As if by the unsought blessings of those above me on the mountain-top seeing to my secure passage. I trekked through the night, a feat I would not have in my wildest dreams even remotely considered. Guided by the moonlight, I swept through countless branches, up under the thicket of some unfriendly ridge, clambering through the dirt and mud—part naked—feeding on berries and streams of snow, chewing leaves in an unworthy attempt at replenishment—wading past thorny foliage, slashing aimlessly at a wilderness of commingling plants and bewildering vegetation, somewhat like a shrub-covered expanse, a primeval wilderness… shrouded in green. An endless scenery of verdure resembling the very beginnings of the Earth, the first rumblings and flowerings of fauna. Here and there, could be seen a small lake but a few feet deep. This was certainly a route that had eluded us on our way up. I scarcely remembered it.

I had abandoned our finds, both the skull and the fibula, in order to lighten the load that would prove wearisome to my back, and also so as not to immediately disobey any instructions issued from the congregation at Ranibaug. What fiery embers their wrath would yield was a matter only my patience would determine. It was their goodwill that was getting me through this journey alive in the first place, and I chose not to test it. The bearded, long-haired and aged dream figures all retreated from my imagination and began to settle in the fog of some distant memory. Even the old lady with whom I had conducted a lengthy discourse appeared no vaguer or more mystical an entity than Swaami Atal-Anivaarya Natija himself. All that remained were the hazy outlines of their presence; scattered dominions of concrete sandcastles, mountains of archipelagos and naked stone, shapes and forms no letters could relate, and that only the drawing hand could confirm. I would attempt nevertheless to communicate to the breathing world, all I had witnessed without the aid of what chance items might consolidate their credibility. I felt no particular urge to produce physical evidence of what I had to report. I would rather not deal with such specimens for hazard of the mental influence exerted by their possession that I had sworn never to endure again.

It was, however, beyond all measure—a great mistake. For no human being in the state of Garhwal, Pratyusha Negi included, paid much heed to my assertions, consigning me to an endless state of official uncertainty and an inconsistent conviction that only the truly derelict would consider. My colleagues at the workplace fancied me mad, and mad I might just have been, were it not for the stark details I was able to recount in my wild and somewhat rambling soliloquy to the masters of my firm. They insisted on my taking a break from the site, relieved me of my imminent duties and provided for my safe but harrowing transportation back to my hometown, Mathura, where I was to be graced with the companionship of my loved ones that strived to enlighten me out of my morbid rhapsody. My name is Barkat Singh Randhawa. Yet, never did prosperity seem so remote from the blasted realm to which I had been a party.

I was visited many months later, by a small board of scientists from the Uttarakhand State Energy Division, an establishment that had already nailed in its placards all over North-Western Garhwal, and proposed a newer and more elaborate power scheme to electrify parts previously unconnected to the electric-mainline on the grid.

There were about four of them, three silent gentlemen and an older lady with a cloud of white-hair that arose over a pair of double-lensed spectacles.

'You do know Pratyusha, don't you?' she inquired, once they had concluded their introductions.

'Why yes Ma'am,' I murmured. 'I do!'

'Well, then,' she settled into her seat in the living room once I was done offering them tea and other refreshments. 'That would certainly make this conference easier.'

'How's that?' I took a seat.

'Well, I just so happen to be her mother,' she stated, calmly and without any expression whatsoever.

'Dr Damini Jain from IIT?' I nearly got up from my seat.

'I'm not with the IIT any longer as you can see.' She waved about at the assembled personnel. The rest of the men just lightly nodded their heads to affirm that. 'The state has assigned me to a sector not previously within the scope of my area of expertise.'

There was a long pause.

'Which is?' I asked.

'Energy!' she stated, gathering her reflections. 'It was merely on account of some recent developments in the state of Garhwal that I was granted this august post as Chairman of the board.'

'Such as?' I asked.

'Such as....' she thought a while, tapping her fingers on her knees. 'Such as Ranibaug.' She took a pause and then proceeded. 'You see, Mr Randhawa, on account of certain electro-magnetic long-wave radio transmissions detected around the peak, the State Energy Division has declared the routes disseminating up from Harki Dun towards the North-Western face of Ranibaug, as out of bounds...'

'Out of bounds?' I mumbled, slouching irreparably.

'That's right,' she failed to nod, or perhaps decided not to. 'Restricted area! From our reports,' here she leaned forward and placed her palms together upon the glass coffee table before her. 'There seems to be some sort of an,' she flounced her hands as if in explanation. 'Irregular power source...or force field, that appears to be lodged in the interior of the very mountain itself. At least that was our initial supposition. Recent seismological readings have determined that there is not only an indefinable power source, but also a sonic radiation that the peak seems to be emitting that has been said to have a somewhat, how shall one say...' she reached for a word, found only a sigh and produced a faint cluck in emphasis, '...*strange* effect on those that have neared it. The mountain has been sealed, and all pilgrimages to Osla suspended till further notice.'

'This...uh...strange effect that you talk of...' I stuttered. 'What reports have you received of this?'

'Well...' she looked around. 'At present only one, from a somewhat singular individual. An astrologer actually. Goes by the name of Atal-Anivaarya Natija, we traced him back to Haldwani under the name of Naveen S. Bhatija. He used to run a cassette store in the old days, one of those roadside market stalls stocked with an array of devotional hymns and bhajans. He proceeded to wrangle his way into Ayurveda, become at one point one of the pre-eminent Vaidhjis in Uttaranchal Pradesh. At first, starting a wandering caravan of botanical products and miracle solvents promising balding patrons their hair back, then once he made the acquaintance of Professor Charan Prakash he started their initiative, in earnest.'

'What initiative?'

'The HRA institute. He's a part-owner of that place. A sort of partner. It gives me ulcers to think that my daughter works under such a person, but I have tried to convince her otherwise. She doesn't listen!'

'She's wiser than you think, Ma'am,' I said. 'She refused outright to come along on our expedition. She's got better sense than I did, I regret to mention…'

At this revelation, she seemed no doubt satisfied. 'Hmm…' She folded her lips. 'Have you ever thought to wonder why?'

'I'm sure she has….'

'There are reasons behind discretion and honest to goodness common sense. Not always altogether what you might call honest reasons, but reasons nonetheless.'

'Suppose you tell me about them?'

The three strange looking men all eyed her from their corners.

'Suppose you tell me first about what you saw up there?' she suggested.

'I asked you first,' I insisted.

'Okay…' she leaned back, drew on a deep breath and said—'There was some talk of her paternal grandmother still being up there, which given the nature of physics, which has been for me something of a specialty, is nothing short of an outright impossibility. Not to mention, lie.'

'How so?'

'If she were indeed alive my dear child, she would be close to one-and-a-quarter centuries old, which—going by the aggregate rate of the human lifespan—is not an option into which anyone in their right mind would willingly enter, unless it was made possible by some altogether different means, some of which seem to be outside the capability of recorded human logic.'

PART FOUR

The Strange Case of the Uttarakhand Electric Division

chapter one

It took close to the better half of the day to explain to them all that I had encountered. They joined my family for lunch, stayed till tea, and departed almost before supper. I spoke to them of the tree, of the skull, of Karma Bodh and the party of sages, that tumultuous drop that glowed from the bottomless pits of the mineshaft. Of how the Professor had attempted to descend it, of how Shera had elected to stay on to see to the Professor's proper retrieval. Of how I had been forced to abandon not only my fellow expeditioners, but also what remote finds and relics we had chanced upon. The absence of the latter still seemed too far-fetched a prospect for them to fathom.

'Are you not sure?' one of the bespectacled men offered. 'That all this might not simply be the result of some sort of extraordinary hallucination, some mental affliction endemic to the uppermost reaches of the peak that forces people to realms of thought not normally considered noteworthy by the natural sciences.'

He stood up from his carefully angled seat, pondering each step before taking it, his feet hesitating from the tiles, looking only at the ground as he spoke and then at his fellow scientists as he reached for an empty cup to attach to its saucer.

'After all,' another one spoke. 'All supernatural phenomena tend to be manifestations of the unconscious mind. To make material what one wishes, or...in this case, fears.'

'Is that not what causes phantoms to be born?' the third one uttered. 'Ghosts to be unbolted, monsters to escape the imagination? Experience—psychological or otherwise.' He clapped his hands together in emphasis. 'Cold hard incident that warps and winds the perception into the nether layers of reality where demoniacal conjurings swim uninhibited by the many strata of rational thought that would shackle such anomalous sights and fancies.'

It felt as if some spiritual seminar were underway, as if the sage that died was talking from the flesh. The three of them glared at me in learned repose, ornate sentences escaping them involuntarily in the manner almost of a lecture. They looked to their superior with each turn of the mouth, as every insinuation that leapt from their tongue found solace in her stare. She continued to look at me, right through me, past me, at the house she was seated in, at the surroundings, the colony, the patterns of the cushion-covers and the colours on the carpet.

'Whatever it is that's up there,' Dr Damini Jain declared, 'will be investigated thoroughly. That you can rest assured, but...' She took a pause that was protracted even further by the anticipation in my eyeballs that now swelled beyond the bounds of a composed expression. '...it will prove beneficial to our programme, if you were to withhold any of your knowledge from the purview of the general public.' She stopped me before I could leap from my seat. 'There are, of course, terrestrial methods for coping with such phenomena!' she pointed out with an elongated index finger that receded from view no sooner than it had entered it. 'Without of course causing the kind of mass hysteria that would doubtless be the logical response to so drastic a revelation.'

'Have you for instance,' one of the men mused, 'visited a psychiatrist? There is a gentleman in the Cantonment. A Dr Prabhat S. Kukreja with the military AnG units, who treats officers fresh out of combat in J&K. I would recommend him! He is known to be of use when dealing with a post-traumatic predicament. He is known to be of assistance in such matters as concern the irrational.'

'Ladies and gentlemen!' I shot up from my seat. 'What I witnessed there and what I have recounted was as real as this tea cup.' I picked up an empty saucer from the table that separated us. 'As real as you or me, as real as the air we breathe.'

'Ahhh…' the same man parted his lips in speculation. 'But is the air we breathe visible to the naked eye?'

I now began to see in full fruition the fiendish design they had envisioned to silence my testimony. The industrial complex of state sanctioned 'truth', the honorable arbiters of *reality*!

'I have nothing to add to what I have already told you!' I stated calmly. 'Nothing of any substance that would count for much in your books. Now, if you have had your tea, you may please leave!' I rose from my seat and started to show them out.

'There's nothing to get excited about Mr Randhawa,' Dr Damini Jain interrupted. 'This is a simple matter of standard operating procedure. What we have been informed by our superiors to relay to you. There's no need to take it personally as any kind of stab at your sanity. We know you are a perfectly rational being, a healthy individual who is complete command of his mental facul…'

'GET OUT!' I shrieked. 'ALL OF YOU! And don't ever step into this house ever again! You are NOT welcome! That goes for you too, Ma'am,' I pointed at Dr Damini Jain. 'And your daughter too. She will tell you all there is to tell about the Professor. About how he schemed to get me to accompany him on his diabolical expedition. That pretense of demonic possession at the temple on the way to Sahastradhara. Hysteria! It was all an elaborate hoax to get me to stray from the path of the rational and the logical.'

'Ahhh….' Dr Damini Jain gasped. 'But as per our reports, you yourself are prone to certain irrational tendencies, aren't you? From what your employers conveyed to us, you seem to have your own innate idiosyncrasies about faith and are prone to what, some might call, compulsive superstitious scruples.'

'HOW DARE YOU!!!!' I screamed. 'I take this as an absolute insult! You prying on my personal records.' I suddenly sat back down and altered my tone of voice considerably so that it would have the desired effect. 'Now, please…' I whispered, purposefully—retracting the display of anger I had impulsively fallen prey to. 'You must leave at once lest my parents get upset.'

chapter two

I resolved at once to get to the absolute bottom of this insoluble mystery, to venture into the very heart of the abomination itself! A visit to the very source of all this menace had to be made. A sojourn into the lair of Swaami Shree Shree Gurudev Atal-Anivaarya Nateeja, located in the back quarters and side-banks of Haridwar where I found myself one summer evening only to be told by one of his attendants that the Swaami Ji had retreated to his resort on the outskirts of the Rajaji National Park for the weekend.

Gathering the address and approximate co-ordinates, I drove off the following morning to a wide stretch of protected forest along the eastern ridge on the fence of the National Park. To encroach any further into its precincts would not be permissible without a slip from the Forest Guard due to a recent development that had been reported to some of the forest authorities. Not the authorities native to the region I intended to visit, but the central forest office under whose radar the territory did fall. As per certain sightings witnessed by the patrolling forest officers deployed to keep the boundaries and perimeters in check, a certain animal (not of identifiable origin) was said to be active and inhabiting the area adjacent to which Swaami Atal-Anivaarya's Forest Guest House was located.

He was said to be a man of some eminence, Swaami Atal-Anivaarya, a doctor of note even—and the seclusion of his weekend dwelling was only legitimized by the secrecy of its activities. It was known in most circles to be an ordinary Resort whose visitors mainly sought its facilities for the purposes of surveying or photographing rare specimens of wildlife that were less likely to frequent the civilian zone. It ran alongside a kilometre-long strip of river making its way down towards the adjoining Dam. There were parts of the property that were said to peep into the innermost recesses of the core area of Rajaji. One could obtain permission to enter the core area of the National Park only through a painstaking process of application, first to the state authorities, then to the forest office, and only by way of a letter of recommendation from any government servant ranging from a member of the armed forces to the I.A.S.

The core area had once been a biodiversity hotspot teeming with fauna of infinite variety. Although technically located within the confines of the Rajaji National Park, Swaami Atal-Anivaarya's Forest Guest House was a private enterprise, and hence not regulated by the government. Apparently, a branch of his family had owned the plot of land since the early 1900s, before the expansive jungle became a protected forest. It lay along the eastern section of the tiger reserve overlooking the precipitous ravines and escarpments blending into the hovering foothills just beyond.

As I drove past the gate, which to my surprise was open, I crossed a small nightwatchman's cabin attached to the right-hand side of the entrance. It was empty, the small wooden door lay open, creakily swinging back and forth at a leisurely pace as if in acknowledgement of an approaching wind. My white Gypsy, its gear adjusted in four-wheel drive, crunched over the gravelled driveway that wound on into three indistinct sectors, bouncing up and down the wobbly road. I glanced all about me at the surrounding property, rocking back and forth in my seat, yet maintaining enough stability to admire the dense vegetation that flanked the onward path. At a junction less than a hundred metres ahead, I could notice a pole standing erect in duty with three obligatory signposts attached to its neck, pointing in three altogether distinct directions. I paid no attention to what the signs specified, gazing instead on across the dense overhanging foliage towards a large colonial bungalow—red-bricked and three-storeyed, that lay rapturously ahead at the conclusion of the gravelled driveway. On approaching closer, I could faintly perceive a large wooden board hung over the front entrance to the bungalow which proclaimed 'SWAAMI: SHREE SHREE—Gurudev Atal-Anivaarya Nateeja WELCOMES YOU TO HIS FOREST GUEST HOUSE', beneath which was etched in clay, 'You are cordially invited!'

The attic above the third floor of the bungalow branched off into a rectangular tower protruding from atop the structure like an observation post. The opaque window obscuring its interior was higher above even the mosaic-tiled terrace that lay beside it. The architecture of the bungalow was irregular in its proportions, with more weight on its gabled roof than its foundation could provide for. The verandahs too spilled out indefinitely from the corners of the bungalow into sub-structures and cottages of their own. One of them housed what I later came to know as the dining area which lay half in the open-air and half enclosed beside the main foyer.

Attached to a wooden pole standing at the tail end

of the driveway was a sign board pointing towards the 'Aviary', beneath which was another sign pointed slightly askew which said—'Pooja Point'. Outside the front porch of the bungalow beyond which presumably lay the reception, stood a signboard next to a small kennel pointing towards the 'Infirmary', and another below it which said—'Rooms 1A to 32B'.

I dismounted my Gypsy and parked it right astern the main house next to the other vehicles clasped on to the gravel path that broke up into four disparate directions to four altogether separate quarters of the property. It was about eight acres in all, bound by a barb wire fence that ran clear along the perimeter of the entire property, replaced in sections by a brick wall with bits of broken glass stuck on top to keep off miscreants. I entered the bungalow after much thought and deliberation, gazing cautiously at the many artefacts and articles of intrinsic collector's value, especially to one in a field similar to my own.

A dining table lay ahead of the foyer in the canteen, covered with a striped linen tablecloth. Delicate cutlery of all sorts from chinaware to ceramic saucers and silver spoons and forks lay stacked next to the placemats. In immediate view of the entrance stood a wooden counter upon which was painted in white calligraphic lettering—'RECEPTION'. In between a disconnected telephone and a rack of magazines and manuals lay the calling bell where I at once placed my hand. A wooden board hung from the back wall behind the reception with all the room numbers. Some room numbers had been crossed, some had been ticked, and those that did not have any signage on them were presumably vacant. An unrolled calendar and map hung from the top of the board and an old grandfather clock ticked away discreetly in the vicinity of the reception, blurting out the seconds and minutes while I searched timidly about for any other living being. The only occupants seemed to be in a suspended state of animation.

The head of a Chital hung above the centre of the back wall. Stuffed birds of all sorts adorned the room. Little animal figurines were to be found all over the foyer which also doubled up as the recreation room with a billiards table and a Carom chest. A leopard carcass was pinned diagonally across the back wall. A seating area had been set up in a far corner of the room away from the dining table where an opulent Kashmiri carpet was surrounded by two sturdy arm chairs overlooking a makeshift bonfire next to which a small side table had an oil fire lamp upon it.

The opulence of the entire arrangement startled me, especially considering the absence of anyone to employ its amenities. It seemed styled to accommodate a royal family, yet wore the manner of some derelict hotel in an abandoned Ghost town. Towards the centre of the room, stood a rock hewn effigy of Lord Ganesha looking ominously into the rectangular distance of the living room. A single beam from an overhead lantern shone upon him, accentuating his deadly features, and filling his contours with shadows that hinted at a latent terror. The basuri he held too appeared as if he were wielding some deadly weapon with which he intended to inflict the severest of blows upon humanity.

I left the foyer at once, retreating to the reception area to commence the formalities that would necessitate my stay. Wearing a cap and shorts with a pouch wrapped around my waist, I looked around—suitcase in hand—at all the furnishings and ornaments out of awe and perplexity. I searched in vain for some occupants, even half-considered calling out but soon abandoned the idea, plonking my suitcase down on the floor instead. I walked up to the reception and rung the call bell two or three times. There was no response.

I looked around bewildered, tried studying the wooden board with the room numbers, glanced through the register even. This time I was rattled by the rumble of some presence behind the counter. A loud knocking was heard. I recoiled from the counter, puzzled—contemplating silently where it could possibly be emerging from. My first impulse was to look towards the front door, but there was no one in sight. The knocking continued, growing more urgent and somewhat impatient. I looked beneath and around the counter as if someone were stuck inside it. I knocked on it a couple of times. The knocking which burst out in response startled me immensely. It was a disembodied call, appearing out of nowhere. But more bothersome was the fact that this was the first contact I had made with any living being on my entire sojourn up till this house.

chapter three

Much to my relief, I did finally manage to identify the origin of the knocking. Behind the counter, invisible to the other end, lay a trap door which had evidently been bolted shut. I went behind the counter and unlocked it. The wooden door rumbled open as a small figure emerged from it. He was a short squat man, barely five feet in height and with a posture bent-doubled to an alarming degree. As he straightened up most laboriously, I noticed a faint moustache sprouting from the semi-circle of his mouth, a balding patch of hair encircling the scalp, and a demeanour given to long spells at the desk. He was barefooted and had a starched off-white dhothi wrapped around his waist. A yellow triangular tikka swam up the folds of his forehead to his widow's peak, and broadened with the slightest hint of expression.

'Namashkaar!' he pronounced, with hands ominously joined.

'Swaami Ji?' I inquired.

'That would be me,' he nodded, wrapping a yellow dupatta across his naked upper torso, and leaning lazily on the counter.

'Are you alone here?' I asked.

He closed his eyes a moment and thought—'How may I be of assistance to you?'

I thought about it a while. He yawningly reached for a beaded necklace of rudrakshes to string up to his neck as if that would restore my memory.

'What were you doing down there?' I inquired with a slight air of impertinence.

A muffled chattering of birds sounded from beneath the trapdoor he stood upon.

'Working,' he replied.

'And who had locked you?'

'Well…' he thought about it a moment before answering. 'I had locked myself. Often, when the work gets too demanding, I have to practice complete and total isolation! Only this time I had asked the door to be locked from the outside, as I had not anticipated to come out before dinnertime.'

'What have you got down there?' I asked, leaning over the counter to inspect the bolted trapdoor.

'Would you like to find out?' He stepped aside from it, a violent flapping of bird sounds thumped at the firm wooden floorboards.

'No thanks…' I demurred.

He made a peculiar squeak of a sound out in reply to the cry of the creatures confined down below. That silenced them, at least momentarily. When they resumed their chirping, it was softer and somewhat subdued. After kicking at the trapdoor one could detect their presences positively vanish.

'My name is Barkat Singh Randhawa.' I introduced myself hesitantly once he stepped back onto the trapdoor.

'Ahh…Barkat…' he smiled, gathering his hands into

mine. 'It was long expected that someday prosperity would pay me a visit,' he jested, or perhaps meant it. 'You come from Ranibaug?' he inquired.

'Indeed.'

'Then perhaps you and I have a little business to attend to?'

I looked around and then whispered—'Indeed.'

chapter four

'Incredible!' he surmised, after a long stroll in the various verandahs and balconies that branched out from all corners of the bungalow in innumerable directions. 'Most incredible. You said the State Energy Board paid you a visit with regard to this? Smt Damini Jain. I happen to know her. Used to advise her brothers.'

'Are you in contact with the Professor?' I baffled myself with the words I uttered, but as there was not a living being in sight apart from him, they were accommodated into reason.

'Not exactly, you see…' he shook his head and frowned. 'It doesn't work like that. It's not so simple. Professor Chaturvedi has arrived at his desired destination, and is out of reach,' he soon admitted after a long pause. 'No mobile phone network will be able track him, let alone some mystical embalming fluid that contains a holy vessel. Aural Morse code!' he scoffed. 'Heh! Nonsense! He's gone!' he rolled his lower lip over his chin. 'Forget about him.' Flicking a hand into the air, he waved it towards the steps that descended into the lawns.

'How can you say that?' I followed him down.

'Because he is happy, and at peace. I know it. I can feel it. I could even bet on it. He's where he always wanted to be. In the very bosom of the mountains. They've taken him. The Himalayas have claimed him.'

'Come on Swaami Ji…' I laughed. 'You don't actually believe that, do you?'

'The history of belief in all its forms has been for me something of a specialty of late. I know what belief can bring, what it can hide, what it can reveal and what it can stall!'

'The Electric Division tells me that I am of unsound mind,' I said. The chirp of some passing sparrow settled mildly into the grassy scenery.

'The Electric Division!' he spat, derisively. 'Hah! Tell them to restore my electricity first. Then they can go off on their errands of mercy! And cordon off that entire mountain if they have to. Seal it up under lock and key!'

'They tell me what I saw up there was wholly of a psychiatric nature…' I continued. 'A manifestation of the psychic state. After all, Ranibaug is said to have a strange effect on the mind of the individual who nears it.'

'What do you think?' he asked me, halting astride the brick margin of the garden.

'I think what I saw up there was as real as anything I've seen before,' I said. 'I know I was malnourished and not in the best shape, but I still retained the capacity to distinguish sight from thought. What do you think?'

'I know what you saw up there was true, beta!' he shut his eyes. 'For I have seen it myself, in my prayers. A land of primeval rock, where insects reign supreme and the snow shuttles past not daring to touch it. I had endeavoured in my entirety to reach it!' he blinked, and then tapped at the thigh of his right leg. 'If Professor Charan Prakash has found it, I say all the better for him! He's managed to do what I couldn't with all my strength accomplish.'

'And what of Shera then?' I asked.

'Shera will find what he's looking for…' he yearned for some sunlight and walked onwards. I followed him.

'They seem to have renounced all worldly considerations,' I told him. 'What would make a man want to do that?'

Swaami Atal-Anivaarya shrugged his shoulders in remorse.

'He said he wants no part of the bright twinkling lights of the city that mock him from down below,' I said.

'Shera said that?' he smirked.

'Yes…' I bowed.

'He who could not spend an evening in Hrishikesh without degenerating into the talk of the town, the laughing stock of every wandering-eyed ascetic fool enough to befriend him.'

'And what of the Professor then?' I asked. 'What of the HRA Institute?'

'It lies in the able hands of Ms Pratyusha Negi,' he said. 'With a little monetary participation from my end, every once in a while.'

'You mean to tell me he's given up his name, all his life's work, his reputation, his business and his responsibilities in order to go off and hunt for salvation in the eyes of the lord? Which lord is this who spares sinners their debts, that dodges workman's wages and provides to those that fail to provide to others?'

'His moral well-being is not my responsibility,' he sighed. 'I tried to do whatever was within the scope of my power to help him. He is quite beyond repair if you ask me. I should have never wasted my time on him in the first place. He is probably meeting his punishment as we speak.'

'And his reward too?'

'His reward shall not be met in this life…' he mused.

'When he is re-animated I suppose…' I added with passing sarcasm.

'From what you described of the processes of death,' he began. 'It wouldn't be unlikely for him to have to endure multiple lives till his retribution is fully served. In the Buddhist context of things, freed only when the soul attains Nirvana. The karmic balance. True contentment.'

'Why go through all that trouble for contentment? There's far easier ways than climbing a godforsaken mountain.'

'Contentment isn't something that's easy to come by, Barkat!' he spoke at length. 'Nor is happiness. One has to earn one's happiness, and if one can't earn it, then one has to find it! Dig it out of the ground, so to speak. In the spirit of the old prospectors and pioneers that built this nation. There's multitudes of people out there who spend their entire lives chasing after happiness. They keep looking for it, in the simplest of things. Like in trees, in leaves, in the flowers and birds. In flies, butterflies, caterpillars, insects. There's happiness in fruits too, in the grass, in the ground in God's green earth. There's happiness in everything, in all of God's creatures.'

We strolled past a sprawl of lolling Monstera leaves to the mango orchard leaning and loping towards a river that curled away past the edge of the property. We trod along the marsh, going all the way along the river bank—across it a vast sweep of wires and electric towers hovering about the distance. The electricity had gone in the entire region that day. When I made known my prior vocation, I was obliged to provide an informed opinion.

Swaami Atal-Anivaarya had suspected that the malfunction was caused due to a broken down electric tower whose wires had not yet been disconnected from the main network of the Dam, thereby blowing the entire circuit. Possibly the work of some disgruntled elephant. All we would have to do was keep following the path of the wires until we found a section that had collapsed from its overhead trajectory.

'Have you ever tried to trace the path of these cables and wires?' Swaami Atal-Anivaarya asked, somewhat reclusively as if to himself. 'It's strange, isn't it? That without these cables and wires any area is unfit to live in! It ceases to be a civilization! Life wouldn't have been the same without these cables and wires!'

They must have been suffering. There had been no electricity for a couple of days in the entire Rajaji area, almost up to Hrishikesh. Since the electricity crisis, the water supply from the Dam had been dramatically altered due to the utilization of overflow for the generation of enough electricity required for the constructional appliances at adjacent excavation sites to go on running.

'You see, what we have out here is a cross-section of a land that was once innocent,' Swaami Atal-Anivaarya pointed out into the distance. 'Villagers flocked the banks of the river. Pitcher on head, sickle in hand and home-grown vegetables for dinner. You know it used to take one village woman a five-kilometre walk to get one pitcher of water from the river, yet they were happy. It was their land. Now the government's moved in. And then, all of a sudden there's no electricity! We're back in the old days again,' Swaami Atal-Anivaarya continued, almost as if he was telling some tale of a distant far off legend.

'How is the resort managing with this?' I asked in humbled stupor.

'And it's all because of the underground,' Swaami Ji

carried on, crawling along the shores of the river like a boundary squirrel.

'Hmmm...' he bent down and touched the ground like he was touching a lover. 'It's fascinating, isn't it? Everything that is under the ground! It's like another hemisphere. A realm of the Earth that is most unexplored. Another world down there. You know there was once a prisoner. He was in for assault and larceny. The judge gave him seven years, but he got out in four, couldn't take it!'

'How?' I trembled.

'He dug his way out through the underground. For two consecutive years, the man dug and dug and dug. I wonder how it must have been for him. He crawled out of that jail cell like a rat. And kept going through with it, until he hit the cemetery.'

There was a ruffled silence. The only sound to be heard was the whistling of the wind, the rustling of the leaves and the croaking of some distant crickets. Almost as though nature itself had responded to the Swaami ji's story.

'Ohh...the horrors the man must have faced! The horrors!'

We walked on through the marsh where tall wild grass was growing irregularly all about the place in haphazard postures and varying states of impenetrability. A small pond or a puddle of sorts had formed somewhere on the bank. Buffaloes bathed in the keechad as birds and amphibians inhabited its mucky recesses. The wires overhead sloped and disappeared over this area, lapsing into a peripheral scramble of cables that lay in the distance ahead of the indefinite grass.

I was stomping through the weeds when somewhere in the marsh and muck and dirt, Swaami Atal-Anivaarya noticed an anomaly in one of the leftward channels of the water pump. A curious amount of water was being discharged from what appeared to be some sort of sabotage in one of the openings of the tubes of the pipes. Water was flowing violently out of it at an alarming rate which seemed to be swelling up the marsh on the bank and accelerating the velocity of the natural flow of the current.

I threw a stone into the water to see it spin off and to count the number of times it would bounce off the water. The result of my attempt stupefied me. The pebble seemed to hit the water at the speed with which it was thrown, then however it bounced off on its own accord at an enhanced rate, and then proceeded to skim off the water, a record seven times, before vanishing into the depths of the leaning current.

In all my years of throwing stones and pebbles into the river I had never known it to bounce seven times before it landed. A sure record considering my vast years of experience. We wondered long and hard as to whether the inherent trajectory of the current in the river was responsible for the damage of the pump and was precipitating this occurrence. We walked up to a rock formation that overhung the river and standing above we could now perceive the minutest details of the current with acute accuracy. We looked on into the river, trying almost to penetrate its surface and configure the route these waters took in their course to the great lakes and reservoirs. We both stood simultaneously stunned a moment, gazing deep into the river to decipher what menace to mankind seemed to be lurking beneath the water.

We shortly walked back up to the pump to take a more thorough look at its configuration. The damaged pipe was partially submerged in the water as its upper channel rose into the chamber connected to the mainline. The apparatus was assembled in perhaps not altogether competent terms, but it did still have the stability to withstand any sort of leak or crack in the metallic pipework. Upon inspecting the damage which had been inflicted upon the cylindrical tube, it was apparent to us that the flow of water within the pump had drastically increased. There seemed to be an external source from which water was being drawn out and then drained back into the river.

Our initial response was to suppose it had something to do with the lowering of the aqueducts and reservoir canals of the dam. Swaami Atal-Anivaarya had been informed of a northward shift of the waters due to the influx, but what we were here witnessing still seemed to exceed any possibility on that count.

'Are the glaciers melting?' I asked.

'The source of this influx,' he scratched his chin. 'Could either be attributed to the bore-well we had dug sometime back when the river had dried up, or even to a third possible additional source that has escaped my notice.'

'Such as?' I wondered.

'An irrigation channel from Rajaji National Park that might have been intercepted, or even as you suggested—the rising of the water level due to the melting of the icecaps. It is summer after all.'

I bent down to taste the water, and as per my worst apprehensions—it was saline, beyond a noticeable doubt. We were now both silent. There was no explanation to be given of this, either by way of assumption or even speculation. Both of us failed to say a word to the other and we both strolled around just a bit longer before Swaami Atal-Anivaarya spun about on his heel and thought out aloud—'That dam was built by the State Energy Division.'

'Hmmm…' I pondered on it, recollecting the signage plastered all around the mountain-ways and uphill roads of Northern Garhwal.

'They've cut off our electricity,' he continued. 'And now as you say—sealed off Ranibaug in search of an indefinable power source.'

'The containing fluid,' I thought to myself before blurting out, 'It seems to generate energy and preserve all organic life. Its own self-sustainable lifeforce. It's saline. Just like the zinc solution to a rudimentary electric circuit. What if they were transporting this very liquid down the mountain in order to utilise it for the generation of renewable power? What if they were saving up all the natural resources there discovered for their very own selves? For all you know, if privatised, some infrastructure development firm or mining corporation might stake a claim and decide to purchase it.'

'What if one were to reach there before they did?' Swaami Atal-Anivaarya murmured.

'It's no good. The place will be swarming with surveyors, government personnel and armed officials. The gold rush is just beginning.' Just then the thought occurred to me. 'What if you were to accompany me up there Swaami Ji?'

'No good,' he shook his head stubbornly. 'I can't make it.'

'With your endowments and special knowledge, there's no telling what we could discover up there,' I offered, in a tone of swiftly mustered sycophancy.

'Hmmm...' His lower lip crinkled up. 'I could send one of my men along with you.'

'That would be no good. I need you Swaami Ji, *you*, with your extra-sensory abilities and special powers.'

'What special powers?' he laughed. 'We are all but human here, after all!'

'Not you Swaami Ji...' I lowered my voice in resolution, still insisting on his divinity. 'It would be a gift beyond measure if you were to come along with me...'

'I cannot grant you that my child.' He clasped a rudraksh

from the string around his neck. 'Not I, nor our creator. You will have to make this journey alone, or accompanied by someone of my choice. Just as you had earlier. Only this time, make sure you don't return alone.'

He left the thought dangling from his teeth, and splashed his hands mildly about in the water to reconfirm its salinity. 'Hmmm…' he filled his palms up. 'What's the closest sea from here?'

'The Bay of Bengal,' I said. 'Oh no…' I corrected myself. 'The Arabian Sea. They're equidistant, except some of the inland channels branching in from around the Sunderbans. Some of them might be saline. The closest from here would be…' I guessed.

'The Gulf of Khambat,' he concluded. 'Or Kutch,' he spat out a spray of water and gaped on into the distance, deciding shortly thereafter that we proceed to the resort for some rest and refreshments.

chapter five

We were now both considerably tired and it was almost four o'clock in the afternoon. Swaami Ji lay down on a cot, the smell of a variety of waterlilies and raath ki raanis swarmed about me as I turned to look on into the garden. The sight of it rather relieved me of all my worries. Just to think that this could as well be a form of endeavour to embrace for the rest of one's life: living amongst nature. Maybe that's what had kept old Swaami Ji so up and about at so tender an age. I had always wanted to be a farmer or a botanist like the Professor, and tend to the leaves. What nobler pursuit, what greater cause? I suppose it gives a person a whole lot of joy to plant a sapling in the ground and watch it blossom.

But I had known of the lesser tranquil aspects of agriculture; the ups and downs, the dependence on forces of nature that lay beyond ordinary human comprehension. The toil, the blood, sweat and tears and the sun—the sun that burnt off all that couldn't withstand it. Be it a flower, a dried-up leaf or an insect; any animate or inanimate object bowed down to that sun. Sometimes it would be a blessing, like the light of day that dawns on the blind man stranded on the street, squeezed out dry. Sometimes it cheered me up to bask in its warmth, and feel its rays soothing my spirit. Sometimes it would be good for the newly planted saplings, sometimes it caused more photosynthesis than the plants required, sometimes it could wither a whole crop before sundown. And the rains! The rains that kept us all a prisoner. In the old days, we used to look forward to the rains as a time of change, when you could wash away all your sins and take comfort in mother nature.

Now the monsoons just came and went like the scent of a sunflower on a dry August noon. I looked around. The petunia petals had wilted before they had a chance to flourish, the soft smell of a row of dried up shrubs passed over the dreary resonance of crickets and other insects beckoning to be heard. The trees bore little fruit this year, and amid the deep recesses of foliage, a Lychee Orchard could be seen somewhere in the distance upon a grove, its bushy dark-green trees swinging wildly left and right. The chirping of the birds too had by now grown painfully restless.

Amid a vast array of Magnolias and rose bushes, there descended a cobbled path that had been carved through a row of Elephant Apple trees on either side, that led directly down to a well to which I soon proceeded. The diameter of the mouth of the well was about eight feet in all. I circled it numerous times, leaning over to catch my reflection flickering at me from down below. The depth however was not a matter that could be accurately gauged from the point at which I stood. Certain rumblings detectable from the circle of still water staring back at me, convinced me it could well have been more than thirty feet in length. Dropping a rock to watch it recede into its depths, I was struck at once by the near absence of a ripple or even a minute disturbance in the shimmering translucent surface. My mind swooped in to plumb the full extent of the bottom of the well, wading past visions similar to ones encountered at Ranibaug, to imagine a bottomless basin; a steep cylindrical passageway down stairs of soil, dropping into a layer of eternal luminescence.

I walked off from the stone rim of the well before my thoughts could lapse any further into its growing underwater opacity. A frog leaped out from a mossy crevice in the stone slabs. I was told to be cautious of snakes in and around the property, and warned not to wander off too far from sight of the bungalow. Dog howls sprung out from between the folds of the ascending shrubbery. A column of Bougainvillea separated this portion from the rest of the property. An ancient banyan overhung the adjacent tract whose topographical features seemed most appropriate for terrace farming. Cultivation of all sorts of cash crops took place. Anything that could be transported to the market in due time. Rice, wheat, jowar, bajra, lentils, pulses, vegetables, fruits seasonal and non-seasonal, tulsi and mint, herbs of all sorts, some of medicinal value, some experiments, saplings collected from all corners of the country tested in these geographical conditions. Some were efforts in vain, some proved fruitful, some were botanical oddities, some were extraordinary outgrowths, some lived on to be many years old and many feet tall, some were inhabited by birds, some provided useful timber, some were just for ornamental and decorative purposes. Some died…but death itself seemed inevitable in this radiance of decay that far and wide encumbered the surface. It stretched out its blessed arms like a blanket, gently beguiling the weak and feeble willed into the dreary depths of oblivion.

Death came as no surprise here, and was to be expected, and tallied along the general head count and nomenclature of each individual plant that was a ritual in Swaami Atal-Anivaarya's everyday existence at the Resort. The plants were his pride and joy. On his weekends here, he would study each plant meticulously according to its exact specifications of soil and climatic type and try to provide sufficient conditions.

The vast and varied assemblage of flora that was a permanent feature of each and every square inch of the landscape were a bit unusual at first, but then they soon began to have a soothing effect on the soul. Almost as though one were in the midst of some verdant maze that man had never trodden upon.

Of late, Swaami Atal-Anivaarya's devotion to his plants had reached obsessive proportions. He did not let any outsiders or trespassers even touch a petal or a branch. Each fraction of his land was guarded by a series of diligent but ferocious watch dogs of the Doberman kind. There were a team of four farmers who worked for Swaami Ji, out of them three were ex-convicts who had been arrested prior to their newfound employment for having tried to break in and perform a burglary in his house in Haridwar. I never understood it, but there was one thing I knew for sure: they worked hard and honestly for Swaami ji and had not once dared to cross him. He took good care of his men and their families and provided adequate means for their livelihood. They in turn respected him and were loyal.

I stayed many days with Swaami Atal-Anivaarya, helping out in the various chores requisite for running an establishment of this size. I recognised some of the camouflage gear and camping equipment as belonging to the HRA supply store. I contributed to the cleaning and cooking, attended prayer, and went on the Safaris with some of the guests that invariably materialised.

It was only on the fourth day of my stay—when I was out in the jeep on my own for, what was supposed to have been, a routine patrol of the woods—that I managed to catch sight of what I had all this while been hoping to encounter. Amid a huddle of bushes that spanned the circumference of a waterhole, I noticed from afar a singular looking creature stooped on all fours to wet his snout, or at least what appeared to be a snout. It was, however, beyond all doubt, a beak. There was no tail. The scaly outline suggested an absence of fur and a reptilian disposition, but the scuttling motions and rigid bearing hinted at a near-simian possibility. It resembled from one end the anatomy of an anteater, yet from another angle assumed the aspect of a mule, and yet from another when upright appeared not to different from a Kangaroo. Its hawkish beak and deformed wings gave it at once a remote kinship to the penguin. There wasn't even a trace of any specie as yet discovered in its entire manner. It was as something entirely novel and inconceivable to the conservationist and paleontologist alike. I immediately produced my camera and began to click away furiously, capturing blurry fragments of what it was actually like. I saw it with my own two eyes and will never forget the hideous glow that emanated from its eyes. The unthinkable anatomy, an outré amalgam of all things natural and mineral.

When I showed these photographs to Swaami Atal-Anivaarya, he shuddered at their existence.

'Destroy them at once!' he commanded me.

'Why?' I demanded.

He flicked hold of the Nikon camera from my hands and immediately ejected the memory card with the smooth adeptness of the technologically literate.

'I will be keeping this.' He held up the slim chip in his thumb and forefinger and placed it into the chest pocket of the white kurta he had worn.

'What was that Swaami Ji?' I gasped. 'What on earth was that thing?'

'It wasn't a thing.' He glared at me sternly, his upper torso wiggling as he placed the memory card inside. 'It's an experiment. Just forget you ever saw it.'

'How can I!' I protested. 'I'm not ever likely to forget

what I just saw. You can destroy my camera, but I always have my memory to rely on. It's gotten me this far.'

'My boy, why don't you understand!' he tightened his lips, finally a bit exasperated. 'If you really want to know what you went all the way up there to find out, you are not going to find the answers here I can assure you, son!'

'At least tell me what that was. I'm entitled to that much. I saw it with my own two eyes, didn't I? It was in my destiny. To chance upon it. Had I never seen it, I wouldn't be asking you about it, would I now?'

'Look, Barkat!' Swaami Ji put his arm around my shoulder. 'What you saw out there was neither human nor animal. It was, how shall I put it…a kind of…eh…' he reached for a word, but his tongue recoiled from it in disgust. 'Ahh…'

'I'm still waiting for an answer, Swaami Ji. And I'm not going to leave without it. I've come a long way from Mathura, as you can see.'

'Very well…' he resolved, taking me aside to one of the verandahs. 'You see, when I had gone up to Ranibaug and injured myself,' he settled into a rattan armchair, 'one of my co-expeditioners had managed to make the trip up all by himself while I convalesced at the campsite above Harki Dun—the ghost-camp you spoke of. He didn't of course manage to make it all the way up there. When he returned, no doubt visibly haggard, he had brought along with him in a gunny sack, a peculiar breed of rodent he had come upon on the route. We had settled at the campsite which contained the belongings of the topographical survey of '71, and were in the process of studying what we found. We had rehabilitated its remains with our own tents and supplies, but the moment the creature was unleashed out of the gunny sack, it began to multiply in numerous forms which ambushed us in all directions, making us flee in the most extreme weather conditions imaginable. We managed to capture one of them, carried it back to Uttarkashi along with us, and at my urging decided to deposit it in my forest resort to observe its activities, and see it propagate. In a matter of few weeks it began to grow prodigiously till it reached the size of a Saint Bernard. When its wings sprouted we had to operate upon them so as to prevent it from flying away…'

'What on earth are these GODDAMNED creatures!' I shrieked. 'I've seen variants of them, in the winged and insectile form. Are they the much sought after specimens of extra-terrestrial intelligence? These monstrous mutations of animal and bird, plant and insect, fish and coral! WHAT the HELL is all this!'

'Get a hold of yourself, my boy!' he huffed. 'You wouldn't want to burst an artery on their account. Those aren't extra-terrestrial entities! They're what the mountain has spewed forth. No one knows just what on earth they are. All we know is that they come from the very pits of the mountain. Some hold strange theories…' his lips cracked apart slyly.

'Such as?' I raised an eyebrow.

'Such as the possibility that the comet or unidentifiable aerial object lodged in Ranibaug is nothing more than a Soviet test flight from after the Second World War which crashed into the peak due to atmospheric irregularities. Some say that Nazi physicists and rocket scientists in South America propelled a craft across the globe filled with an assortment of genetically modified animals, to cause wide-scale panic, if discovered. The assumption being that when found, it would no doubt be thought of as concrete evidence of alien life.'

'Some sort of diversionary tactic,' I supposed.

'The experiments they conducted on the livestock produced startling effects on the flesh, and also invariably on the landscape in which they were administered. They were in search of the Holy Grail, after all. Firm believers in the occult. High ranking generals of the SS. Wanted to execute a plan of total world domination by altering the magnetic poles of the earth.'

There are mysteries which yield enigmas, discoveries which disclose the unconscious forces that propel beings in action, into order, into conquest, and down quests unquenchable till they reach the ends of the earth no wiser than when they had started. Such as was my lot in this life!

The more I sought a solution to all I had witnessed, the more entangled I found myself in some abject theorising, in the presence of those whose wishes were not drastically different from my own. Those who sought to unravel the vaulted information that tormented us, that lived in morbid contemplation of Ranibaug and its Queen Goddess.

'There are parts of the earth uncharted for all of eternity.' Swaami Anal-Anivaarya stated. 'Designs that our creator intended not to share with us, thoughts he schemed to leave out of our experience. And perhaps it is better that way! Or so it may seem…' he mumbled to himself.

I turned an ear to listen more clearly to what was being said.

'This…' he waved his palms about himself. 'Garden of Eden is not the spawn of alien intervention. It is the fruit of human will. Of dedicated care, and careful study. The taming and cultivation of this wilderness is no more a product of superior intelligence than the mere sparrow's nest, constructed meticulously over the course of countless days and weeks, twig by measly twig at a time. But they have managed to get inside your head and convince you of its mystery…' he pointed at me. 'Of its divinity, even! And I say you are a fool for it!'

'Who?' I said.

'The people you met up there. The pagan lot, barbaric, uncouth. An aghora cult of madmen and witchdoctors reigning supreme over one of our own mountains. One of God's own creations.'

I now slowly began to see the full purpose of our expedition.

'I had sent you there to clean up that whole lot, to purge the peak of the demonic influence, and mark a location for the building of a new temple. A temple that would cleanse the damned mountain itself! The Forsaken Wilderness that drives people insane with its winds and its atmospheric abnormalities. God has yet to make his presence known at Ranibaug. As of now, it is our imminent duty to rid his Himalayas of all improper elements. That includes unconventional faiths and random religions of any sort that could spring up and populate parts of the neighbouring villages, and cause undue influence on the mountainfolk's way of life. Which is why I have created for myself here, a sort of private ecosystem where I may attempt to evaluate the effect that one of those creatures might have on the natural environment.'

'And?' I gazed about the expanse of green, glowing a burnt fluorescent with the glaring sunlight. 'What are the results?'

'It hasn't managed to mate or reproduce as yet.' He shook his head in disappointment. 'But we are working on it. After all, we do have to be discreet. It was sighted the other day by some of the forest guards. They have put out an alert across the area. You see, if this thing turns out to be harmless then we can rest assured that it is not imbued with any special capabilities, let alone extra-terrestrial or supernatural properties—that it is indeed nothing more than a bizarre state experiment by some country from some corner of the globe. That it was dropped into our lap by chance and contains no real significance, certainly not cosmic and least of all *divine*!'

PART FIVE

Return to Ranibaug

chapter one

Some years hence, I journeyed back up to Harki Dun with a team of ex-colleagues from around the Garhwal region. We made it no further than the rock face that shielded Ranibaug from the tread of the ordinary human foot: the obstacle we had once so effortlessly overcome. Even with the varieties and store of advanced mountaineering equipment and cordage at our disposal, we found no anchor on the sprawling base of the tree trunk. The protruding rock too had become merged with the toes of its roots. It was as if a spike had been placed upon the head of a hurdle to prick the foot of he who leapt high enough to cover it. Climbing the rock face inordinately meant climbing the gigantic tree trunk that spanned its ledge.

It was now no longer a tree, it was indeed a monument, having grown considerably since when I had last seen it, and having stretched itself imposingly upon the horizon. It could be spotted from a mile away, and was by now something of a landmark for lost parties.

We produced our photographs before the state authorities and also shared our findings with the Wadia Institue of

Himalayan Geology in Dehradun. Swaami Atal-Anivaarya Natija was summoned by the military to the Dehradun Cantonment. A private conference was held with the Office of Army Intelligence. Several generals were in attendance, and it was said that Swaami Atal-Anivaarya was compelled to disclose all information currently at his disposal regarding Ranibaug and the fate of the expeditioners there vanished. What he revealed is still classified, but one can only assume that he did not share his true impressions, and by all means must have composed an account to fit the official story, bereft of any speculative apprehensions that were otherwise characteristic of his opinions on the subject. He was not, however, to my knowledge, called upon to present before the authorities the strange animal I had sighted at his Resort, the presence of which I had made known in my brief but very public statement to the police.

I was never called upon by the army. A reporter working for the *Himalayan Traveller Biweekly Journal* got in touch with me for a story he was working on about the HRA Institute of Mountaineering and Research, and the unaccountable disappearance of its founder—Professor Charan Prakash Chaturvedi and his ex-employee Shera, a known mountain guide from Hrishikesh. I furnished him only with the rudimentary details of our expedition to Ranibaug, the hardships and storms and so on, reserving the more alarming implications for my own account later to be shared with the public.

chapter two

It was several months later, when in the process of penning my account of the incidents there witnessed, that I was contacted by Ms Pratyusha Negi, who it seems, had had a sudden change of heart regarding the fate of her ex-employer. Swaami Atal-Anivaarya's donations notwithstanding, she had been experiencing some difficulties with the maintenance of the HRA Institute and requested my urgent assistance. I wrote to her that I was at present engaged in a rather serious matter, a matter which neither she nor her mother had deemed fit for consideration, but nevertheless an experience, which I felt compelled to account for.

She wrote back several weeks later, a complaint—somewhat in the tenor of a formal letter or legal brief—of Swaami Atal-Anivaarya Natija's recent usage of the Institute grounds for certain occult rituals and midnight mass ceremonies, where an assemblage of sadhus was sighted by one of the chowkidaars deputised to guard the premises at night. He spoke of a large, somewhat oblong looking animal that had been shackled to a pole. An animal he found entirely impossible to identify and whose form he did not in the least recognise. It seemed they were in the process of training or manipulating the creature into the motions they desired. It was first made to climb up a mound, then made to trot upon its hind legs, then propelled from a ramp into an airborne squeal. It was strung up to a lattice work around a jungle gym that was under construction, and suspended from its top bars. It was made to produce a wide variety of raucous sounds that repelled the chowkidaar at once from the scene of the atrocity. He failed to catch sight of much through the bushes. The sound of a horn or shankh finally deafened him into retreat and eventual hiding.

Once the night passed, he arose from his cabin to find the campsite empty, and devoid of any signs or stains of the nightly activity that had eluded his understanding, and had vanished right before his eyes before he could provide evidence of it.

Pratyusha Negi alone believed his story, as she had supplied the Swaami Ji with the keys to the establishment, given that he was a supposed partner in the absence of the Professor, and knowing fully well that he was capable of anything outside the ordinary, having been responsible for the Professor's disappearance in the first place, she proceeded to investigate further into what had been reported to her.

We decided to rendezvous at a dhaba on the old Khathauli Bypass route. She was guarded and hesitant at first, but as the afternoon progressed she grew thoughtful and dazed. She appeared not to have slept for many nights, and had great big craters under her eyes that blackened with the slightest bulge from her sockets.

'Would you like some tea?' I at length thought fit to ask.

'I wouldn't mind a cup,' she sniffled into a polka-dotted handkerchief she produced from her denim jacket.

I called for a cup of tea and a glass of sweet lassi. The

young waiter disappeared into the kitchen with the order and in fifteen minutes emerged, balancing a tray on the heel of his palm while swatting flies off the rim of the tandoor with the ragged cloth wrapped around his other hand.

'Have you been to his resort?' I asked, once the lad had delivered the two glasses onto the table, and pranced off.

'I haven't,' she took a sip, stirring the thick liquid about in its cup and applying the warm edge to her temple. 'Have you?' she placed it back onto the wobbly wooden table imbalanced with one leg shorter than the other.

'I have,' I said, inspecting the sweet lassi before delving into it. 'It's an eight-acre medical farm, in which there also happens to be a greenhouse, laboratory, and private aviary. A collection of indigenous birds, caged up and confined at night and allowed to roam the premises by day.'

'There has been talk,' she informed me, almost confidentially, 'in various prestigious scientific journals in Delhi of a startling new technique discovered by Swaami Shree Shree Gurudev Atal-Anivaarya Natija.'

'A technique?' I took a sip of water before proceeding to slowly stir the lassi with a tablespoon.

'A technique by which any animal can be cured of any ailment, wound, disease or injury that might have been inflicted on it in the wild, and be brought back to health.'

The lassi nearly entered my windpipe. 'I'm sorry?' I coughed.

'Some kind of miracle botanical cure!' she stated, straight-faced as a stonewall. 'Found in his plants.'

'Is it legitimate?'

'Seems to be.' She blew into her cup.

'Have you seen its results?'

'The Professor claimed to have....'

'Ahh...I see...' I almost got up from the stool I was

precariously balanced on. 'The Professor's area of expertise happened to be the botanical sciences.'

'Why do you speak of him in the past tense?' she frowned.

'Okay *happens* to be…' I corrected myself. 'Does that make you feel any better? It doesn't give me any joy to refer to him in the past tense, Pratyusha. I only hope to God that he is still alive. I wish it as much as you!'

'You could have stopped him, like I did,' she squirmed. 'You had the chance to. You saw me. Blocking the wheel of that jeep with my foot,' she paused, sort of spitefully. 'But you didn't. You went along with him…'

'Now that's an instance that certainly ought to be referred to in the past tense. And left there too, if you please. In the past. It doesn't do anyone any good to bring it up.' I hushed my agitation and drew close to the table, hunched up under my jacket. 'I think we'd do better to focus on what ought to be done about this, not what has been done and has happened. If Swaami Atal-Anivaarya is experimenting on animals and birds, and has indeed synthesised some sort of a concoction, which he claims came right from the bosom of Ranibaug itself, then we may have some clarity as to what links him to the Professor's disappearance. If the Professor had been sent on some sort of recovery mission by Swaami Ji, then it might make sense taking this up before the authorities and doing whatever we can to see to the Professor's safe retrieval.'

'But the case is closed,' she snapped. 'The Uttarakhand authorities have declared it a simple open and shut missing person's case. The area is restricted. They can't send up a search party.'

'You mean to tell me that no one has gone up since?'

'How am I to know?' her forehead creased up in thought. 'All I know is that the Swaami Ji's claims are all a lot of nonsense! Claims to be imbued with special capabilities. How on earth could *he* have possibly come up with a miracle cure to treat all animals. By magic?' she almost laughed, or it was at least the closest she came to a laugh. 'You see, I had at one point even studied to be a veterinarian, and I've never heard of such a cure to this date.'

'Were you studying to be a doctor for humans or animals?' I asked.

'Both.' she said. 'I was sitting for my M.B.B.S., M.D. and M.S.…'

'What do you think Swaami Ji keeps doing out there on the weekends?' I interrupted her before she had fully answered my own question. So impatient was I, that when the cheque arrived I scarcely paid it a glance, causing her to reach for it in an involuntary attempt at courtesy; an act I took strong objection to, as it was I who had asked to meet her here in the first place in light of the sudden revelations that had baffled and upset her.

'What do you think?' she finally asked of me.

'I don't know,' I exhaled. 'I was there for a couple of days, and I couldn't make head or tail of his activities.'

'The Patwaari and Forest Ranger are going to be arriving there for an inspection,' she whispered. 'We'll soon see what comes out.'

'How do you know?'

'My mother,' she breathed faintly. 'She reported him to the authorities on multiple occasions for spiritual malpractice. Brainwashing, she claims.'

'What?' I sat her back down once the table had been cleared. I called for another cup of tea, this time for myself.

'I can only guess what Swaami Ji keeps doing out there in that forest,' she sneered, dragging the foot of her stool up to the table with a screech. 'Research! Discovery.' She spun her bent palm up around into the air in disbelief. 'At least, that's what he says.'

'What else does he say?'

'He once professed to have developed a fantastic method,' she almost smirked. 'A method by which he can communicate with any form of mammalian, reptilian, amphibian, bird, or even aquatic marine life.'

'How?' I nearly choked on the cup of tea that was shortly brought to me.

'Just how a dog trainer tells his dog how to sit, when to bark, how to flip, whom to attack. Or else, how a ringmaster in a circus manages to tame the most terrifying lion into harmless submission, and presents him before the crowd as sedate as a vegetable.'

I wondered a while without saying anything, rattling the cup of piping tea up to my mouth, and burning my lips with the approach of its contents.

'Since the dawn of existence!' she began, now finally mustering up her long suppressed classroom manner. 'Since Adam and Eve, mankind has strived fanatically to try and understand our fellow living creatures. How to tame them, how to breed them, how to kill them, how to make use of them when required. Till now, only the attempt to communicate with the dolphin has been successful. With the others…it is safe to say that there are many creatures on this earth that we will perhaps never be able to fully understand.'

A long silence loomed over the empty tabletop, lapsing sullenly into the adjoining murmurs. I had very little to add to such a thought. It had never occurred to me in my wildest and most adventurous thoughts, to think that this very trick had been mastered by a member of the human species. It would be nothing short of a leap for the sciences, not to mention the administrative possibilities inherent in such a harmonious reorganisation of nature.

'It has been said that with the assistance of some equipment in his laboratory, he is able to communicate with any living creature,' she continued in a bewildered and also slightly frightened tone. 'He can grasp any frequency not normally perceptible to the spectrum of the five senses, and can hear and understand what they are trying to say, and indeed in some cases, can talk back to them.'

chapter three

Any further attempt to disentangle the wealth of incident that had transpired within the course of the preceding years, found me plunged neck-deep into the ruins of state survey records, ancient files and documents stacked away in the cabinets and drawers of some government office, the police station in Uttarkashi where the missing person's report had been originally filed back in '71 of the topographical survey team that had failed to return from their expedition to Ranibaug, the endless drama of unbelieving friends, relatives and acquaintances with their morbid hypotheses.

There was only one course left to be taken. For the last and, what was supposed to have been, final time, I ventured back up to Taluka in my white Gypsy this time accompanied by Pratyusha Negi. The first two days passed steadily, up until we reached Osla, beyond which our mental state began to rapidly deteriorate. Once we crossed Harki Dun and had made it tirelessly up to that gargantuan tree, neither of us could trust our eyes. We had carried along a surplus of provisions in the event of such unaccountable fatigue—twelve sachets of Electral, a box of Glucon-D, an assortment of chewable and non-chewable vitamin and calcium tablets, energy bars, dry fruits, apricots, and so on—but found ourselves unable to consume even a bite, and forced to return to Taluka, dazed and confounded, this time swearing to make a vivid spectacle of the photographs taken by us of the monstrous tree that had cut off all routes in the ascent to Ranibaug.

Pratyusha had already made arrangements to sell the photographs to *National Geographic*, a plan of which I strictly disapproved, but nevertheless felt impelled to comply with. When we did finally manage to locate representatives from the magazine, they had a litany of questions for us to answer regarding the photographs before they could proceed with their publication. Some thought it manmade, a product of some bizarre cult intent on blocking access to Ranibaug (a site which had eluded even some of their most adventurous photographers) and thereby consolidating its exclusivity. Others proclaimed it to be a geological abnormality, an archaeological find: not a tree but instead some accumulation of aberrant earth that defied explanation, akin almost to the adobe formations unearthed at the ancient city of Petra.

Once disclosed to the readership of the magazine, the photographs had the desired effect. A team of geologists from the Wadia Institute immediately detailed an expedition. An elaborate boring device was constructed to stir its unshakeable constitution which blended into the very base of the cliff itself. It seemed to them to have sprung directly out of the rock face, like some solidified geyser of wooden flesh.

Several excursions were made to the land where that enormous tree stood. Some by routine survey personnel, some by scientists, some by mining expeditions, some by logging and timber enterprises. But no one succeeded in getting it to budge an inch. Each party warned their successors of the evil that lay within the Tree. Some said it was haunted, and planted there by some deranged sadhu, and that each person who attempted to destroy it was in turn destroyed. Some said it was an evolutionary experiment forged by some quasi-simian civilization that predated even the early Cenozoic age, and that it was waiting to emerge in its full form from subterranean caverns near the Earth's core, where it had been stored for centuries. Some said that its glandular secretion consisted of a series of complex multicellular organisms comprised of compounds whose elements could not be identified and were possibly of alien origin. They assumed varying chemical properties in the gaseous, or liquid form.

No one could really come to terms with the mystery of this Tree. The more scientists studied it, the more they were perplexed by its properties, and the less they could account for what they witnessed. One thing was for certain—it was growing at a phenomenal rate.

chapter four

Our next stop several months later was Swaami Atal-Anivaarya's Forest Guest House, where we found ourselves inadvertently snooping around for a few days, stumbling out into the adjacent forest for the supposed purpose of collecting sturdy samples for the rock-climbing wall to be constructed at HRA as per Swaami Ji's instructions.

Swaami Ji was not in attendance when we made our visit—it being a weekday after all—and so, with the exception of the four caretakers immersed busily in their chores, there was only a single sadhu present, an aged fakir of sorts, with approachable eyes, and a friendliness of bearing that shone in sharp contrast to Swaami Atal-Anivaarya's marked air of authority. His name was Somdev, and he claimed to have survived solely on tea and water for the last couple of years. He had arrived only the night before last and was eagerly awaiting the Swaami Ji's presence. When we learned shortly after making his acquaintance that he came from Ranibaug, we took him into confidence, and spoke of our previous visit, even shared with him photographs of the Tree that had stirred the public's imagination.

On one of our excursions, we took him along in my Gypsy to scan the neighbouring premises for any trace of the indefinable creature we were in search of. He even offered to guide us back up to Ranibaug through an alternate route if we so desired. He, however, failed to answer any of our questions pertaining to the more troubling matters at hand, feigning ignorance or perhaps practicing a caution neither of us were aware of. He did know of the Tree though, and spoke of it with musing regularity, in a stillness and wonder most befitting its incommunicable features. Of the temple, he had not the remotest desire to converse about. The plight of his fellow exiles he would not touch upon. It was perhaps too severe a subject for casual discourse.

'I happen to have seen those blasted things!' I reminded him, steering clear of a ditch as he wobbled about in the backseat clutching on to the hand rest for dear life.

'So you have…' he bounced up, and then remained almost upright in his seat as if standing over it.

'Are you comfortable at the back?' Pratyusha inquired, leaning her shoulder over.

'N-n-not exactly…' the sadhu stuttered, then changed his mind—'I'm fine! Nothing to worry about.'

We halted beside the water hole where I had previously sighted it. Pratyusha quickly assembled the tripod for her camera on the bonnet of the jeep, and peered into the shrubbery through a pair of binoculars. The sadhu sat silently in the back seat, keeping a sound lookout, and resting his flute sulkily on the lowered window. I insisted he abstain from playing it. He cupped the palms of his hands around his mouth and made a variety of sounds which I suppose were intended to draw or attract whatever it was that we were after. Pratyusha sat cross-legged on the bonnet, camera in hand, attention still peeled on anything that could be possibly skulking around in the foliage. I stepped out of the jeep, slamming the door shut.

'Shhh...' Pratyusha squawked. 'Be silent, will you!'

She hunched down low to peep through the viewfinder and fastened her index finger around the flat, trigger-like button, aiming the muzzle of the lens into the waterhole. She tried to hold the contraption steady but her forelimbs trembled, and just as she adjusted the footing of the tripod, I heard something move in the foliage circling the waterhole. She looked at the sadhu, who nodded in response. It was apparent that something had caught his attention. She handed over her binoculars to him and whispered an instruction into his ear, on account of which his expression turned frightfully pale and alarmingly uncertain. In a matter of seconds, the creature emerged from the undisturbed surface of the waterhole, and swerved across the bushes to pounce into the underlying shrubbery. Pratyusha swung the camera around and clicked twice. The sadhu, gathering his wooden flute, jumped out of the backseat and tiptoed over to the undergrowth it was hiding in. He prodded the flute at the vegetation four times with his upper torso turned away before he managed to startle it from its refuge.

It bounced out in an instant, and staring at us dumbfounded with open-mouthed terror and harrowed eyes, stumbled about on its hind legs before crouching on all fours to scurry across into the surrounding forest. The 'WHIR'—'ZOOM'—'BING' of the assembled Nikon photo camera whizzed away within a fraction of a second. Pratyusha kept readjusting the focal length and clicked furiously on until it had vanished off into the all-encompassing tangle of green.

The sadhu and myself huddled around the camera to inspect the photographs Pratyusha had captured. There was one in sharp focus where one could gather in resolute detail, the incongruous features that spanned its shambling form. It looked more or less the same since when I had last seen it, only its head had grown a considerable amount in the intervening years, almost disproportionate to the dimensions of the rest of the anatomy. As if the bulky head of a bear had been planted atop the timid neck of a cow. The tips of its limbs were neither paws nor hoofed nor webbed, they resembled neither a claw nor a hand, but were outstretched with a plumage of innumerable ingrown nails and protruding scales sprouting a mess of fur and feathers. Its skull was determinedly ovoid in shape compared with the rest of the rectangular body, bereft of a tail yet humped with an irregular bulge weighing upon its back.

'Hmmmm…' the sadhu purred, as we stumbled back along the rocky pathways up to the Guest House.

Pratyusha turned her upper torso around over the backrest on registering the sounds that escaped him. 'Hmm?' she crumpled her brow.

'Hmm…' the sadhu nodded, his head poking out of the open window like a puppy bracing the air.

'If you've got a sound that belongs to the Hindustani language, then spit it out!' Pratyusha ordered. 'What are you saving it for, Dusshera?'

'Hah!' the sadhu cackled, his mouth wide open and his jagged teeth looming like white glacial mountains over his blackened tongue. 'I have nothing to say about what we just saw, my child!' he looked her dead in the eyes, then proceeded to stare out of the window. 'I have not seen it before, and I don't think I wish to see it ever again, even in the pictorial form.'

'Well, you don't have to see it again,' Pratyusha wobbled about in her seat. 'No one's asking you to examine it. But now that you *have* seen it, what do you have to say about it?'

'I don't have anything to say about it,' he said.

'You saw it up close even, with the pair of binoculars I gave you.'

'I scarcely even know how to work these.' He held up the strap and handed it back to her over the partition that split up the jeep.

'But you did see it with the naked eye?' she persisted.

'I did…' he swung his head up and down, slightly flustered. 'As did you.'

'And?' she opened only half her mouth.

One of my tires spun over a crater in the kachha-raastha, lobbing us leftward as the car curved along towards the front gate of the Guest House.

'I have only one thing to say about it…' the sadhu crankily decided. 'And it shall be said not here, in these unholy grounds, but amidst the hallowed graces of Ranibaug.'

chapter five

There being no internet at the Guest House, and certainly no perennially available electricity, we had to wait out a torturous night before we could transfer the collected data over to our point of contact in *National Geographic Magazine* and depart smoothly without suspicion being aroused in the hearts of our unpredictable caretakers.

Dinner was served at eight as per scheduled. The sadhu of course abstained from any kind of solids, opting instead for a glass of water boiled in mint and cinnamon to ease his throat. The four caretakers, clad in sleeveless khaki camouflage jacket and army cap, were silent as ever. Not a word occurred to them, or ever a point of common interest broached.

'When is Swaami Ji expected?' I asked, breaking the morose silence.

'On the weekend.' One of them answered without eye contact, the voice came as if from a disembodied spoon shovelling a pit of daal amid a heap of rice.

'I see…' I took a bite of the carefully prepared cauliflower which had been soaked in nothing more than mustard oil as per my knowledge, and thereafter fried in mustard seed, exerting an inordinate influence on the sinuses.

'I hope you have prepared the bill for tomorrow morning,' Pratyusha spoke with her mouth half-full. 'As we intend to depart at the crack of dawn.'

The four caretakers all turned from their bowls in a collective glower which caused her to cough out loud—'You see, we intend to miss the early morning traffic on the highway.'

'And you too Babaji?' one of them asked of the sage.

'Oh no…' he took a sip of the lukewarm liquid he had been nursing. 'Not in the least. I intend to stay here until the Swaami Ji's return.'

Holding his flute up like a sceptre, he arose from the long wooden dining table and hobbled over on one leg to the defunct fireplace. Pratyusha wrapped one arm around her camera case, watching his every move carefully with dead-eyed precision.

'Is that a Sony Ma'am?' one of the men addressed her without looking up from his plate.

'No,' she exhaled. 'It's a Nikon.'

'Ah…' the man munched away. 'I see…' he cleared aside another spoonful from the mess of rice and daal on his plate. 'Rakesh, could you pass the salt!' he asked one of his co-workers.

On being handed the salt shaker, he dug out a patch of plain rice from his plate and catapulted it off into the verandah for the Dobermans to feast on. 'We have a lot of wildlife photographers coming out here,' he said, without looking at either of us, his gaze still hovering about the squalling dogs fighting over a speck of rice in the verandah. 'Some from *Sanctuary Magazine*,' he continued. 'Some from WWF, Project Tiger, trappers, nature clubs, students, zoologists, especially ornithologists. Bird watchers, we had a party of four ladies just the other day, in fact. Bird Watching Society from Dehra Dun. Golden Wings, I think they were called.'

'Gilded Wings!' another one correctively grunted.

'Gilded Wings! My name's Sankalp by the way.' The talkative fellow finally introduced himself. 'This is Anshuman.' He pointed at the man who corrected him. 'And that's Rakesh and Parshuram.'

The two that remained saluted with their spoons, tipping their caps faintly at the Madam.

'What do you do?' Sankalp abruptly turned towards me.

'I'm sorry?' I gulped.

'What's your line of work?' he leaned forward and raised his voice ever so slightly.

'Oh…' I took another bite. 'Engineer,' I said.

'And you Madam?' he turned back to Pratyusha.

'Teacher,' she spoke without opening her mouth.

'At the institute?'

'That's right.'

'I see…' Sankalp smiled. 'Then I take it that photography is merely a hobby for you people? Not exactly a pressing vocation, is it?'

'Oh no…' I said. 'As I said….' I took a long pause over which I chewed my food. '…we went out to collect rock samples. We barely took any photos even.'

'Really?' his eyes lit up. Pratyusha's wilted.

'It wasn't working properly,' I bluffed.

'What?'

'The camera.' I lifted another spoonful from my plate and dallied around with it before sinking my teeth in.

Pratyusha caught Sankalp's gaze swishing over to the camera case in an instant. 'Really?' he flattened his eyebrows. 'Maybe we could fix it for you?'

'No need,' Pratyusha promptly answered before he had even finished framing the proposition.

'As I said,' he laughed, showing his teeth. 'We have a lot of wildlife photographers come up here, Ma'am.'

'I heard that.' Now that the eye contact was being belatedly returned, she spoke without deigning to look at him.

'We happen to know a little about electronic repair work. It's part of the job. A sort of necessity. How to repair a torch, a watch, a radio, a walky-talky, an invertor, a boiler, a telephone, even a camera or television set.

'No thanks,' Pratyusha affirmed. 'It's not working because there isn't a plug point to put its charger in…' she took a pause, then thought up a reason. 'The electricity being gone and all.'

'Ahh…but that's where you're wrong, Ma'am!' he got up from the table with his plate significantly emptied. 'You should have told one of us. We would have gladly provided you with such a plug point, or power source. You see, the electricity may be gone.' This he addressed to me. 'But we do have provisions for what to do in the event of an emergency. There had been a bit of an electricity crisis a couple of years back.' Here he looked to the sadhu. 'Ever since, the electricity has been a bit…uh…what's the word… erratic. Comes and goes! Which is why we had to install an invertor which also happens to have conked out at present. But you see there is a small cabin in the property where we have a small generator…'

'Generator?' I chewed.

'Runs on fuel. If we keep the motor running you can leave your camera to charge there for the night, and by the morning have it equipped to capture any souvenir that might catch your fancy on the way out.'

Pratyusha and I quietly finished our dinners, ignoring the young man's malicious design to the best of our abilities. He kept insisting though as if it were his duty as our hospitable host and caretaker. The other three scarcely paid his persistence much mind, but it was apparent from their mildly indifferent manner that they were not altogether uninterested in the plight of our batteries.

'This is, after all, Swaami Shree Shree Gurudev.' He joined his hands together in abrupt solemnity. 'Atal-Anivaarya Natija's Forest Guest House and Bird Sanctuary. Where people come to learn about the animal kingdom, to observe them, to click pictures of them! In that regard, it's a sort of goldmine, with prospectors flocking here with camera case and belt pouch, ever ready to snap a sight fleetingly witnessed by them in the never-ending wait. It's like being a chowkidaar!' He laughed.

The sadhu sat silently all this while on the floor by the fireplace, his eyes closed shut and his forehead smooth and untroubled.

Pratyusha and I both simultaneously looked at each other as Sankalp spoke—'The first to click a sighting is the first to sell it off to a magazine and earn a bundle of money for it. Not a bad deal!' he rolled his lower lip up in admiration. 'And so they fight. Wildlife photographers. Scheme and cheat to keep their colleagues misdirected, send diversionary reports on the walky-talky, so that they can lay their eyes on the real goods.'

Parshuram started slurping somewhat impolitely at his bowl of daal, and buried his head into the rice before he was through with it.

'Don't mind him!' Sankalp smiled. 'He has his peculiar eating habits! Isn't exactly a master of dining room etiquette. Something the Swaami Ji tried to school him in even!' He suddenly smacked the bowl off the table with the back of his left hand, leaving Parshuram gaping into the table mat, stunned. 'Now go and pick it up!' He instructed the no doubt considerably younger, Parshuram.

Parshuram slowly arose and did what he was told to do.

'The animals keep track of who makes money off of their hides. Exploiting their appearance and cuddly facades. Don't think for a moment that the animals aren't clicking pictures of our guests. In the mind's eye. They all say animals do not possess the capability for abstract thought. But who knows?' he pondered. 'Who really *knows* what goes on inside of their furry little heads. They remember everything, they especially never forget a face! They can see everything, even in the dark, at night, in the deadening silence, they can even hear everything. They can hear us right now, talking about them. What we cannot perceive, they can hear. What is not visible to our naked eye, they can see clearly with both their eyes. Day and night. Watching us like ghosts!'

It was only then, at this rambling change of direction in the conversation, that Pratyusha made the mistake of inquiring into Swaami Atal-Anivaarya's supposed newfound technique of communicating with birds and certain animals.

chapter six

This revelation was greeted with astonished eyes, and a slightly bewildered silence. It failed to endear us any further into our hosts' confidence and only ignited their suspicions.

'It is not impossible to communicate in any form the mind may wish to.' Seemed to be the party line. It was the only explanation we received for the startling claim put forth by Pratyusha Negi. It, however, only increased his enthusiasm to provide for a plug point should we require the services of the camera on our way out.

'You should take back a souvenir,' Sankalp insisted, guiding us out the backway of the bungalow, down the cobbled path, past the well and up eventually to the boundary wall where a small laterite block squatted among the lychee trees and newly planted Gulmohar saplings.

A single 40-watt bulb with a one-armed filament hung from the ceiling. Sankalp, with the aid of his torch, pumped on the motor with a few windings of its wheel till it provided all the dim illumination available in the dingy room. And rusting amid the cracked and splintered walls, was a small three-point triangular socket that looked not like it had been used in over a century.

A squirrel wound its way along the edges of the floor and disappeared into the cracks of the night. The soft squeal of a rat sounded somewhere from amid the corners of the cavernous cabin. The three holes of the plug point stared on at us in a kind of statuesque frown. The shadows emanating from the dangling bulb obscured the insides of its cylindrical apertures. As Pratyusha neared it, charger in hand, she recoiled momentarily from it in fear of an electric-shock—but when assured by Sankalp that it was safe for her—injected the three pins slowly into the wall with the little finger on her left hand pressed gently at the switch that lay beside it. We watched as the little red light on the camera came on, detecting a current.

'You got some choice goods in there?' Sankalp grinned, pointing at the uncovered camera with its lens cap still on.

'I beg your pardon,' I intervened.

'You storing anything you wish to hide?' he smirked.

'I don't see what you mean,' I shook my head in forced bafflement.

'Look, Mister!' Pratyusha finally snapped. 'I've had enough with your nosing around. Why don't you just mind your own goddamned business for god's sake.'

'You don't seem to have a mighty high opinion of God, Madam.' His smiled vanished. 'Referring to him in vain the way you do. We're a God-fearing lot out here and do better than to use the almighty's name to settle our own personal scores. God doesn't have time for that! He has to see to more important things.'

She pulled the plug of the charger out in an instant, and began bundling up the wires to stuff them into the camera case.

'You don't have to get upset, Madam. You can still use our electricity. Please. By all means. Be my guest. The

Swaami Ji has given us strict instructions, to see to the ultimate welfare and care of our guests. We do whatever we can to provide you with a pleasant stay!'

Just then, as we were about to exit the cabin, we were at once arrested by the rumbling of some motions from within the plug point. The rotations of the motor grew more vigorous, the bulb wobbled to a spark, the walls began a tremble and before we could even detect the violent shriek of rats rising steadily from inaudibility—OUT SPRANG a profusion of crawling caterpillars and centipedes, growing longer and more lurid as they poured out of the holes of the plug point! They scattered about the floor as they fell and began to encircle our footsteps. Pratyusha stamped at them maniacally. Sankalp shone his torch beam at the floor, spinning back the wheel of the motor into silence and darkness. Once the generator went off, we leapt out of the cabin covered in earthworms and leeches, reaching frantically for a pair of matches stolen away somewhere in the multiple compartments of Sankalp's cargo trousers.

We managed to light a few and ward off the writhing vermin from our bodies, burning our own skins in the process. The application of a lit matchstick to the human forearm can produce the most bewildering results. At once, the sensation of a burn prolongs itself into insensibility, and strikes like a snakebite when the senses are alert for even a fraction of a millisecond. The absence of a strong wind allowed for the burning of multiple matches and their easy waving to and fro in the darkness to scare out the insects from our person. We ran our arms vigorously through our bodies, clearing off every speck of dirt or dust that felt like an insect. Their snake-like motions poked at the soles of my feet. I rubbed my calves, felt the inside of my socks, and dusted my shoes for any trace of vermin.

Scratching furiously, we made our way back up the cobbled path in a dizzying flight from the cabin. Thankfully, the camera case had been strapped along to Pratyusha's shoulders. But the charger had been left inside in the panic, and was probably by now being devoured by the insects. Pratyusha contemplated whether or not to turn back and retrieve it. We had about thirty-two per cent battery left in the device, and an entire night and drive back to the city to wait out.

chapter seven

None of us slept that night. We sat by the semi-enclosed canteen area at the dinner table, occasionally waltzing off to the verandah for a brief stroll. But none us, the sadhu included, thought it fit to leave the confines of the bungalow, at least on that particular night.

'If only we could have grabbed some photographs of those things.' Pratyusha thought out aloud before smacking her own head clean of such an unwarranted consideration.

The four caretakers had by now called it a night and retreated to their quarters at the back of the house. Even Sankalp, who perhaps exhausted from all his talk, refrained from staying on in our company any longer.

The three of us were now alone around the dinner table, and spoke whisperingly with one eye slanted in the direction of the reception.

'Are you coming with us?' she asked Baba Somdev.

He simply bowed his head in reply, and then wondered—'Where?'

'Ranibaug!' she said.

'Do you wish to go back, my child?' A ripple of concern spread upon his eyes.

'That's where we're going after we've rightfully deposited those photographs.' She looked at me, clutching tightly at the camera case, not letting it out of her sight for even an instant.

'If that's what you wish, I shall accompany you!' he murmured.

'What about the Swaami Ji?' I asked.

'That can be saved for later…' he decided. 'I will meet him when I so desire. In the near future. When he graces this Guest House with his presence.'

'Can you get us past that tree?' I wondered.

'Ahh…' the wrinkles on his face all collectively came together as if to join in a smile. 'The tree…' he mused. 'I know a way around that tree…' he pointed a finger to the sky with professorial aplomb. 'I even happen to know what that tree is…'

The dawn hesitated to oblige us with its arrival, it broke instead into a streak of red, unnoticeable amid the distant clouds. As the three of us gathered around the rear of the jeep to load up our luggage, one of the roaming dogs nearly threatened to tear loose on old Baba Somdev. On hearing the deafening howls of the Doberman, Sankalp hopped out of his shack looking considerably dishevelled in his torn and tattered vest as he put on his camouflage t-shirt and denim jacket. He buttoned up his trousers, slipping on a pair of Caterpillar boots without socks and rushed up to answer to the summons of the dog.

'Brunooo! Shhhh!' He rubbed the dog's neck, catching hold of him by the collar. 'Noooo!'

We had done our last checks on our respective rooms; all that was left in mine was a tissue paper, a tooth pick, some plastic wrappers, and a couple of used batteries with a half empty bottle of whisky. Both of us left our room doors open as we were certain we had not left anything of value inside, and after having freshened up, strolled up towards the reception, taking in the scenery before preparing to bid it goodbye. Baba Somdev did the odd Surya Namaskar here and there to welcome the sun, one of the caretakers was gargling furiously by an outdoor washbasin, the dogs had been tied back to their kennels, and the jeep stood loaded by the gravelled driveway, ready to depart after we had paid the bill.

At the reception behind the cash counter, Sankalp began handling the transaction with Pratyusha, who tried her level best to smile back at him, expressing our gratitude for their kind and thoughtful hospitality. While going over our bill, he noticed he had charged us with an additional sixth meal as breakfast time was approaching, and since neither of us had breakfasted as yet, he insisted we join the staff for a plate of bun-omelets Rakesh had painstakingly prepared for our delectation.

I was a bit puzzled at his intentions for doing so, for surely it seemed to me that we were the kind of company the Resort could do without.

'That's very kind of you, Sankalp!' bowed Pratyusha. 'But I am afraid we must be on our way if we are to make the highway before sunrise, and we have already packed and loaded our jeep.'

'That's perfectly alright,' said Sankalp. 'I can easily get Rakesh or Anshuman to mind your belongings while you eat. I'm sure you must be famished and weary from all your travels and excursions. You have a long drive ahead of you. A tiresome one too, through those rugged mountain roads. It is better to get some strength in you before you proceed. And I hope you haven't placed any objects of value in the bags, say cameras, for instance. Although none of our staff including Parshuram are known to steal, it is better to avoid providing temptation.'

'That's quite alright, Sankalp,' Pratyusha assured him, losing the last thread of patience. 'I'm afraid we will have to be on our way!' she stressed.

'But we have made breakfast for all of your party. If you don't eat, then it will go to waste.'

'I am sure the four of you accompanied by those fine Dobermans will do justice to the spread you seem to have prepared.'

'How about you, Babaji?' all of a sudden he turned to Somdev who came in to check if he had left his flute in the dining room. 'Didn't you say you were going to wait till Swaami Ji's arrival?'

'I have some work in Ponta Saahib,' he said.

'In Ponta Saahib?' Sankalp smiled.

'That's right!' he nodded. 'I shall be back later.'

'How? You won't be able to hitch a ride with the water tanker that brought you here day before yesterday. Babaji, you are beyond where the buses go!' he laughed.

'Water tanker?' I thought to myself. 'What for?'

I glanced out through the window to the river trickling away into the low horizon illuminated in the distance. The water level had definitely risen since the last time I had strolled about its shores with Swaami Ji.

Sankalp went off towards the dining verandah, barking out orders to Parshuram—who was doing a lousy job of mopping up the wooden flooring—and took a right turn to enter the kitchen.

The two of us just stood alone at the reception desk while the sadhu went out to guard our belongings by the jeep. Pratyusha was visibly apprehensive of Sankalp's intentions. From inside the kitchen, we could hear him yelling out instructions to Anshuman to lay the table for breakfast.

'Let's just finish our breakfast and be on our way!' I suggested. 'There's nothing to worry about.'

chapter eight

It was about a quarter to seven when we set off from the Guest House, shuffling hurriedly past its unlocked entrance, not even deigning to shut the gate once we had successfully exited it. The watchman who was supposed have been minding the gate was again nowhere to be seen. Perhaps he was on leave.

With some nourishment in us, the drive proved effortless. The sadhu had had his customary cup of tea and that seemed to suffice. The two of them dozed off as we touched the highway, and awoke with the blare of traffic that greeted us on the old Hrishikesh Bypass route. While stuck in the congested tollway, I searched my phone for network, the internet had returned. I immediately awoke Pratyusha and told her to get to work on transferring the data at once with the aid of her laptop resting in the storage compartment at the back of the jeep which the sadhu soon passed over.

The pictures took some time to load. The battery was dropping down to an anemic thirty per cent. The cable to connect the camera to the computer was a part of its charging device that was now no longer with us. She had inserted the memory card right into a slim rectangular port on the side of the laptop, and was depending solely on the force of the internet from our phones for their courier. On nearing Dehradun, we thankfully chanced upon a roadside Cyber Café and Xerox Centre, where we immediately pulled up. From outside in the car, I could see Pratyusha arguing agitatedly with the Sardaarji behind the counter, convincing him of the urgency of her situation. The computers were all occupied, and as a timid college student exited she leaped over to one of the desktops and settled her camera case on the mousepad.

I waited with the sadhu outside in the car, trying to strike up some conversation. 'The pictures will be printed the following week.' I informed him. 'In the next issue. If there is any monetary reward to be gained from this, I assure you we will split it three ways! You can rest assured you will have your full share before this is over.'

'How much did you get for the tree?' he asked in a sudden shift of tone.

'How do you know about that?' I said.

'Everyone does,' he shrugged, reaching for his flute. 'At least anyone who has anything to do with Ranibaug. And is aware of it. And knows of its unique characteristics. They printed that story a few weeks ago, didn't they?'

'Who told you?' I turned to look into the cyber café. Pratyusha was typing furiously away into a keyboard tray.

'Just because I roam the forests, doesn't mean I can't read or write,' the sadhu laughed. 'We're not illiterate. On the contrary. Some of us are quite well read. More so than even you city-folk that boast fancy college degrees. We happen to know things of which you have no knowledge. Like take the tree for instance,' he supposed. 'You printed the story, brought it to light before the whole world, revealed it, are supposedly an authority on it, but what can you tell the world about it that your photographs already can't tell us.'

'As in?'

'Same goes for the animal you captured photographic evidence of. What do *you* know about it?' he said. 'What special information have you to offer on it? What makes you an authority on what you have witnessed?'

'The fact of my witnessing it!' I said.

'Hah!' He leaned back in his seat and stared outside his window at the sun beating down on the dotted line at the centre of the road. 'I will show you a way around that tree,' he said.

Pratyusha stepped back into the passenger seat with a pronounced 'THUD', gathering the camera case onto her lap. 'Move!' she snapped her fingers at the steering wheel.

'Did they go through?' I asked.

'They have been duly received,' she adjusted her head in the affirmative.

'Any response as yet?'

'We'll be hearing from them soon. Take it to a petrol pump. We better fill up. We have a long drive ahead to Taluka.'

chapter nine

'In the year 1975,' the sadhu began, on our long and winding drive up the spiralling roadways, and vertiginous passes beyond Uttarkashi. 'One day upon a small hillock in the glaciers of Gaumukh, an old ascetic decided to set his feet in the ground, and settle there for the rest of his days. He tied his hair into a long pigtail, his white beard glistening in the sunlight, naked without a scrap of clothing on, he stood there! He set his roots into the earth, and raised his right hand up into the air. Like this!' he demonstrated with a similar action. 'He's been standing in that position ever since. He hasn't moved till today. Some say that he gradually began to turn into a tree. Grass began to grow from his weathered skin, and his bones began to protrude from beneath his sinews like wood, wound up by a network of veins and arteries that appeared as if embedded in stone. His entire anatomy resembled that of a skeleton. He began to rot like an old banyan tree. He is still alive in some state of consciousness hovering halfway between life and death. These days he's even presented in various fairs and carnivals like a sideshow freak or like some mutant. In the numaaishes of Bastar in Chattisgarh, in Madhya Pradesh, even once in the state of Uttarakhand. He was presented to the public in an act that was known in some quarters as the "Silence of the Tree". Like the two-headed chicken or the three-legged man who crawls along the floor like a spider in front of everyone. Our tree is the wellspring of life. It is there to provide us with infinite support and shelter. For eternity. Nature's own artificial intelligence, that can supersede both the human and animal kind and outlive and outwit both!'

This was now my fourth visit up to Ranibaug. We were still stocked with the mountaineering gear and tent-kits from our previous trip a few months ago. They had been stowed away in the storage hold of the jeep and were unloaded once we found a safe spot to park the vehicle. Taluka seemed bleary and laden with gloom. It was sundown when we reached. The tall tale of the tree had settled upon my fancy, and occupied most of my subsequent meditations. The sage Somdev was the most navigationally adept companion I had enjoyed thus far. He knew his way up the mountain-sides like the sadhu we had first encountered at the campsite up in Harki Dun who had lead us up to that troubling rockface, and abandoned us shortly thereafter.

We were able to cover the trek up to Harki Dun in a matter of a day and a half, as opposed to the two days it had taken us one our first trip. Pratyusha proposed we carry on and conspired determinedly to prevent all possibilities of a halt. She was the fittest of the lot, with an inexhaustible endurance that bordered almost on the fanatical! In the manner of certain P.T. instructors—competing perhaps only with Shera's athletic vitality. So intent was she on beholding her grandmother with her very own eyes, that she seemed to possess a near-militant devotion to completing this journey.

We would not fail this time! And indeed, we didn't. We made it easily past the rock-face through the same precipitous ledge I was previously taken along by the sadhu that found me in a condition very nearly resembling death. Somdev tracked each route with an almost extra-sensory keenness. He knew which rock to step on, which path would provide for the dubious passage of three adults, which platform would collapse with our weight, which branch seemed steady enough for support, and each broken route up the jagged, rocky formations that surrounded us—the ones that yielded a dead-end, and the ones which gave a clear-entry up to a more walkable pathway.

The sadhu led the way, but Pratyusha overtook him eagerly at every opportunity, her lungs squeakily huffing past us at an alarming pace, the mud beneath her trekking boots displaced with every assertive step. She had even carried along her cushioned Reebok running shoes in the event that they were required for a more daunting terrain that had to be fleetingly covered with a lighter foot. It took only the ruins of the tattered campsite we crossed to finally stall her from her unflappable march up the steep slopes and boulders.

She was, no doubt, struck by its presence. This time, we managed to unearth certain files from the bottom of one of the old rucksacks that lay hidden below the heap of belongings in the torn tent-hold. There were identification cards dating back to the year 1970, a log-book filled with scribbled entries for the purpose of documenting the survey expedition to Ranibaug, passport-sized younger renditions of the faces I encountered there. Even the late sage whose hour of deliverance we had been called upon to witness, bereft of shaggy hair and beard, a cleaner-cut smile than the one that had greeted me by his funeral pyre. One of the faces sighted in the antiquated rashan cards seemed also to belong to the older sadhu that played the marine-shelled shankh from within the temple. A late convert it seems to the ascetic way of life. Many of the Swaami Ji's belongings too appeared secretly to occupy the floor; the stray rudraksh, a book on bird anatomy, a burnt-out agarbathi, scattered remnants of Pooja samagri, the odd crepe bandage.

Pratyusha sifted through all the dusty disintegrating papers, in search of some sign of her grandmother's documentation. Even a name or a signature on some worn out file. Baba Somdev walked up to the lone rucksack that still stood upright near the rubble of a bonfire. He poked at it first with his flute, then opened its laces slowly to peer inside.

'All we have here are some goddamn trigonometrical drawings,' Pratyusha threw aside a stack of sheets. 'Nothing of any consequence.'

'Wait just a minute,' I bent down to gather the drawings from the pebbled floor. 'I've seen these before…there's one that stands out.' I hurriedly leafed through the triangular shapes and graphs, even unbound a loose contour map with wriggling curvilinear forms nearing imbecility. 'Here it is!' I spotted the pyramidal tomb at the bottom of the pile. 'What do you make of this?'

She studied it in the torchlight, her eyes swelling serenely as she ran her gaze along its intricate geometry. Before she could place an association, my eyes began to roam the lower nooks and corners of the tent. When we had previously been in its confines, our principal aim was to find food of any sort—we scavenged the sleeping bags and gunnysacks for any trace of even a crumb, emptied the rucksacks in search of a spare packet of biscuits—and so had neglected to chance upon what I then discovered, which was to my wildest astonishment, a vintage photo camera.

I brought it out from the sea of belongings the back of the tent-hold provided shelter to, and showed it to Pratyusha from whose hands the diagram of the pyramidal tomb promptly fell.

'Give it to me!' she snatched it from my hands. 'Where did you find this?'

I remembered the photographs we had recovered, but a camera had eluded us on our previous inspection.

'AAAAAHHHHH!!!' Baba Somdev called from outside the tent.

We rushed out to find before his feet, a corpse of the same indefinable animal lying twisted and gnarled on the ground—only half its upper torso spilling out of the rucksack. The hump at the back was visible, it was considerably smaller though. We had a chance now to study its face, to let each feature sink in, and examine its relation to any other species of animal kind as yet discovered. The closest association we could come up with was that of the hedgehog. Its scaly surface also bore a remote kinship to the Iguana. Its head seemed made of the same humanoid skull, its limbs wore a similar design to the writhing branches and tentacles of the Tree. It was quite unlike the winged-serpents spawned by the mountain. Apart, of course, from the shape of the skull, which seemed uniform on all accounts, even when considering the multiplying insects that had swarmed me now on two occasions—which seemed pregnant with a similar lobe about to emerge from their swelling tops. The shape of the temple, the grotesque deportment of the Tree, the pyramidal tomb, the oblong slabs at the bottom of the water body, the glowing orb-like luminescence mysteriously inhabiting the bottom of the mine. They all seemed to constitute some remote design.

'How far is it from here?' Pratyusha asked, checking the time on her wristwatch.

'About two hours,' I supposed.

'One,' Baba Somdev stated.

She hoisted up her rucksack and strung it up onto her shoulders without as much as a thought. 'We better be on our way then.'

chapter ten

The message received on Pratyusha's mobile phone from *National Geographic* had arrived when we had spent the first night in Taluka itself, it being the closest spot to connectivity we were likely to enjoy—a fact that had been carefully concealed from me till we were to set foot in Ranibaug, were its contents a potential deterrent to my enthusiasm regarding the expedition.

'Startling new discovery!' it read. 'Come back to our offices at once. We will bear the expense for your travel. Please revert at the earliest.'

In light of this deception, my first steps up the terraced ascension to the familiar drone of the temple were marked with a slightly ill-tempered assurance. This time we were struck by none of the mental incapacities that had plagued our prior expeditions beyond Harki Dun. The unsteadiness of sensation that was a constant feature of this part of the journey had escaped us; owing possibly to the sadhu's proficiency up the steep mountain walls. With the exception of a light wheezing on Pratyusha's part, the result no doubt of her inordinate exertion, none of us were ridden with any species of fatigue, either bodily or mental. We were well nourished this time, having carried along a shamefully lavish amount of food and beverages that ached our backs but quelled our moods. The sadhu consumed none of it, adhering to his strict principles—leaving the lion's share of the spoils to the two of us. We enjoyed them with a heartiness that bordered on gluttony. On the first night itself we had, Pratyusha and myself alone, gone through three tins of baked beans, an entire can of Dak Luncheon meat (something the sadhu would not in his wildest moments consider), two packets of Maggi Veg-Atta Noodles, two of Top Ramen-Oats, and a sprinkling of salted crackers. It kept us in good stead for the better part of the morning, as we were to not enjoy a break till at least lunch time, when we set up the stove and prepared a reasonable portion of MTR Rajma Chaawal which we had with a generous helping of Cuppo Noodles. A few biscuits and dry fruits were consumed on the trek, and we had with us a more than ample store of water. Pratyusha's rucksack contained two bottle-holders on either side which were filled to the utmost breadth of their circular capacities. Sometimes on the walk, one of the large water-canteens would fall from her back, and one of us would invariably have to pick it back up and drink from it before handing it back over to its allotted holdings.

The temple stared at us from up above, its two square-shaped apertures brooding like angry eyes. Baba Somdev bowed at its appearance and caressed the very earth that stretched up to its feet. Pratyusha was affected by its architecture. She recognised the wholly alien and uncanny nature of its aspect, so remote and cut off from anything constructed in the Hindu world, in the name of any deity this side of the Indian Ocean. She thought it Druid or Celtic in shape and form. It reminded her of the unnecessariness of the Stonehenge and other such inexplicable structures that loomed over the earth like an insult to manual labour. From what she shared, it seemed to bring to her mind 'hermetical shrines built by madmen to an invisible goddess'.

'What?' I questioned.

'A mermaid coral kingdom!'

'I'm sorry?' I asked again.

'A lofty sandcastle!' Echoes of images spun before her mind. 'The bottling of the Aurora Borealis. Gigantic hillocks with harrowed expression! Town planning. Cityscapes constructed from Jenga built with legs of Lego! Blocks! Bricks! Baking a cake…' her babblings now deteriorated to the infantile. 'Bah-Bah Black Sheep.'

'Pratyusha!' I shouted. 'Get a hold of yourself.'

'Yess doctor!' she began to chew on her fingernails. 'I'm sorry!'

'You're what?' I frowned. A wind was now beginning to blow our way.

'Sorry…' she said.

'What on earth has gotten into you Pratyusha? Are you feeling okay?'

'I'm feeling fine!' she said.

'Then?'

'It's just that I'm….' she thought long and hard. 'Sorry…'

'What the hell are you talking about Pratyusha?' I caught hold of her hand and began to guide her away from the temple. The sadhu, ignoring shrewdly this demented display, entered in with eyes closed, not even looking our way.

'What the hell!' she snapped herself out of it. 'Where's the camera?'

'Which one? It's in your bag.'

'N-n-no the other one…' she stuttered. 'The one we found.'

'Here.' I unhooked a strap of the rucksack from my left shoulder. 'I have it!'

I had wrapped it in a bundle of woollen pullovers, and placed it carefully right at the top of my clothes above the stove. I brought it out delicately and handed it over to Pratyusha, who then proceeded to store it in her own rucksack as if mine was somehow lacking in dependability.

'I'm going to check the negatives in a lab once we get back,' she explained.

'*If* we get back…' I swayed and sort of shook my head.

A ragged band of mountainfolk emerged from the stone-arched entrance to the temple, greeting us in their incomprehensible dialect. Baba Somdev seemed to speak it fluently and conversed with a few of them near the altar. They watched us in their woolly garments and mountainous layers of shawl with a sort of bemused fascination. One of them offered to exchange his ornate Fez for my HRA cap, which I gladly did. Baba Somdev whispered something into one of their ears, on account of which they all turned frightfully silent and visibly grave.

'What's the matter?' I asked, as we took off our footwear and stepped in. No one answered. They just gaped on at Pratyusha in awe.

'Have any of you seen Shera?' I then ventured to inquire.

'Shera?' one of them cackled.

'The lion!' Baba Somdev told them. 'I know of him. Your friend and guide. He is with us.'

'And what about the Professor?' I asked. 'Any word from him?'

'Not as yet,' declared Baba Somdev, mournfully.

'Where is everyone?' I asked.

Prayusha stood silent all this while, helplessly trying to recover her faculties. I could feel her starting to sway. The wind reduced for a flicker of a moment, and one of the gathered bunch simply spread out his hands and laughed. 'But everyone is here!'

'I mean Karma Bodh!' I said out loud.

Everyone now turned pale, the silence thickened, the air quivered, the walls hissed—Baba Somdev pressed his forefinger to his lips and motioned my way, placing his hands on my shoulders to take me out of the temple. Pratyusha followed us out. We put on our shoes and headed up to the edge of the peak.

'We don't refer to her by name!' Baba Somdev then informed me.

'I see…' I apologised as we descended the step ladder beyond the cliff.

Pratyusha hesitated to enter the cave complex once we found ourselves on that ledge. Something about the potential for claustrophobia frightened her.

'There's plenty of space inside,' I assured her. 'You won't feel claustrophobic. I promise you. I've been in there.' I pointed my neck in towards the entrance. 'You can trust me.'

Something about my words seemed to settle her, she placed her rucksack by the entrance and took a few deep breaths, then picking it back up and heaving it on her back, exhaled—'Let's go!'

We silently crept in, the three of us, feeling in the darkness for anything resembling an opening. Pratyusha finally shone her torch in to illuminate the distant corners and bends of the corridor we were slowly walking through. Baba Somdev then took the front, taking hold of the torch from her and wagging his index finger in a leftward direction. 'Here,' he whispered. 'This way!'

He proceeded down a passageway bedded with the pointed spikes of numerous stalactites. It was like walking on a Fakir's bed of nails.

'No wonder you only survive on tea and water,' I jested. 'You don't seem to feel pain,' I halted. 'This isn't the way I came in before. This is a different route. I can't be sure of where you're taking us.'

'Come with me,' he frowned, a harrowed impatience erupting on his otherwise friendly features.

'Just go!' Pratyusha shut her eyes and started to walk.

It took us exactly forty-one steps to cover that tract of thorns, I counted each one of them. The curving walkway descended down another flight of finely-chiselled steps leading us to a platform that overlooked the waterbody I had been submerged in. Not a soul occupied its pebbled shores. The hearth was empty of logs, and very sparse illumination provided by the odd torch or lantern made visible the entry to the mine-shelf.

Baba Somdev, however, had mapped an alternate route that lowered us after a long downward climb to the very stalactite covered doorway I had conversed with Karma Bodh at. The winged cocoons were gone from the ceiling. Nowhere was any member of the survey expedition in sight.

'WHERES IS SHE?' screamed Pratyusha.

'They have all proceeded down below,' he said, glowering into the depths of the pit from over the edge of the shelf.

'How?' she glanced over.

'By way of a vessel,' he said. 'It can be descended by rope too, if you wish.'

That was all the prompting she needed to remove a thirty-five-feet long roll of elastic wiring, which she fastidiously strung up to the edges of the rocky entranceway in multiple knots, each intended to anchor the fastening of the other. This prolonged anchorage occupied a good seven to eight feet, after which it dropped over the wall of the mine-shaft, leaving us with only a descent of some twenty-seven feet. We put on our gloves, knowing the need would arise for another one, which I swiftly produced from my rucksack, having foreseen the need. My rope provided another twenty-four feet, granting us a total length of a little over fifty feet, still negligible in the scheme of things, yet sufficient enough to provide us with a closer view of whatever it is that was down there. Perhaps when down there fifty feet below, we would come upon a possible fissure or if lucky, a shelf, which we thankfully did.

Once down there, Pratyusha rummaged through her rucksack, practically emptying it of its contents to unearth from one of its zips, another wire of a similar sort with a span of some thirty feet. The tip of our joined elastic wire and rope dangled over our heads. With a jump of a few feet, without hazard to the knees, we found ourselves on a four-by-six foot mine-shelf carved into the sloping wall. We began to shovel a pit in the rocky floor of the shelf with our bare hands, so as to devise a burial where the anchorage for another rope could be interred.

It took us about half an hour but we managed to cover it with enough rock and slabs of stone unpeeled from the wall of the mineshelf. There was sufficient weight on it to hold it. We even placed our heavy rucksacks on the covering just to be sure it granted us enough support till we reached another thirty-odd feet below the shelf, testing the stability of the rope. It nearly crackled a few times as we lowered ourselves down another thirty feet onto an eroded protrusion from amid the grizzled contours of the mineshaft.

Balance was of the essence here. A stance, or single toe in the wrong direction and the precarious platform we found ourselves on would stand us no longer.

It took multiple tugs with both of us pulling with all our might—our feet firmly planted on the jutting rock—to even begin to displace the anchorage we had moulded from the previous shelf. We had to yank at it incrementally, it being elastic, over the course of about fifteen minutes to forcefully loosen it from its curiously conceived holdings. There was one pull where I felt my feet slipping over the narrow edge of the eroded platform. I stumbled over a few loose rock fragments before Pratyusha grabbed me by the wrist and held me back as I watched the stones slowly tumble into the depths of the pit. The sound of their landing did not occur, or at least was not heard by us.

Having safely unfastened the rope after another ten minutes of vigorous pulling, we saw one of the rucksacks slide down the wall of the mineshaft, nearly knocking us down with it. It fell violently from the edge of the shelf, taking down with it a large globular rock, having probably unsettled the ground beside it. Some of the stony dust hit our faces as it powdered down into the drop, swimming languidly in the air as it receded—its particles illuminated vaguely by the all-encompassing glow of the mineshaft.

Pratyusha bound one end of the rope across the bulging rock formation beneath our feet, then stringing it up to our carabiners, began to proceed down an entirely vertical and featureless stretch of the wall. In the last instance of the climb down we had had to proceed one at a time, as the sturdiness of the anchorage was not sufficient enough to hold for the passage of two persons, even without the rucksack.

'Nails!' I shouted out, in a sudden burst of recollection.

There are moments when the speech uttered by one's tongue does not necessarily correspond with the contents of one's thoughts.

'What?' Pratyusha's head spun up at me from down below, her body still balanced tightly on the rope. She slid down another twelve feet, systematically loosening the grasp of her gloves.

'Nailssss!' I almost began to weep.

The mind was swirling with unthinkable details of the drop that awaited us.

'Naaaaaa…' I growled.

Pratyusha suddenly froze on the rope. 'There's nothing down here!' she called out, in a ringing echo. 'I think I better come back up!'

'Naaaaaaaaaahhh!!!!' I began to produce a sound, unidentifiable even to me. 'Wuuuuaaaaaahhhhh!!!'

'What the hell is wrong with you!' Pratyusha's head bobbed sideways as she tried to look up, swinging back and forth on the elastic rope.

'Waaaaaaaaaaaaaaaaaa!' I began to pound the edge of the eroded rock in protest.

'Nooooo!' Pratyusha wailed. 'Don't! You'll break it! Barkat Singh! What are you doing? Are you crazy! Have you gone mad?'

She climbed back up a few feet with a grimace of almost paralytic exertion.

Her teeth clenched, she pressed the soles of her boots against the wall and began to ascend up almost horizontally. Her forearms bulged as she tried to reach for the projected edge of the rock I was trying to dismantle. We were a good eighty to eighty-two feet below the mineshelf from which our joint wiring still hung, its tip lying from us now at a height of approximately thirty-odd feet. How we would attempt to cover it I could not even begin to think. We were stranded on a lone protrusion from the eroded minewall, like a mountain goat who unknowingly ventures onto a step in the rockface from which there is no return. I tried calling out to the sadhu, who had by now perhaps abandoned us.

Pratyusha heaved herself onto the edge of the rocky parapet around which the rope was tied, and produced a pick-axe from the inside of her jacket which she swung wildly at me, three or four times before I stopped trying to sabotage our spot. The point from which there was no return, only a passage to the infinite depths of the journey. The journey that knew no end!

She unhooked the rope and tied it around her waist, after which he hurriedly began to fashion a wedge in the ascending wall that would allow her easy access to a fissure which lay some eight feet ahead. She clung onto the rocks with her left hand and with her right dug the pick-axe into a more porous portion of the plateau, where she placed her foot to lift herself up another three feet. The next step was to be found in the form of a narrow indentation along the wall, where only the side of a foot could fit. Gripping the rock forms now with her right hand, she buried the pick-axe another two feet above her, deep enough into the wall to provide support for another lift up to a bend in the fissure.

My mind was still reeling with sheer vertigo, and as I watched her attempt that impossible climb, drew nearer to total *madness*! Each step she took caused in me a flurry of terrifying palpitations. She was now about twelve feet above me, and clinging to the wall with all the life in her.

'Back!' I screamed, in a state approaching utter lunacy. 'Nooo!'

'Shut up!' she echoed back.

There was place scarcely for her toes in the next step she was attempting. One arm locked on the pick-axe, she scanned every inch of the rocks to which she was clasped—glued motionless for an instant, which seemed to last an eternity—before leaping up to a wild grab she had planned which, thank but for the heavens, turned out to be an actuality. Her left hand slipped from this curvature on the rocks, though. It was too risky a proposition in the first place: being suspended solely from the support of a mere pick-axe. She should have never have attempted it! Were it not but for the grace of God, she would have surely lost grasp of that proposed hinge, whose unsteadiness summoned in her, a strength which at that point was her only saviour. One could sense her entire body tightening up and discreetly trembling before she finally struck her pick-axe into another corner of the wall, and hoisted herself up onto what appeared to be a depression in the ascending contours, which provided her with a further step up to what she managed to chisel into a thin parapet, where she could place some of her weight in order to relieve her limbs of the vigorous efforts they had expelled.

She rested for a moment, catching her breath, still as a stone statue, loosening her muscles, yet still rigidly stuck to her corner of the wall. Hacking away at the contours to fashion a full-fledged foothold, she managed to cover the last few feet up to the shelf where one of our rucksacks lay with much ease and dexterity; an acrobatic proficiency that came as no surprise given her illustrious achievements in the field of adventure sports.

She swung one of her legs onto the edge and dragged the rest of her body up with half her torso hanging from the shelf. Having heaved herself up, she arose from the ground in an instant, and before I could even applaud in weary sarcasm, began to arrange an anchorage for my secure passage up the same portion of the wall. The conjoined rope was now within reach, and hung just a few feet above her head.

She tied the elastic wire around her waist to the remaining rucksack, and even chained it to the roping above her, improvising a sort of elaborate pulley system by which I would have enough weight on the anchorage to climb up to the shelf.

'Come on!' she flicked her fingers at me from up above, and then tossed down the rope.

Her neck craned up to navigate the last stretch of fifty feet we would have to ascend before returning to safety. I still hesitated to reach for the rope she had flung down to me, it caressed the jagged wall she had traversed, and lay still along the shadowy rock forms I was supposed to press my feet against. Rappelling down was certainly easier than having to climb up a rope with nothing but the use of one's own innate strength, a reserve of mine that I could only now sense the depletion of. I staggered about the narrow ledge, looking up at Pratyusha who was busily preparing another weighty anchor, a pursuit from which I soon discouraged her by yanking at the rope with half my will and all my might, thereby stealing possession of the rope in its entirely. It escaped nimbly from each of its slips in the pulley that hadn't as yet been tightened and fell cleanly right by my feet.

'Don't be silly!' she shouted, her hands placed firmly on her hips, and her expression baring not the slightest hint of patience. 'Throw it back up here,' she offered out her hands. 'Come on!' she blew a fuse, awaiting a reply. 'BARKAT!' she screamed.

I reconfigured the same attachment she had tied up to the rock below my feet, my motor skills not having thus abandoned me—but found myself unable to answer to her shrieks which grew in urgency as my task was fulfilled. When I realised I was lowering myself down the featureless rappel of about thirty feet to which the rope extended, I caught sight of her from down below waving her arms wildly about in the air, all sounds escaping her diminishing gradually as

I went deeper and deeper into the pit. Grey concrete walls as if constructed for a vertical tunnel abounded below me, I could have even sworn I caught the MDDA (Mussoorie-Dehradun Development Association) emblem stamped on some remote square of the near-cylindrical shaft. From what I calculated we were crossing the hundred-foot mark, or at least I was. Pratyusha's harrowed face still shone above me, her contorted features devoid of sound, distorting at me in senseless silence.

PART SIX

Rainfall of Horrors

chapter one

I was about as close to a dead-end as I had ever been through my numerous voyages up this mountain. This was *it*! The last step to be taken, the final drop! All reason abolished, only the sensory apparatus in command, and in determined pursuit of the wonders it had long-waited to behold in the flesh, in their very physical form. Not as thoughts or images, but living, throbbing things that startled the eyes and invigorated the spirit.

I went! Down in the forsaken drop through whose vast expanse I flew at the speed of sound, which was incidentally also the first sense to desert me. The sight held, the speech could not be heard, the sense of smell and touch embraced the air into which it was plunged. Just when I let go of the rope I cannot accurately say, but it happened as if in a flash, wholly devoid of impulse like an involuntary response—the shutting of one's eyes at sunlight, or the closing of one's ears at a noise. To my muscle memory it seemed the logical thing to do, to unmoor myself from all the earthly apparatus that shackled my every heavenward movement; to let go... and just fall, freely...

Down I went, turning over backwards, sometimes somersaulting, often head-first, eventually straight as an arrow as the trajectory of gravity spun me around. I was now in stable motion, and looked about me to see the endless outlines of the walls of the mineshaft. The rocky features only grew more ornate and vivid as I descended deeper, and deeper, and then deeper still…till I again felt myself tumbling forward with a sudden jolt of air which threw me aside numerous times causing me to sway towards the rock-wall. I even feared that I might crash into its hideous dimensions and die before my time had come to approach the light, which only grew more distant the further I fell, as if in a mirage. The depth of this cavity in the mountain however seemed infinite, and as the mountainous moulds which contained it distorted into distressing patterns and designs hewn out of the rock bed—I felt certain at length when my heart had ceased to pound at my brain, and my nerves were significantly steadied, that the ray of light was appearing to dawn closer, and closer still as I fell another hundred feet. I was diving headfirst into its blinding flare, and only excited my prospects of finally coming face to face with the enigma, when the illumination around me split into crepuscular fragments of dazzling colours that propelled me faster and faster, as if exerting the influence of a turbo boost, or some vast centrifugal force. The light drew closer, and expanded into all that was around, filling up every stark feature of the mineshaft with the deadliest meaning, enshrouding all available matter in a spectral luminosity. The orb-like source of all this emanation grew faintly perceptible beyond the glowing cataract I was soon able to penetrate. When I fell into the epicentre of all this unendurable light, I broke through a threaded layer of unknown material, and then passed into a dark well of the most frightening malevolence. It was here that sound was somewhat restored when deprived of sight. The human body has provisions that exceed our own understanding. I could discern the gush of a waterfall, and then the howl of a furious wind which toppled me again in the air, whirling me around and this time sending me almost up to the solid stone wall that was now smooth as marble, immaculate beyond belief—and grey as an obelisk, with myriad etchings inscribed with characters unrecognizable that were detectable to the touch, almost framed in braille.

When propelled back into sight after tumbling along the grey wall, and falling through a water body through which gravity seemed to operate—conducting us keenly through the liquid barrier—I looked up to see, the water suspended in the air. I was now closing in on an even deeper section of the illuminated portal. For a moment, all went golden, then purple, and yellow and then a faintly perceptible white intruded on by scattered starbursts such as one sees in the invisible black of the eye sockets when one's lids are closed. Polygonal petals of colours forming and reconstituting, then dispersing with the flash of a blink. Time itself had ceased, space had been blotted out, I sank into a vacuum of endless luminosity, such as could not be conceived, as might be emitted from the sun, or a nuclear reactor—a singularity, conjuring with all its might, a black hole: the dark matter that exists outside of the knowable universe. Was all existence derived from a dot, as the Hindus say with the must-contested Bindu theory? Did we arise from nothingness? And if so, are we headed in the same direction as we speak? Some say that there exist mirror universes, where times spreads backwards in an inversion of our natural temporal laws. In our path to obliteration lies their passage to the beginning. Death and birth exchanged in some cosmic folly.

It were as though landscapes were capable of motion, trees were capable of travel, settlements capable of existing intact in inertia with the gift of mobility; objects alongside floating freely in a sort of indifferent serenity presented themselves intermittently, depending on the nature of the tonnage—adobe hutments with thatched roofs, vast corrugated aluminum warehouses, cement blocks and quarters of construction mass, even some obsolete machinery was seen to trickle by in this primeval rainfall of objects. I saw men, and women, and children scattered in the wind; cattle, and goats, and chickens, horses even, great stags, herds of wild dogs, and birds myriad and multi-coloured with wings deformed. Insects, invertebrates, plankton, microscopic marine ooze from which we all formed and reconstituted and evolved. The collective unconscious of nature. It all stared before me from the abyss that awaited my presence as I dropped lower into its incalculable depths, perhaps beyond the depths of the very Earth's core itself, into some place deeper and darker still than all that inhabited its natural laws; deep into the heart of the dark matter that envelopes and threatens to close up on all existence.

Was it there that I spotted the anthropoids? The half-conscious remnants of that black pool, the neither human nor animal products of the vast wastelands of the universe. I couldn't quite say whether they were the products of the imagination made fruit, or whether they were merely a manifestation of the psychic state, or whether they were indeed the constituents of a separate reality! Neither science nor faith could say. There were all kinds of creatures beckoning for existence, begging to be made a part of the natural order, or of even the human kingdom. The tentacular mass of crawling vegetation—insectile and insensate, broadening into the mineral realm—writhing and squirming to and fro from their incomprehensible flesh and phlegm. The primordial ooze might itself have been but a marginal spectacle in the vistas that proceeded with deranged promise into another land, a lineless plane, a circularity which folded and unfolded into prisms unendurable. I imagined perhaps, even in the nethermost regions of the mind, a kind of vast orbital spaceship, an all-encompassing craft that could account for all that I had witnessed and felt. Images of extra-terrestrial entities rather confounded than liberated my brain, all that the earth had fed us in its illimitable search for the unknown. Tentacles, antennae, orb-like skulls, ovoid eye sockets, sheer-skeletal anatomies, all the imagery invoked by the myriad associations implanted in the receptacle that is our consciousness. I could have died in a second and not known the difference.

But, the terrifying velocity lasted; preyed upon all my instincts, derided my intuitions. I was conscious of life, but could grasp not what living entailed. I felt as if I spun, or more appropriately swooned through a loop of the same unending extensity; blasting all notions of time and space held dear—it were as if I was back in that godforsaken water body, down in the slumbering depths of slimy opacity. I strolled into the dark, as if by means of a magnetic pull: The true primordial blackness that begat all! From which we extracted the light, from which we grew, from which we became…

The primeval night. The essential darkness that enshrouds all. Where does it exist? Would we exist without it, if existence be merely a process, like death, that the mind, body and soul wanders through, unwittingly? Bereft of choice, and the divine doctrine of free will…

But hark! something calls in this wilderness of propelled flight…a voice, a hearing, a sharp being of conscious intent—

something that endeavours in all its entirety to reach, or approach…to speak and touch…I paid nary a glance at my fellow passengers that were lowered with me into the bottom of this mount! It was as if a vision spoke to me: a voice from the depths that announced what I was experiencing, a tumultuous descent into the inferno of existence, the swirling magma of neither solid nor liquid mass in which we found ourselves; inhabitants of some nether lair, truly uncharted and untenable.

Were we not all as one? A mass of cells and molecules moulded by our creator into what we are now? Good and evil, absolute! Within and without lie all potential for kindness and humanity, for cruelty and contempt, the divided soul and self that wanders at will through our unforeseen existence. I gaped on at all the infinite flaws of a humanity mutated, of an existence distorted, and a reality propelled into unreality…

'Gaze not at what you see!' the vision commanded. 'Nor at all that you hear, or feel or touch…every sensation is as but a mere satellite to the senses devout, the feelings withheld, the goodness foresworn, the evil unrepentant. Being is what one would want it to be, even without…if mere being could determine what the onward mass of time made measurable into actuality.'

I had heard of instances wherein the roots of a plant could communicate with that of another, where the cells of a non-existent human being lasted in one of its offsprings as the spirit everlasting. Was it the Professor that was in communication with what I was undergoing? Did he know? Could he see? Was he too falling endlessly?

The Goddess of all the Himalayas beckoned, the mountain itself stirred, the ocean from which it was spawned seemed still and higher than us now. The focal point of all this energy, this magnetic velocity which sucked me down at a furious speed, grew more distant to the eye the closer it seemed to the other senses. I floated serenely on into this bottomless chasm, crossing rivers and streams that seemed stuck to the wall, flowing against gravity. Settlements which appeared to exist on a vertical plane, vast expanses of meticulously cultivated landscape defying all laws of physics, motion that appeared inert, vegetation that grew sideways—an entire wilderness frozen in space. An infinity of the same winged creatures inhabited its intricate topography.

A few of them flew past me, swooping and flapping pointlessly in circles till a flock of them formed a bed of wings under my flat and floating body that carried me along in the fashion of a magic carpet back up against the tearing gravity. The violent alteration of air pressure nearly made my head explode as I was swept back up over the bewildering expanse I had flown freely past; the dark patch of perennial night, the suspended lake, the glowing magnetic force field of intolerable brightness, the yellow, blue, and purple profusions of sparkling shapes and patterns all blending in to the receding twilight. The creaky primeval whirring or whistling sound emitted by the creatures I was rested on encompassed all sensation. It grew louder and shriller as we gained altitude, and in a matter of mere minutes I was thrown back ashore onto the stalactite covered edge of the mine, which I could from a distance behold Pratyusha attempting to climb with the aid of the string of rope anchored at its entranceway. She nearly lost her grip on the rope when she caught sight of my pterodactyl-like avian accompaniment. She clambered up the last few rocks in a hurry and with both hands placed on the edge, drew her entire body weight up with the preternatural strength of a gymnast—undoing the knot around the entranceway, and walking tentatively up to me, with palms cast outward as in caution.

I was covered from head to foot in a strange sooty material, which left a greenish residue all across my person. As I later came to know, the rucksack which had fallen into the pit was mine; a stroke of providence I had not in the least suspected. Thankfully, the one belonging to Pratyusha was in our possession and had been securely recovered from the ledge some fifty feet below us. It contained the vintage camera we had found at the campsite, and was also amply provisioned to see us through two days of trekking back downwards, which we would have to accomplish in this instance without Baba Somdev's invaluable assistance.

I showed Pratyusha the water body in which I had dived with a snorkelling mask provided to me by her late paternal grandmother, the hearth around which the ceremony had taken place, the winding labyrinthine tunnels which proceeded in all directions through the cave complex, one of which we employed on our path back out to the stepladder that hung outside the entrance to this grotto. No one was to be spotted in any of the caverns on our way out, not even Baba Somdev, he had vanished into the ghostly shadows of the mineshaft, perhaps to join his fellow-exiles in the bottomless descent, perhaps to leave us to our folly, perhaps to join the congregation of mountainfolk at the temple. Who knows?

All I know is that when we reached the temple they were gone. Nowhere to be found. Only an ooze of insects inhabited the insides of the temple, an interlocking mess of recumbent earthworms twice their natural size, scorpion-shaped tails and flowering gnats and beetles exceeding their wildest everyday proportions. This had probably driven away the rest of the company, as there was no rifle within reach as there had been earlier assisted by the marksmanship of Karma Bodh. No one to save the people from the incomprehensible spillage from the basements concealed just below the temple. I took her by the hand and rushed out of the temple! Her rucksack nearly fell off her shoulders, I tripped once or twice over the irregular rock formations strewn all about the sloping tracts of terrace. The downhill stride propelled us into a sprint, our feet were operating now out of our command. The tumultuous drop at the edge of the approaching cliffside stared at us from some twenty metres on. There was nothing we could do to deaccelerate our tumble, we were in rapid motion and as I caught from the corner of my eye the bending stairway of rocks creeping down the base of the terraced-steps, I saw that there was only one choice.

I pulled her arm with both hands and leaped towards the turn as we neared the drop. We somersaulted into a quarry of rocks, and rolled downhill some seven metres before falling back at the top of the abandoned campsite.

chapter two

We plundered every article from that wreckage of campsite that could be of some remote use to us in the arduous descent. Mufflers, monkey-caps, some of Swaami Ji's shawls, also certain books and magazines of the time that might hold the mind on a leash, along with a musty .32 Long Barrel Revolver. I searched all the jacket and trouser pockets for a round of ammunition, came upon a few stray bullets in one of the outer compartments of a rucksack, hidden away in a matchbox.

'I think you'd better give it here!' Pratyusha placed an outstretched palm before me.

'I found it!' I told her.

'Still…' she insisted.

'No!' I refused outright. 'You were the one that made me find the camera so you are entitled to keep it, same rules apply for the firearm.'

'Barkat! I don't think you are well-equipped to handle a gun right now! I think you'd better let me have it.' She rolled her fingers up into her palm.

I handed her the gun, but held on to the bullets. 'If you insist!'

We were making our way towards the bottom of the same rockface through that frightening path charted by the sadhus along the narrow parapet, bypassing the tree and arriving at the patch of flat land where I had once dug our rations—when I noticed from the top of the slope, trudging up along the harsh hillside from below—a pair of policemen, or at least uniformed officials. One of them was a policeman, and the other donned some kind of a black-green commando attire, unrecognisable to either of us, especially to Pratyusha who was from a defense background, which was all the more disconcerting.

'Yes?' The policeman asked, in a tone of casual insolence—his right hand making motions and shapes in the air. 'What are you two doing here?'

'My mother works for the State Electric Division,' Pratyusha frowningly answered, a bit dismayed. 'Her name is Damini Jain Negi. You can check. Ask anyone!' her tone degenerated into an affront within one syllable.

'Your mother?' the policeman's frown curved even lower than hers.

'That's right!'

'What did you say your name was young lady?' the other gentleman inquired.

'Pratyusha Negi!' she snapped. 'I'm with the HRA.'

'The HR what?' the policeman whined.

'Could I see some identification please.'

'Look…please…' I intervened. 'We work with the government.' I fetched up a bald-faced lie.

'So do we,' was the policeman's gnarly retort.

'We work *for* the government,' the commando stipulated. 'You work with them…' his mouth crinkled up in thought. 'That makes you our seniors!' he decided.

'Them?' the policeman gasped, in forced incredulity

'That's right,' the commando smiled, taking off his pair of dark glasses. His face was shaped like a cement slab, his hollow eyes acting as handprints. 'And if they happen to be our seniors,' he carried on, in mischievous pursuit. 'They certainly would be aware that there happen to be some rules implemented and in place regarding the area from which they have, it seems, just returned. And well…' he rambled on. 'If that just so happens to be the case, then what we have out here are a pair of deliberate rule-breakers who possibly harbour some ulterior motive for being out here in the first place. But then, if we were to give them the benefit of the doubt, we might also suppose that they could possibly be one of the select few that are permitted to visit the peak. But if that were the case, they certainly would not be in the condition in which they now appear.'

'Who else is allowed to go on top?' I asked.

'We are not privileged to lend out that information to you, sir. Our job is to keep all passes up to the peak sealed, at all costs! In the interest of public health. Now, if I may ask, what exactly is *your* job sir?'

chapter three

We were escorted back down by the two grumbling officials whose custody proved to be an unintended deliverance of sorts. Were it not for their firm hand, and adept navigational manoeuvers I doubt we would have made it back to Taluka in one piece.

We were, however, arrested and did have to spend a couple of nights in an Uttarkashi jail-cell until Pratyusha's mother was able to travel up from Dehradun to pay our bail. The vintage camera was handed back to us wrapped in the depths of the rucksack as its presence had not been revealed in our modified official account of the incidents. We were subjected instead to a thorough questioning by the two personnel from Army Intelligence who seemed more interested in what the mother had to say for her daughter than what her daughter had to say about all that we had discovered. We, of course, claimed to have been lost in the wilderness on a routine trek to Harkidun, and guided up there by a pair of malicious sadhus.

'You better be careful of those sadhus,' Lt Commander K.P. Barnwal politely smiled.

We were seated in the DIG's secluded cabin.

'Aghoris, tantrics, you don't know what kind of stuff they've got up their sleeve!' he now grew serious, imparting a measured assessment of what might have possibly led the supposed sadhus to take us up to Ranibaug. 'You can't stop them!' he complained. 'Even if you block all access, they can still come up with a route. Through the bushes and rocks, they're like goddamn termites. They can walk through wood! By the way…' a more serious thought fleetingly passed his memory. 'Weren't you the one?' he looked at Damini Jain Negi just to be sure. 'That got those photographs of the Tree across to the *National Geographic*.'

'That's right,' Pratyusha answered before her mother could.

'Mmmm…interesting.' Lt Commander Barnwal looked at the tiles that spread out across the floor. 'All on a routine trip to Harki Dun heh?' he got up.

'I keep going up there,' Pratyusha said. 'It's a kind of a place of…' a word occurred to her which she refrained from using. 'Pilgrimage,' she chose instead. 'For me, at least!'

'Worship?' Lt Commander Barnwal's eyes lit up.

'Oh no!' Damini Jain Negi shook her head agitatedly. 'She comes with me to the temple every once in a while. There's nothing wrong with her like that!' she assured him.

'And…' he settled back down into his chair. 'What intrigued you about this tree?'

'I'd never seen anything like it.' She explained without any expression whatsoever. 'I don't know,' she finally snapped out of her stupor. 'What intrigues you about it?'

'We've tried to chop it down!' he blankly stated. 'Applied mechanical buzz saws, a wrecking ball even. Nothing seems to work to get it to budge an inch.'

'Perhaps that's the way it was intended,' Pratyusha said.

'By whom?' all eyes in the room suddenly spun around at her.

'Whoever it belongs to?' she shrugged her shoulders.

'What?'

'The Tree.'

Lt Commander Barnwal exchanged an indiscreet look with one of his sub-ordinates. The three of them sat still in their chairs, waiting for another word to be spoken. I decided to take up the rest of the questioning with concocted anecdotes; incidents which seemed plausible enough yet which tested the patience of their collective credulity. We were soon ushered out, while they had a final word with Pratyusha's mother in our absence.

The two of us stood outside the gate of Uttarkashi Police Thaana, taking in the petrol air, the soothing sounds of earthly chaos and commotion taking on an ethereal quality. It seemed real! Undisputed.

'What are you going to do with the negatives?' I asked, after a long and still silence.

'I don't know,' she looked on into the distance, her eyes roaming celestial freeways and distant ruins of outer space, then falling back upon the world around her and stumbling into sense. 'I suppose…' it occurred to her. 'It might be one way of meeting my grandmother. If not in the flesh, then at least through the eyes!'

'Hmmm…' I nodded my head along with her thoughts and meditations. 'Perhaps you might get to see that Tree.' I suggested. 'Fifty years ago! What it looked like. What it might look like.' I thought to myself before thinking out aloud. 'Fifty years from now. Why fifty, maybe a hundred-two hundred. Entire centuries beyond! Centuries, and millennia and ages ago and ahead. It stood there. And Pratyusha you were the first to bring it to light before the world.'

She smiled hesitantly, or at least it was the closest one could expect of a smile from her. 'That animal too!' she looked beyond into the future. 'And if what I find in this camera is of any value, who knows?' her eyes flitted across to mine. 'A name to be made. A place in the history books. An entirely new profession from rock-climbing.'

I smiled at the prospect and wished her luck as her mother collected her from the driveway of the Police thaana. The two state-issued government ambassadors crawled out with the officials behind Damini Jain Negi's Ford Endeavour. I bid them all farewell and got into my Gypsy parked outside the gate. It had lain without attendance for a number of days now, and had to be wiped clean of all the bird droppings and mud and dust that coated it.

While washing up the mudguards, and polishing the windscreen, I had to borrow a cloth and spray from the back of the jeep where the jack and wrench lay—and while doing so came across the issue of *National Geographic* from the week before with the vivid portrait of that deformed tree gracing its cover.

A seated sadhu by the crumbling wall of the police station, noticed me from the roadside. He shone at me from his haggard posture, a toothless smile brimming with an intangible camaraderie. I returned his warmth with a wink, which he just nodded at, and rested his head against the wall—gazing up at the mesh of wires wrestling overhead—then slowly shifting his head in my direction, as if in indecision, he nodded again at me and slowly winked back—the same smile lighting up his landscape of a face.

I threw the magazine back inside the trunk, and slammed the door shut, waving him goodbye—to start up the ignition and warm up the engine before I could be on my way back to Mathura.

It was a long drive, proceeding through lush acres of green, smoky highways and peripheral forests, past many Mofussil towns, and truck-stops, hotels, petrol-pumps, food courts, providing regularly for all the daily amenities of everyday life. The Tree constantly danced before my mind as I cruised through another wilderness at top speed. It was a discovery! By all possible means, a real find. And it would forever determine my onward path, now that I have explicated the details of my account.

The photographs of the animal are to arrive on the 23rd of June in their Summer issue. What Pratyusha might find in way of evidence of that archaic expedition still unsolved, only time will tell. In the meantime, I would urge the keen reader to pursue any means possible of trying to help better the understanding of that unexplainable botanical lifeform.

It has been something of an object of obsession for me of late, as I had once prayed to it, feared it even, and bargained with it to alter the outcome of the doom that lay waiting in my destiny. And it *had* provided! In the form of that sadhu who was my only saving grace, my only guardian from death and starvation. Was it *real*? Had it exerted the divine influence?

This question has been plaguing me recently, and causing in me a wild array of psychological maladies and morbid afflictions. I request, at once, the urgent assistance of anyone that might be aware of how to dispel the situation I am undergoing.

chapter four

The Tree has begun to occupy my every thought. I pray to it twice a day, once in the mornings and another time at night before going to bed.

My condition has only grown worse. I am given to spells of manic-depressive tendencies, I sometimes even talk to myself, falling asleep between sentences. My family members feel I have grown more reclusive since my last expedition, often wishing to be left alone and not disturbed. I loathe the company of people. The only thing I take comfort in is plants. It has even become mandatory for every visitor that comes to our house to arrive accompanied by a sapling of some sort. In ordinary circumstances, my family would never have allowed it, but once convinced they agreed to make an exception in this case, and accommodate the plants provided they did not grow too large for my room.

I lie in bed all day, surrounded by ferns, cacti, conifers, touchmenots, money plants, and the ivy creeper which now extends to the neighbouring bedroom. I speak to them, tell stories, ask them questions, plead with them, even eat them sometimes; sometimes I regret to mention, I even become violent with them. On many an occasion a visitor to my room has found a smashed flowerpot next to the toilet.

These peculiarities of behaviour are a cause of much alarm to all those around me, who by now are convinced that the ailment which plagues me is a strictly psychological one—and after having observed my recent incivilities towards the plants, are quite sure of their supposition.

I speak to a psychiatrist from New Delhi, every now then, over the phone. It is in these long phone conversations that I am able to open up about my fixation on the new discovery disclosed by *National Geographic* in their previous issue, with which the doctor is currently unfamiliar. He did not take it seriously at first, and when informed of my part in that discovery—considered it to be a delusionary lapse of reason, because as one can rightfully imagine—instead of paying attention to the matter of what I was saying, he was placing more emphasis on the manner, which was by any means—far from normal.

What *was* that tree? Where did it come from? When did it begin, can it ever end? To what does it owe its existence? And what do I owe it?

I pondered many a night upon these questions, wondering constantly what duty I still had towards the Tree. Whether I ought to go *back*? A proposition unthinkable now. I have spoken to numerous experts in the field of botany, and have managed each time to alienate rather than interest them with my observations. But I know one thing for certain. It is growing at an alarming rate and might even one day cover the peak of the mountain, doing the government's job for them to seal off the secret buried in the earth's bosom.

Was it the face of *God*? An arrow-glance at the heavens. Or was it the face of Satan? All that is unknown and unthinkable, the hideous aspects of humanity from which one's eyes automatically avert. Death, delirium and the dance of the Grim Reaper! What lies beyond that unreachable gulf? I find myself down a horrible vortex of thought. The incurable incomprehension of those that *know*. Down the sordid crevices into the uncharted regions of the psyche. I find the brain itself imitating the motions of the Tree, with roots extending as far underground as they can go.

Perhaps, it was some hitherto inextricable life form from another, inconceivable universe, obstructing the march of any mechanical invention that could possibly conquer it. Or perhaps it was simply Mother Nature's answer to the wheels of progress that are constantly trying to overtake her and leave her behind, stranded on the washed-out shores of the cosmic race against time.

THE END

ACKNOWLEDGEMENTS

I would like to thank Simar Puneet for being a constant source of encouragement and support, and for putting me in touch with my dear friend and editor the brilliant Sayantan Ghosh, who I would also like to thank for his belief in this book.

I would like to thank Jahaan Subrahmanyam, Divya Jagdale, Jaimini Pathak, Joy Fernandes and Denzil Smith for being such magnificent sources of inspiration to me, and for being kindred spirits and fellow travellers in the land of Edgar Allan Poe and Ambrose Bierce.

I would also like to thank the wonderful and brilliant writer Indrapramit Das who had worked on an edit of a previous incarnation of this story in novella form that was to have been published in 2016 under the title 'The Whispering Skull'.

And finally I would like to thank my good friend the amazing writer Carlo Pizzati who took the time out to read some chapters of an early draft of this book and was kind enough to give me feedback.